KILL THEM COLD

HIDDEN NORFOLK - BOOK 7

J M DALGLIESH

First published by Hamilton Press in 2021

ISBN (Trade Paperback) 978-1-80080-854-6
ISBN (Hardback) 978-1-80080-982-6
ISBN (Large Print) 978-1-80080-749-5

EXCLUSIVE OFFER

Look out for the link at the end of this book or visit my website at
www.jmdalgliesh.com to sign up to my no-spam VIP Club and
receive a FREE Hidden Norfolk novella plus news and previews
of forthcoming works.

Never miss a new release.

No spam, ever, guaranteed. You can unsubscribe at any time.

KILL THEM COLD

PROLOGUE

FOR ONCE, it was a relief to escape the chaos. The music, the laughter and the boisterous behaviour. Though muted, the sound still carried to her as she walked. The fresh air made her dizzy. Had she really drunk that much? The sound of waves crashing against the beach, of insects chirping in the nearby brush, reminiscent of Mediterranean holidays. If not for the lack of dust underfoot she could easily imagine she was in southern France or on a sparsely populated Greek island.

The night was clear, the moon looming large in the sky, illuminating the path. A gentle breeze passed over the sea of reeds, whispering to her politely, feeling cool on her skin. Brushing aside the hair clinging to her forehead, still clammy with sweat from the packed pub, she looked back. Movement from within showed the party was in full swing and didn't look like ending anytime soon. Usually, she would be in the thick of it.

But not tonight. She'd had enough.

There were those who would be pleased she'd ducked out early. The jealous ones. Those who smiled sweetly but would actively savage her the moment she turned her back. It wasn't her fault they were being ignored. They should look at themselves in the mirror before shooting daggers in her direction. Men were visual creatures. More so when they drink. Even the intellectual ones, not that they'd admit it if asked.

Men were curious beings, so easy to entertain and so quick to convince themselves of their unique qualities. Despite observing the experience of others, their rise and subsequent fall, when it came to themselves, they were convinced that this time would be different. They were different. Therefore, it followed, as their delusions manifested, that the outcome would also be different.

A quick smile, wide-eyed and welcoming. The occasional flirtatious touch. It didn't need to be anywhere intimate, just a casual stroke of the back of a hand or forearm and a pulse of electricity would pass between them. This was usually enough. She felt it too. The promise of excitement. The anticipation of something new, intoxicating, rebellious. Their eyes would follow her around the room for the rest of the evening, pretending not to, watching as she interacted with people and silently hoping she would return and make good on her promise. And it would be different. Of course, it would be. Other men didn't possess the same appeal. When she flirted with the others it meant nothing, and when she came back to them it was because they had what she needed. Each man thought he was special. He was the one.

They were all wrong, of course.

The older men were an interesting challenge. Having done a few laps of the track already, they knew the rules of the game far better than the twenty-somethings. Not that they were immune. They were easy to draw in, but much harder to convert. They knew better. The risk was greater, for they usually had more to lose than merely a bruising encounter with their pride. But a man's ego can take on its own mischievous character, whispering plausible narratives in otherwise deaf ears.

The attention was nice and all but, contrary to popular belief, it wasn't attention she craved. She wasn't mistaking male company for the displaced love of her childhood or whatever pop-psychology was thrown at her this time. No, the high came from the feeling of power. The thrill of watching them react to her, male or female, and playing one off against another without making it too obvious. The physical thrill was fun too, most of the time. But she wasn't looking for that tonight.

A stick cracked nearby. She half turned, expecting to see someone approaching. She waited, watching the bushes intently, listening hard against the backdrop of the sea. A cloud passed in front of the moon, causing a shift in the light, offering new shadows to her overactive imagination. Conscious of holding her breath, she absently toyed with the braid tied around her wrist. Satisfied she was alone; she resumed her walk towards the beach.

Footsteps.

She started and spun.

This time a figure stepped from the brush alongside the path. Putting a hand on her chest, she smiled as she took a deep breath.

"Oh, it's you." She could hear the relief in her voice. "You startled me."

"Sorry, I didn't mean to scare you."

"That's… what are you doing out here?"

"I saw you were alone. I thought you might want some company."

She was on edge. The clandestine approach. The casual words. The easy smile. She felt her own smile fading as she looked back to the pub, a beacon of light amid the houses in darkness dotted around nearby.

"No… no, I don't," she said, hesitantly. This offer wasn't on her terms. For once, she felt out of control. "I wanted to be alone for a bit."

"Really? Who wants to be alone?"

She backed up, trying to put some space between them, registering a change in demeanour. It didn't work. Her instincts asserted themselves, screaming at her internally, and she turned, thinking to run only to catch her footing and stumble. Putting out a hand to break her fall, she still hit the ground hard. She may feel like she'd sobered up, but clearly her body disagreed. A figure appeared over her as the clouds cleared and they were bathed in silver light.

"Here, let me help you."

A hand was extended to her, and reluctantly she reached up and took it. Rising to her feet, she dusted herself down.

"Thanks. I...I don't know what happened there."

The smell of cigarette smoke was dominant, overpowering that of beer. They were close to one another, closer than she would like.

"So, do you want some company?"

She shook her head almost imperceptibly. "No, thank you. I'd rather be alone tonight."

"No. No one wants to be alone."

CHAPTER ONE

"EXCUSE ME, WOULD YOU?"

Becca rose from her seat and glanced across the bar before looking hopefully towards Eric, who smiled at her warmly as she lingered. Tom Janssen sat forward and gestured behind her to the right, rescuing his detective constable who was still oblivious to his partner's needs.

"They're just the other side of the bar, in the far corner."

Eric flinched. "Yes," he said, the smile vanishing, and he pointed to where Tom had directed her. Becca offered Tom her thanks and set off. "I should have guessed."

Both Tamara and Alice smiled in Eric's direction, just as his face reddened. This was only the second occasion where Eric had brought Becca along on a social event, and Tom felt as if her acceptance within the group mattered very much to the young man. On his part, Becca had proven to be quite a hit. She was confident, outgoing, and very easy company.

"She's lovely, Eric," Alice said, sitting next to him as she was and gently patted the back of his hand. Eric appeared relieved as both Tom and Tamara made approving sounds.

Tom looked around at the number of empty glasses, finishing his orange juice.

"Same again?" he asked. A general murmur of agreement followed and he rose. Eric followed suit.

"I'll give you a hand."

They headed for the bar and Tom glanced back over his shoulder at the DCI sitting opposite Alice. The two of them were engaged in conversation which was nice to see. They would never be close, he was sure of that, but as to why he couldn't say. It was easy to say their last case had put a strain on all of them, Alice being a suspect in the murder of her ex-husband, but Tamara hadn't pressed that angle of investigation and had seen through it quickly enough. To be honest the likelihood of the two of them being friends was low, even before those events, but tonight seemed to be going well.

He attracted the attention of the barman and waited to be served. Eric was nervous, more so than merely the worry of his colleagues liking his partner.

"Just make mine a half, please," Eric said. In response to Tom's raised eyebrow, he said, "I need to keep a clear head."

"Penny for them?" Tom asked. Eric looked at him quizzically. "What's on your mind, Eric?"

Eric's face split into an awkward smile. "Is it that obvious?"

"I'm a detective."

Eric laughed. Tom waited patiently, Eric organising his thoughts.

"You've been married, haven't you?" Eric asked.

Tom nodded, his eyes flicking over to Alice. It wasn't his favourite topic of conversation.

"So... how did you go about... you know, asking?"

"Proposing?"

Eric fixed him with an expectant look, nodding. Tom took a deep breath.

"I'm... probably not the best person to ask," he said grimacing, remembering his ill-fated proposal to Alice and reliving the trauma in an instant flashback. Eric was crestfallen. "Do you have something in mind?"

"Well, yes…. several," Eric said, frowning. "But every time I think of something, I end up talking myself out of it."

"The idea of marriage or just the proposal?"

"Just the proposal," Eric said quickly. "Whenever I think about it, I think it's just not good enough… and I want it to be right, you know?"

Tom empathised. It was a big step in anyone's life. After all you only plan to be married once – at least most people do – and the pressure to make it memorable could be intense.

"I mean," Eric said, "a friend of mine proposed to his girlfriend on holiday. They both like hiking and they had booked this amazing trip to the Alps. He planned it all out perfectly, she hadn't a clue. They hiked to the summit of one peak, him carting his new drone all the way up there on the premise of filming from the summit. Then he proposed to her while the drone circled overhead filming the entire thing." Eric shook his head, dejected. "It was the most beautiful thing I've ever seen. The backdrop, the sun on the snow… incredible! They'll remember that day for the rest of their lives."

Eric let the conversation drop as the barman took their order.

"What was Becca drinking, vodka and tonic?" Tom asked.

Eric shook his head. "Just a mineral water."

"Driving?"

"No, we walked here from her place," Eric said, glancing across the bar as Becca reappeared from the ladies' and moved through the throng towards them. "She has a lot of prep to do tomorrow ready for the new term starting on Monday. They've given her Year Two this time around which is great."

Tom recalled Becca was given primary year one as a newly qualified teacher and now, entering her second full year, she had moved up a grade.

"Is that significant?" he asked.

"Absolutely! Becca says they put the NQTs in Years One or Three."

"Why do that?"

"Because the children sit their SATs at the end of Years Two and Four, and they count towards the school league tables," Eric said as if it was obvious. Tom had no idea what he was inferring. Eric noticed. "If the NQTs mess up, then the school has time to get the kids up to speed in the following year leading up to the exams."

"Ah right, I see," Tom said, silently wondering how teachers not recently qualified would feel if they were allocated years one or three in the future if this was common knowledge. Presumably if Eric knew, then so did everyone else. Becca reached them, smiling broadly, and Tom responded to Eric's fearful look in such a way as to reassure the young man his secret was safe. Eric greeted her affectionately and she slipped her arm around his waist, placing the other gently on his chest.

"How are you coping with all of Eric's workmates?" Tom asked. "It can be overwhelming."

"Not at all. I've been on at Eric for ages to arrange something. It's nice. You are all …' she tilted her head to one side thoughtfully "…much more normal than I expected."

Tom grinned. "Stick around. It won't last." His eyes drifted to the door spying Cassie's arrival with another in tow. He caught her eye, beckoning her over with a twenty-pound note in his hand, signalling that he was getting the drinks in. Cassie hurried over.

"Sorry we're late," she said on the half turn, allowing space for the woman alongside her to come into the group. "This is Lauren," she said, introducing them. "DI Janssen—"

"Tom," he said pointedly, offering Lauren a welcoming smile.

"Tom," Cassie said, emphasising his name. "And this is Eric, and…" she raised her eyebrows as she turned to Becca.

"Becca," Becca said, smiling.

"Of course," Eric said, firmly clenching his eyes shut. Tom felt for him. Eric was at his absent-minded best tonight, surely a result of his preoccupation with something he couldn't share with anyone. Introductions complete, Tom added two gin and tonics to the order.

"Tamara and Alice are at the table in the corner," Tom said, indicating the far side of the pub.

Becca led the way. Cassie, taking Lauren's hand as they went, fell into step behind her. Eric seemed transfixed by something. Tom followed his eye. Eric met his gaze.

"Are they?" Eric asked.

"What?"

"Cassie and…"Eric nodded in their direction.

"Lauren."

"Yeah, the two of them… are they…?"

"Looks like it," Tom said. He didn't sense Eric disapproved, just that he was surprised. "Considering you're a detective for a living, perhaps we need to schedule you some observation training. What do you think?"

Eric's brow furrowed momentarily before he returned Tom's smile. "Anyway," Eric said, double checking they were alone again, aside from the barman lining up their order on a tray in front of them, "what do you think… about the proposal idea?"

"I haven't heard it yet."

"Oh, right. Well, as I was saying, I came up with these ideas – like chartering a small boat out of Wells and doing it out at sea. You know, the moonlight reflecting off the water as we bob about. I could take food and a nice bottle of… well, whatever."

"Sounds special… romantic."

"Yeah, right. That's what I thought," Eric said.

"But?"

"But what if it's cloudy that night or it rains? And you know what the swell can be like if the wind gets up. It wouldn't be great proposing whilst trying to keep my lunch down. Then there's the food, it'll be cold. You can't have a special proposal meal of sandwiches… that wouldn't be romantic at all!"

In the corner of his eye, Tom caught sight of the barman

suppressing a smile. Eric wouldn't be the first man to grapple with this predicament. To be fair, Eric's discomfort was quite comical.

"You're overthinking it, Eric," he said, handing a couple of notes across to the waiting barman and glancing in the direction of their table where the five women were deep in conversation. Turning back to Eric, Tom grinned. "Look, whatever you do it will be memorable. Trust me, you don't forget where you propose, and Becca will remember it for the rest of her life. What you intend is far more important than what you say and where, or how you say it."

The advice didn't seem to hit the right note. At least, the visible weight of concern contained within Eric's expression hadn't lifted at all. The barman returned with Tom's change and the two men shared a knowing look as Tom took the coins and put them in his pocket. Eric glanced towards Becca and the table, checking that no one was looking, and produced a ring box from his pocket.

"I've been carrying this around for days, in case I got spontaneous."

"In that case, why not do it tonight?"

"Really? You think?" Eric said, his expression lightening.

Tom shrugged. "As good a time as any. It's still warm; a clear night at the end of summer. If you fancy taking a little boat out in September, you're a braver man then me. And this weather won't hold forever. Unless you have some annual leave to take? You could go away somewhere nice."

Eric shook his head. "Nah... used all of it when Mum fell ill, remember?"

"It's just my opinion," Tom said, picking up the tray. "And as I said, my track record in proposals is a bit of a car crash."

"Plural?" Eric asked. "I thought you'd only been married the once."

"Yes, plural, Eric," Tom said with a sigh as he made to walk off.

He stopped. "And as of now, I've only had a fifty percent success rate… and that ended in divorce, so take my advice with a pinch of salt."

Eric frowned and Tom moved off. He heard Eric mutter something under his breath and the tone suggested he hadn't helped much.

Tom set the tray down on the table and Alice helped him pass out the drinks. Meanwhile, Eric brought over a couple more unoccupied chairs from the neighbouring table for himself and Tom. The others shifted their seats to make room. As they sat down, Cassie pointed to Eric's half pint of beer.

"I see you're still using the children's glasses."

Eric smiled sarcastically, scrunching up his nose. It was a long-running joke between himself and DS Knight regarding his height: she was taller than him even though she was not considered particularly tall for a woman. Lauren slapped Cassie's arm by way of a telling-off and everyone smiled.

"I just want to keep a clear head, that's all," Eric said defensively. "Besides," he glanced at Tom, "we've got something on later, so we can't stay late."

"Have we?" Becca asked, looking confused. "What have I missed?"

Eric flushed, his lips moving but seemingly not able to form words.

Cassie laughed, casting a sideways glance at Becca. "Well, if you don't know then he's probably about to propose!"

Eric's mouth fell open and the skin of his neck flushed to match that deepening in his face. Cassie read his face, her eyes flitting to Becca whose smile faded as she registered Eric's horrified expression. Eric stumbled through an incoherent arrangement of sounds. Nobody spoke.

"Anyway!" Tom said loudly, drawing everyone's eyes to him and breaking the awkward silence. He raised a glass, angling it in Lauren and then Becca's direction, "a toast to new friends."

They all raised their drinks in salutation, knocking one another's glasses together and the moment passed. Alice leaned in close to Tom and whispered in his ear. "Nice save."

CHAPTER TWO

Tom Janssen pulled the car up onto the verge at the edge of the police cordon at the entrance to the field. He waved a greeting to the uniformed constable who was coming across to meet him. Eric's car was parked next to the liveried vehicle and with a quick glance through the gate, he could see several figures at the far side of the part-ploughed field where the hedgerow marked the boundary. A tractor was parked up nearby; another uniform speaking to who he guessed was the driver.

"Morning, sir," the constable said. Tom reached back into the car and retrieved his coffee cup, acknowledging the greeting as he shut the door. He stifled a yawn. The sun may have risen in a clear sky, but it wasn't yet seven in the morning on a Sunday. Ever grateful for being virtually teetotal, Tom allowed the constable to guide him to the gate, the line where no members of the public would be allowed to cross. Not that there were many people around at this time. Brancaster was a little village situated on the Norfolk coast between the Brancaster Manor marshland and Scolt Head Island nature reserve, roughly three miles west of Burnham Market. Aside from the early risers walking their dogs, there was precious little movement here, unsurprising with this village and the two others making up the parish registering fewer than eight hundred residents in total.

"Is that who found it?" Tom said, gesturing with his coffee cup.

"Yes, sir," the officer said, glancing in the direction of the man standing with his arms folded across his chest as the constable he was talking to made notes. From leaning against the tractor, he lifted himself upright and looked in Tom's direction. Perhaps it was the man's sixth sense alerting him to Tom's attention, because his gaze lingered on Tom and they stared at one another. As far as he knew, Tom couldn't recall having met him before.

"Farmer?" Tom asked. The constable nodded. "Working overnight."

"Apparently so. Trying to get ahead before the forecasted rain comes later in the week."

"Right."

Tom was surprised. He knew farmers would work through the night if under time pressure but usually that was to bring in the harvest before the weather changed rather than preparing the soil. Although he was hardly knowledgeable on the subject. He slipped through the five-bar gate, leaving the constable to close it behind him, and headed across to where Eric stood. The detective constable looked like he hadn't slept; dark patches hanging beneath the point where his eyes met the bridge of his nose.

"Good morning, Eric. What have you got for me?"

"Morning, Tom," Eric said, his tone was light but he sounded as tired as he looked. "Farmer turned this up overnight." Eric beckoned Tom over to an area of the field close to the boundary which was separated by a drainage ditch with a thick hedge beyond. The soil, despite having been recently turned over, was still fairly solid underfoot; a result of the clement spell they'd experienced at the tail end of what had already been a dry, hot spring and summer. It was a shame it was all supposed to come to a violent end in the coming days. Tom stepped over the deep furrows before dropping to his haunches. A bone was sticking out of the soil. To an untrained eye, it could easily be considered an animal bone but the joint immediately struck Tom as belonging to a human femur. Part way along the length of the bone it was crudely broken ensuring the lower part connecting to the knee was missing. What was in no doubt was the left side of a cheek bone and lower section of an eye socket visibly protruding from the soil less than a foot away. Tom's brow creased. "Obviously, the driver didn't see it from the cab at the time, even with his running lights on."

Tom looked up over his shoulder towards the tractor and then scanned the field. It was probably two-thirds turned over. "When did he see it?"

"His dog found it," Eric said, grimacing.

Tom's eye rolled to the cab of the tractor seeing a dog with its snout pressed against the glass, watching events. He couldn't be sure but it looked like a Hungarian Vizsla. "Nice." Tom stood, looking around and once again catching the eye of the driver. He turned to Eric. "The medical examiner?"

"Fiona is on her way," Eric said. "I spoke to her this morning. I think she was about as happy to get the call as you were."

"That's okay. I was up anyway," Tom said.

"Were you?"

Tom smiled and shook his head. "No, Eric." He lowered his voice. "How did it go last night, after you left?"

Eric couldn't refrain from displaying his obvious delight as his face split a broad grin. "She said yes!"

"I'm pleased for you, Eric. Congratulations." Tom stepped away, clapping Eric on the upper arm as he passed, heading for the man who discovered the bones. "When did you say Fiona will arrive?"

"Any minute."

On cue, another car pulled up in front of the gate. Tom recognised Dr Fiona Williams' silver Discovery. Leaving Eric to fill her in, he crossed to where the constable was taking down the farmer's statement. She broke off as he approached, introducing Tom.

"DI Janssen, this is James Green. He was working the field overnight and it was his dog who alerted him to the whereabouts of the remains."

Tom acknowledged the man and looked up at the dog who registered his interest by barking at them.

"Calm down, Cogey!" Green shouted and the dog was silenced but still pressed its nose against the glass. "Sorry about that, Inspector. You can't get him out of the cab when I'm in it but he doesn't do well cooped up."

"Is this your field?" Tom asked.

"Tenanted, but yes. It's been mainly used for livestock these past years but we're rotating things a bit which will see us planting this year. A lot of rain is forecast for the end of the week and I was getting ahead."

"When will you plant seed?"

"Next couple of weeks. All this grass will get turned over, put it below the surface and give it a chance to decompose before sowing." He looked beyond Tom to where Eric was watching Dr Williams begin her inspection. "I guess that won't be happening anytime soon, will it?"

Tom followed his gaze. "Once we know what we're dealing with we'll have a better idea of how long it will be roped off."

"Do you think it's more likely than not to be Roman?"

Tom found his curiosity piqued, looking around. "Roman?"

"Yeah, this field is the site of the old Branodunum Fort," Green said. Tom was surprised he'd not realised this was where they were. Green looked around. "Not that you'd know to look at it."

Tom recalled there was just a metal sign at the entrance to the field, precious little to denote the archaeological interest in the site.

"Do you think it might be then, ancient I mean?"

"Too early to say," Tom replied. The last thing he wanted was to initiate a rumour mill.

"They say weird things go on around here."

"Such as?"

Green shrugged. "Well, there's been sightings and the like... apparitions... that type of thing. Strange goings-on."

"You've seen them?" Tom tried very hard to keep the incredulity out of his tone.

"Well, no. Not me personally... but people talk."

"We'll bear it in mind."

Tom headed back over to stand beside Eric. Dr Williams looked up from where she was knelt examining the femur.

"Good morning, Tom."

"Hi, Fiona. Early thoughts?"

"Well, it's human."

"Medical school served you well."

She winked at him.

"Can you date it with the eye?" Tom asked. "We're on an archaeological site here."

"Roman?" she asked and Tom nodded.

"You know your local history."

She laughed. "I saw the sign when I parked the car, it reminded me. Fifteen-hundred years old? I doubt it very much, just from the depth of the remains alone." She thought about it momentarily, her brow furrowing in concentration. "It would be interesting to know how close to the surface the Roman layer was when previously excavated. I wouldn't rule it out but there's no real way of telling with the naked eye. We will have to have the lab analysis of the bone and the surrounding organic matter to be sure. Speaking of which, I do hope there's more than a skull and a partial femur to work with?"

"Male or female, Fiona? Any idea of the age?"

Fiona Williams tutted at him and he smiled. "I'm a forensic medical examiner not Mystic Meg. I might be able to hazard a guess once your CSI team clear away most of the surrounding material. Judging from what's already visible I would expect to see further significant damage to the crown of the skull, possibly down to your man's plough blades," she said, pointing towards the tractor. She cast an eye along the furrow. "The rest of the skeleton might take some finding if it's equally been chewed up and distributed nearby."

"Forensics are on their way," Eric said.

Dr Williams scanned the earth at her feet, taking in the partially revealed skull. "If we aren't looking to bring Time Team onto site, I would say the skeleton has been in the ground for quite some time. It is fully skeletonised, there's no organic tissue on show which indicates it's been underground for a number of years."

"That's what I was thinking," Tom said, drawing a deep breath.

"Better dust off your missing persons' files, Thomas."

He nodded slowly, glancing at Eric. "Once CSI have the site squared away, you can make a start gathering those files together. Start with locals who were reported missing from three years ago and work backwards. There won't be too many. I doubt this case will be recent, probably from much further back, but let's be diligent. Once we know more about the remains then we can start to narrow the time frame down."

"Will do," Eric said, making a note in his pocketbook.

"I'm confident we can already narrow it down with regard to the victim's age," Dr Williams said. "I'm just looking at the wear on the head of the femur and the overall condition of the greater and lesser trochanter. I'm not seeing any evidence of osteo or rheumatoid arthritis. I reckon you can rule out anyone in the older age bracket. This person was much, much younger."

"What about the break in the body of the bone, Fiona?"

She cast another eye over the scene, her expression a picture of concentration. "Looks later to me. I doubt they went into the ground like this. There's every chance this isn't the first time the remains have been disturbed by a plough. Only this time something has come to the surface. Purely speculative on my part, mind you."

"Duly noted," Tom said moving closer to examine the skull.

The call of crows circling overhead made him look up. Attracted to the freshly ploughed soil they were still wary of the human presence. They came down in the outer reaches of the field, well away from where they were. A white van pulled up at the gate signalling the arrival of the forensic technicians. Tom was hopeful they would soon have more to work with.

CHAPTER THREE

It took the bulk of the day for the team to painstakingly excavate the soil from around the exposed remains and uncover more of the skeleton. By early evening, a four-metre square section of the south-eastern area of the field had been roped off, and the heat of the day replaced with a warm, sticky humidity. The team, clad head to toe in their white coveralls were looking forward to some respite from the environment. They'd worked methodically, carefully removing thin layers at a time and gradually revealing the secrets long hidden from prying eyes. Tom Janssen remained present throughout the day, only sending Eric back to the station to begin compiling a list of potential names.

A small group of onlookers waited patiently at the edge of the field, curious as to what was going on. The numbers had risen and fallen periodically throughout the day as word spread locally. A local journalist had already been on the phone requesting details, details that were still scant at best. Tom was about to call Tamara, his DCI, and give her an update when Fiona Williams beckoned him over. Slipping the mobile into his pocket, he crossed to join her.

"Have you made progress?"

"We have," she said, inviting him to step within the cordon.

Initially they had set up a tent to cover them whilst they worked but by early afternoon, they knew this would no longer be sufficient. "We needed to widen the search area in order to find the rest of the skeleton," Fiona said, stepping down due to the sheer volume of earth they had shifted. Tom followed. "But we're confident we've done so."

"Is it complete?" Tom asked, taking in the scene. Up until now he'd been content to stay out of the way and allow the team to do their work, conscious that his presence may only hamper proceedings.

"I should say so," Fiona replied, frowning. "It's always possible that we are missing something but as near as possible, I am confident."

"What can you tell me?"

Tom scanned the ground. There were numerous numbered crime scene markers denoting where parts of the remains were found, each was made from moulded plastic, yellow and with black type. Aside from the skull and the femur, that were visible from the surface, the remainder of the skeleton was broadly together. However, it was not laid out in the form of a burial, Roman, medieval or even modern. The bones were assembled awkwardly. Fiona read Tom's expression as he assessed the finds.

"I would say the body was dropped into a hole, head or legs first I couldn't say for certain, but she was unceremoniously deposited."

"She?" Tom asked. "You're sure it's female?"

Fiona tilted her head off to one side. "Not for certain, no, not until the bones can be reassembled in the lab but that's my initial reaction to what we can see. Look here," she said, stepping forward and lowering herself to her haunches. Tom did likewise. She indicated to what was clearly, even to a lay man, the bones of the pelvic area. "You can see the flared ilium."

Tom raised an eyebrow in her direction.

"Sorry, the hip bone." Tom nodded. "In the female it is more rounded. Couple that with the wider angle of the pubic arch," she said, charting the angle with the tip of her pen, "and I think it is likely to be female. Running an eye over the vertebral column – just a cursory measurement, so please don't quote me just yet – I think your victim is probably not much taller than five-foot-four or five at the most. I know we grow our men, those born and bred in Norfolk for generations, on the shorter side, but even so..."

"Likely to be a woman," Tom said, finishing the thought.

Dr Williams agreed. "And I would speculate that she wasn't very old. Matured, certainly, so we are not talking about a child but a young woman, perhaps late teens to late twenties. I'm not seeing any of the shotgun pellet-sized pockmarks lining the inside of the pelvic bone caused by the tearing of the ligaments indicating—"

"That she has given birth," Tom said. Fiona nodded. The thought of her age perturbed him. A child disappearing provokes substantial interest but once a missing person reaches adulthood it becomes far easier for them to drop off the radar without raising many questions, depending on the circumstances. Those people who have careers, expanded contacts in the area, spouses or children of their own are noticeably missed whereas people without those ties can easily vanish, and sometimes people barely bat an eye.

"Any indication of trauma?"

"Potential causes of death? No. At least nothing obvious."

"What about the broken leg?" Tom glanced back towards the road but his view was obscured by a line of wind breaks staked into the ground at the edge of the dig site to shield their finds from the onlookers. "I'm thinking of the potential for an accident on the road there, and someone panicking and dumping the body here?"

Dr Williams shook her head. "We located the patella end to the broken femur but I think that was a break that happened long after death, so more likely a result of the ploughing as opposed to the point of death – a collision with a car or something. No visible injury to the skull either, aside from the recent damage done by the plough's blade, or to any of the other bones as far as I can tell. Once the remains are catalogued and photographed on site, we'll bag them up and transport them back to pathology and x-ray them. If there are any abrasions, scrapes or similar that could be the result of a knife blade or another weapon, that's when we will find them. There is more to see though," she said, gesturing for him to move to his right.

Tom did as requested and Fiona pointed to some remnants of fabric to be found beneath one of the hands and an arm.

"Clothing?" he asked.

"I would say so, yes. Much of what is here has degraded beyond use in terms of identifiable fashions, brand or retailer, probably due to the high volume of peat in this area. It retains water and rots the fabric, particularly organic fibres but we haven't found shoes, which I would expect to, seeing as they are often substantial enough to ensure long term preservation ahead of light-fitting garments for example. However, that's the least interesting of all that I wanted to show you. Look here, at the wrist." Tom moved closer. There was a braided cord looped around the forearm, perhaps only five millimetres thick with a circumference suggesting it must have been worn around the wrist. Despite being covered in mud, colour was visible beneath the grime. Tom could see braids coloured blue, yellow and green, all intertwined to form a colourful rope. All three met at one point where they were tied, leaving a loose mix of tassels hanging free.

"Just the one wrist?"

Fiona nodded. "Nothing on the other."

Tom frowned. "They don't look robust enough to be used as restraints."

"Agreed. Man-made fibres as well judging from the lack of decomposition. Coloured nylon strands braided together. Simple, cheap. Easy to mass produce, and definitely not Roman."

Tom scanned the area seeking more tell-tale clues as to how the victim came to be here.

"I sense you have more to tell me."

"You know me well," she said, pointing to his left.

Beneath what he thought was a shoulder blade he could see the unmistakable texture of black plastic. It was discoloured through a residue of dried mud and Tom wondered if their victim had been wearing some black PVC clothing, a skirt perhaps, but it didn't seem to be connected to the body with a layer of earth in between.

"Tarpaulin," Fiona said. "And that's definitely not branded Hadrian or otherwise."

"Used to wrap the body in prior to transportation and dumping?"

She shook her head. "Doubtful. It stretches out beyond where we found the body, two metres in each direction. More than one sheet as well. A second overlaps the first but neither was found on top of any part of the skeleton."

"Sounds weird. Have you ever seen anything like it before?"

"No. I can't say I have. Certainly, a bit peculiar but clearly puts your victim in the modern era."

"Is it basic tarpaulin or are we talking that which is used in construction, say, as a damp-proof membrane?"

"It's thick, certainly much thicker than the grade used for domestic refuse sacks."

"Speaking of the modern era, can you hazard a guess as to how long she's been in the ground?"

Fiona thought on it. "Judging by the lack of soft tissue remains, I reckon you're looking at fifteen to twenty years. The lab techs can run a soil analysis on the surrounding organic material and give you a far more accurate figure to back up the dating of the bones, but I dare say I won't be far off."

"Okay, thanks."

Tom excused himself and walked away, leaving the team to catalogue the finds. Taking out his mobile, he called Tamara Greave. She answered immediately.

"Hi, Tom," she said. From the sound of her voice, he could tell she was not in the house, most likely she was in her garage tinkering with the car as she often did on her days off. "I guess you're not calling with good news."

"I'm afraid not. This is looking very suspicious to me. Fiona Williams has it as a young woman, put in the ground at some point in the last fifteen to twenty years."

"That covers a lot of ground," Tamara said.

"It does. No indication of foul play yet—"

"Other than having been concealed in a field... which doesn't speak to devoted love and affection."

"Agreed. I have Eric compiling a list of unresolved missing persons as we speak. We are probably looking at someone in their late teens or possibly through to their late twenties. We'll have to wait for the full autopsy assessment to be sure."

"Right. Anything else?"

Tom turned to look back at the scene. The sun was low in the sky and a warm breeze drifted across him. "It would appear she was dropped into a hole, deep enough to keep her from being uncovered until now and I think that only happened through chance. No ID, handbag and scant clothing remains. No shoes either. All of which suggests to me she was killed elsewhere and brought here. You could slip in here without anyone seeing you. It's a small village, easy terrain."

"Local?"

Tom thought on it, eyeing the perimeter of the field. "Not necessarily. The location is readily accessible to anyone passing through. There is another thing I've yet to get my head around."

"What's that?"

"I'm not sure of the significance. Let me think on it," he said, turning his mind to the black plastic sheets found beneath the body. It seemed out of place, odd, and yet there must be a reason.

"Okay. I'll give Cassie a call and meet you in ops."

"Yep. See you soon," Tom said, hanging up. He touched the mobile to his lips, looking back at the crime scene technicians hard at work, the scene lit up by irregular flashes of their cameras. "Let's find out who you are," he whispered.

CHAPTER FOUR

ENTERING THE OPS ROOM, Tom found Eric standing before a white board adding information. He knew the team were coming in and had made a start on setting up necessary equipment. The detective constable didn't hear Tom's arrival and was startled as he came to stand behind him, reading the first name, underlined, at the head of the board.

"Claudia?" Tom asked.

Eric took a breath, stepping to one side.

"I thought Jane Doe was too boring... and seeing as she was discovered at the Branodunum site..." Eric said, looking sheepish. "I can change—"

"No, don't worry. I like it."

Eric smiled.

"But she's not Roman. Fiona thinks we have a time frame of fifteen to twenty years," Tom said. Eric's face dropped. He was disappointed. "But she's still dead and needs a name. And we also need to find out why she's buried there."

"Yes, of course... Sorry," Eric said, stumbling over his words. "It's just, I sort of hoped Fiona Williams was wrong. I like history, you know. I thought it was exciting."

"Still is, only in a different way," Tom said. "How did you get on with compiling the list?"

"Four possibles," Eric said, gathering a sheet of paper from his desk and passing it across to Tom who accepted it.

Tamara and Cassie entered ops together, Tamara making a beeline for them while Cassie went straight to the coffee machine – a recent addition to the ops room they were all grateful for. Both Tom and Eric acknowledged them, and Tom indicated for Eric to continue. He turned back to the white board where he was entering the details of the missing persons. Only two names had been added so far.

"I started with the local missing persons who were in the age bracket Dr Williams defined – late teens through to thirty –and that gave me four," Eric said. "There are more but the others are likely either older and not particularly close to here or men, which I think we are ruling out?" He looked at Tom who nodded. "If we strike a blank with these four, then we can return to those names later."

"Can you give us the headlines on the four please, Eric?" Tamara said, perching herself on the edge of a desk. Cassie came over, passing a cup of steaming black coffee to Tamara and pulling out a chair for herself. Eric looked at the sheet in Tom's hand and he passed it over. Eric smiled his thanks.

"I'll start with the furthest back, which is Tina Farrow. She was nineteen, local girl, went missing in 2001," Eric said, reading from his notes. Tina wasn't up on the board yet. "She had a fractious relationship with her parents, a bit of a chequered upbringing. Flitted from job to job, all casual work and was prone to pulling a disappearing act every once in a while. No evidence to suggest anything untoward happened to her at the time."

"Who reported her missing?" Tamara asked, reaching for her coffee cup.

"Her sister," Eric said, glancing down at his notes. "Angela Farrow."

"Not the parents?" Tom asked, surprised.

Eric shook his head.

"Next up, Marta Kowalska. Polish national, aged twenty-six, moved to the UK in the late nineties and eventually settled in Hunstanton," Eric said. "She was reported missing in 2006 by her partner, Pavel."

"Investigated at the time?" Tom asked.

"Yes. Nothing was considered out of place. The couple had few friends, having not been in the area for very long. She worked in one of the local supermarkets and he was a mechanic. Both were well regarded by their employers and liked by their colleagues."

"And the boyfriend, Pavel, where is he now?" Cassie asked, before sipping at her drink.

"Still local. On the electoral roll, at least," Eric said. "No arrests or convictions."

"We'll need to have a word with him," Tom said. "The other two?"

Eric pointed to the white board where two names were already added: Sophie Reading and Harriet Croix.

"Both of these can potentially be ruled out because they went missing in the last decade, so don't necessarily fit the timeline."

"But they do fit the age profile and location," Tom said.

Eric nodded.

"We need to follow up on each possible, contact the relatives and see if anything uncovered can point towards them. What happened to Sophie and–?" Tamara asked.

"Harriet," Eric said. "Sophie was twenty-eight when she went missing. She was already estranged from her family and was known to us."

"What for?" Tom asked.

"Petty crime: shop lifting; that type of thing. The file implies she was a known drug user stealing to feed her habit, spent time in an addiction clinic and was on the methadone register."

Tom stepped forward, folding his arms across his chest and scanning the board. Pointing to Cassie, he said, "Look up her old haunts, known associates and see if any of them are still on our radar."

Cassie made a note.

"Users tend to have unreliable memories," she said without looking up.

"Do the best you can," Tom said. "What about the last?"

"Harriet Croix," Eric said. "Twenty years old, working as an au pair for a family living just outside Holt. She's a dual national, French and British. She had been in the country for two years, living and working for the family in the eighteen months prior to her disappearance. Seemingly upped and left one day without warning. The family returned from a long weekend away to find everything cleaned out of her room, all her clothes and belongings were gone. No one's heard from her since."

"Family?" Tamara asked.

"Erm..." Eric looked down, scanning through his notes. "Parents living in the south of France, sister in London, at the time of her disappearance. Not sure where they are now."

Tom gave Eric an appreciative nod and drew breath.

"Okay," he said, turning back to face them, "we will be able to extract DNA from the remains and if we can obtain samples from family members then we will be able to identify our victim. What I don't want to do is offer anyone false hope that we've found their loved ones. To offer them closure and then immediately dash their chances a few days later would be cruel. Eric, Cassie, I want the two of you to make contact with the next of kin, or closest family member you can track down if the registered next of kin have moved on and try and find a link to what we've found at the Branodunum site. Tread lightly, note it as a follow-up call if you like. Reassure them their relative's case is still very much active. If you turn up anything useful to match the missing person then we can follow it up with a personal visit. While the two of you are making headway with them, I'll look into the choice of the burial site."

Tamara met his eye as Eric and Cassie went to their desks to begin their unenviable task: contacting families and reopening old wounds that may not have healed, but the passage of time could harden emotions. A telephone call out of the blue could undo all of that in seconds.

"You think it is particularly significant?" Tamara asked.

Tom scratched absently at his cheek. "It could be an abstract place to dispose of a body but... something came over me when I was out there... I don't know. Maybe it was the isolation, a *good* choice by the killer. After all you'd have to be really paying attention to see something going on out there. It could be that simple but, then again, there might be more to it. It just struck me as an odd location. There are plenty of hollows, or ponds around these parts that are virtually inaccessible. If you stashed a body there, they would be unlikely to be found—"

"You're assuming the killer is local. From what I can see on the map it is just off the through road. Anyone passing could have seen it as a decent dump site, so as not to run the risk of carrying the body further. Statistically, killers try to minimise the length of time they spend with the body in tow, thereby minimising their chances of being caught with it," Tamara countered. "And you're also assuming that we are dealing with a murder, while you're at it."

"Murder or not, someone disposed of a body for some reason. It's a historical site, one likely to be revisited. A body is likely to be discovered, so it's not a clever choice in my opinion."

Tamara thought about it for a moment, looking over at Cassie and Eric on their phones.

"You make a good point. Perhaps the killer didn't realise. Any idea when the site was last excavated? Presumably, it has been previously."

"Next on my list," Tom said. "It's a National Trust managed site, so you'd need to apply for licences to dig there. Should be easy enough to find out when the site was last dug."

Their attention was drawn by Eric raising a hand and snapping his fingers enthusiastically, followed by his beckoning them over to his desk. He was trying to dampen his excitement because he was still on the phone but it was clear he had something. Cassie hung up on her own call and pushed off her desk with her feet, allowing her chair, on casters, to slide towards Eric. Tom and Tamara came to stand beside his desk.

"And where would she have got the wristlet from?" Eric asked. "Can you be sure?" He listened to the reply, looking up at Tom and then Tamara and nodding furiously. "I see ... right, yes. Listen, I know this is short notice but I think we need to come and see you, discuss it further so to speak. Would that be okay?" He nodded again to his silent audience. "Today, preferably. Can you do that? Great ... can you confirm your address for me."

Moments later Eric thanked the recipient and hung up. Slowly putting the receiver down, he turned to the expectant team and grinned.

"If you don't say something soon, I'm going to brain you, Eric," Tamara said, gently tapping the back of his head.

Eric brushed her hand away, still smiling. "The braided cord on the wrist. She thinks it was something purchased, or handed out, at a music festival the week before her disappearance. If she's right then we may well have a name for Claudia."

"Who?" Cassie asked.

Tom waved away the question. "Who might it be?"

"Tina Farrow," Eric said, glancing at the phone. "That was her sister, Angela, I was chatting to. She says Tina came back from a festival wearing something similar a few days before she went missing. She described it perfectly; said her sister was buzzing from the experience for days."

"And Tina went missing when did you say?"

"2001," Eric said. "It was late summer, at the end of August to be precise. The telephone number I had for the parents rang out. Angela says both parents moved house when they split, getting divorced five years back. But her mobile, Angela's, was on the file, so I tried her. She still lives nearby in Hunstanton."

"Good work, Eric," Tom said. "And she's happy for us to drop by today?"

He nodded. "Yes, she has the day off work, so she's home. We can call in whenever we like. I got the impression she was keen for us to do so."

"Come on then. You and I can head over there. Make sure you've got a DNA sample kit, then we'll have something for pathology to compare with."

Tom looked at Tamara for confirmation and she agreed. Tom went back to his desk to retrieve his wallet, mobile and keys. Cassie patted Eric on the shoulder as Tamara moved away.

"Nice one, Eric," Cassie said. He grinned. She leaned in closer so only the two of them could hear. "Listen, I gather I dropped you in it last night. I'm really sorry if I'd known you were planning—"

"It's fine." He held up a hand to stop her apology. "I was working myself up about it and decided the best thing was just to ask, so I did."

"You did?" Cassie said, failing to hide her surprise. Eric frowned.

"Yes, I did!"

"And ... what did she say?"

"Yes, of course," he said, although his attempt to make it sound like the answer was a foregone conclusion didn't have the confidence he desired. Cassie squeezed his shoulder.

"Pleased for you, little man."

She moved away just in time to avoid his backhanded swipe.

"When you're all grown up your arm might reach further," she said over her shoulder with a grin, walking away. Eric laughed, seeing both Tom and Tamara were amused by the exchange.

"Ready?" Tom asked him.

"Absolutely."

CHAPTER FIVE

HAVING RUNG the bell for a third time, Tom stepped back and looked up at the windows of the flat above the shop. There were no window coverings to obscure the interior but more importantly no indication of anyone present. He looked at Eric inquisitively.

"Are you sure she said she would be home?"

"I'm certain," Eric said anxiously. "Maybe she's just popped out for a minute?"

Tom nodded, looking around. Angela Farrow's flat was located above one of the shops in Hunstanton's small high street, accessed from the rear. They were standing in a tight parking area behind the row of shops, little more than a few spaces for residents and only if they parked their vehicles at odd angles to make them fit. The outer reaches of the town boasted wide streets with grand three-storey Victorian houses or apartment buildings overlooking the sea but, here, the modernity of twenty-first century life was squeezed into a nineteenth-century footprint. The high street consisted of a variety of cafés and restaurants, both national franchises and independents owned and run by locals, all largely geared towards the tourists who flocked to the seaside town every year.

They didn't have long to wait before a figure rounded the corner heading in their direction clutching a plastic supermarket carrier bag awkwardly across her stomach. She hesitated when she caught sight of them, but resumed her approach, eyeing them warily. She was in her thirties, Tom guessed, but her hair was lank, tied back, and her face lined beyond her years.

"Angela Farrow?" Eric asked when she came close enough. She nodded, her eyes furtively glancing between the two of them. "We spoke on the phone. I'm DC Eric Collet." He indicated Tom. "And this is Detective Inspector Janssen."

Tom smiled and she returned it with one of her own, although hers was forced out of politeness.

"And you think you've found our Tina?"

Eric exchanged a glance with Tom who indicated for the constable to take the lead. After all, he had already broken the ice with her over the phone.

"That's what we are looking to determine." Angela's smile faded as quickly as it had formed, her expression turning fearful. "May we talk inside?"

"Erm ... my place is a bit of a mess." She looked at the entrance, as if she could see through the door. "Maybe we could take a walk?"

Eric and Tom agreed. Angela opened the door, just enough to put the carrier bag at the foot of the stairs leading up to her flat. The sound of glass bottles clinking together gave away the contents. She locked the door and glanced between the two of them once more.

"We can walk along the promenade if you like?"

They set off to their left in the direction they'd come. Once at the end of the alleyway, they turned right and walked towards the seafront. It was still busy. The summer season was coming to an end but tourist numbers were undiminished and the bars and restaurants were preparing for the evening footfall. The snack bars and ice cream parlours were shutting up for the day while the amusement arcades were experiencing their quiet spell as day trippers headed home. The promenade was busy as one would expect on a rather warm evening with dog walkers, joggers and those out for a stroll mingling as the tide gently rolled in against the sea wall. The shrieks of excitement and fear carried to them on the breeze from the nearby funfair, the neon lights would only get brighter once the sun went down.

"Can you describe the wrist band to me again?" Eric asked as they walked.

"Sure … vaguely though, it was years ago. It was multi-coloured, braided … don't ask me which colours, mind you."

"But you're sure Tina was wearing it when she went missing?"

Angela nodded. "She'd only just got back, wouldn't take it off. It was like a badge of honour for her or something. I wondered whether it would become like her necklace; something she would never take off."

"Necklace?"

"A silver chain with a heart pendant … a gift from our aunt. We both got one exactly the same," Angela said, reaching up and pulling the neckline of her blouse down so she could produce exactly what she was describing, holding it out for them to see. "It's nothing special … valuable, I mean. Aunt Sarah was our godmother. We liked her so much. She was everything our mother wasn't but I guess it's easier to be the fun aunty as opposed to the parent. This was a parting gift, sort of." Angela read Tom's enquiring look. "She died. Cancer. The same year Tina went missing."

"You said Tina wore the wrist band as a badge of honour?" Tom asked.

"Yeah. Mum and Dad went mental at her." She looked at Tom, a smile creeping across her face followed by a brief shake of the head, as if she was dismissing a memory. "She was never supposed to go."

"To the festival?" Tom asked.

"Yeah. Mum forbade it; said she was too young to go all that way by herself. Not that it stopped her." She grinned at Tom. "I think that's why she went. She wasn't that bothered if I remember right, but when Mum threw her weight around it only made Tina more determined to go."

"Your parents were quite strict?"

Angela shook her head. "Not so as you'd notice. Tina just liked winding them up. She seemed to take pleasure in it."

"Why?"

"No idea." Angela absently kicked out at a stone near her foot as they walked by. It bounced a couple of times before splashing into the water.

"Which festival did your sister go to?"

"Isle of Wight," she said, meeting Tom's eye.

"You didn't go with her? You're a similar age, aren't you?"

"Only eighteen months between us, yeah. Although, no one ever recognised us as sisters. Chalk and cheese, Dad used to say, in both looks and personality."

"You didn't get on?"

"It wasn't like that." She laughed without any real humour. "We got on okay. Festivals … being around thousands of other people who were all off their—" She shrugged. "Just not my type of thing."

"What can you tell us about that day, the day Tina went missing?"

Angela stopped, turning to face the sea with a faraway expression.

"She was still on a high from the festival, figuratively speaking, although Tina was never shy of getting a little *other-worldly* if you know what I mean?"

"She took recreational drugs?" Tom asked.

"Yes, often. Not that she had a problem; don't think that. She just liked dancing … being out till all times of the day and night, you know? You can do that with a few drinks in you but … but it's not the same."

"That day?" Tom asked.

She shook her head. "Not as far as I know. She was heading

out; it was Friday night after all. Mum had just given her a rocket; fallout from the whole festival thing. She'd upped and left for the previous weekend without telling anyone she was going. We all guessed, obviously. When she turned up five days later, still buzzing, literally, from the experience, Mum went mad."

"When you say *buzzing* you mean—"

"Off her tits, yeah." Angela smiled, running a hand through her dark shoulder-length hair and pushing her fringe to one side, tucking it behind her ear. "Mum was apoplectic. The day she came home wasn't too bad, I mean, you can't have a stand-up argument with someone on a high because they'll not take it in, will they? But you can imagine how badly it went when Tina was coming down ... not that Mum spared her in the least."

"Do you want a drink?" Tom asked, indicating the café on the promenade. It was still open. Tom gave Eric a note and sent him in to get them a tea and coffee along with whatever he wanted. Tom sat down with Angela on the sea wall. The crowd was thinning a little here and it seemed like a decent spot to sit and talk. "Did she go on a bit, your mum?"

"I'll say. Her and Tina were always going at it over something or other. Dad reckons the two of them were so alike and that's why they clashed." She smiled then, clearly a thought tickled her. "Not that he can talk. He had frequent run-ins with her, too, and she was nothing like him."

"About what?"

"The usual: lifestyle choices, boyfriends."

"Was she involved with anyone at the time?"

"Boyfriend? No. She wasn't into anything serious. That applied to relationships, jobs, college ... you name it." She shook her head, frowning. "You know, that was the strangest thing about Tina. She was smart, attractive, more than capable of doing anything she set her mind to but ..."

"But?"

She exhaled, her face a picture of concentration. "But she never applied herself to anything. Nothing constructive anyway.

Dropped out of college, drifted between jobs. Tina ... it was like she wasn't interested in taking anything seriously. If only she had then, whatever it was, I reckon she'd have been a success at it. She was that sort."

"You sound regretful."

Angela dropped her hands into her lap, her shoulders sagging. "If only I had a bit of that myself, maybe ..." She left the thought unfinished.

Eric returned with the drinks, handing them polystyrene cups hot to the touch and placing sachets of sugar on the wall between Angela and Tom. Tom thanked him, peeling off the lid and blowing on the steaming contents.

"You said she was heading out for the evening. Do you know where she was going?"

"Not at the time, no," Angela said, stirring two sugars into her tea with a disposable plastic stirrer. "But afterwards I found out she'd been at the pub; the one where she worked, you know?" Tom shook his head to infer he didn't. "The Crown Inn. She worked the odd shift there, more so when they were busy. Other times she worked casual shifts at the amusements; the ones at the old pier."

"But not that night?"

"No, not that night." Angela sipped at her tea. "Maybe if she had been working this might not have happened."

"Do you think it's her, then?" Tom asked.

"I wouldn't be surprised." She snorted a laugh, raising her eyebrows. "Just as I wouldn't be surprised if she walked into my place tomorrow, sat down and cracked open a bottle of prosecco as if the last twenty years hadn't happened!" She met Tom's eye. He was wondering what to make of Tina's description. "Please don't get me wrong, Inspector. I love my sister and miss her dearly ... but she did what she wanted to do regardless of what me or Mum and Dad wanted her to do. The Isle of Wight wasn't the first. She'd been pulling that sort of stunt since she was fourteen or fifteen if not younger."

"Doing what?" Tom was sure to keep his tone neutral and not judgemental, now finding his coffee at a drinkable temperature.

She shrugged. "Taking off ... with God knows who to wherever she damn well pleased. Tina didn't seem to care what it put us through ... me, Mum and Dad. It was always about her. Hell, I only went to your lot after she'd been gone a week. After Mum laid into her for a couple of days, we all figured she'd just taken off for a bit until the heat died off."

"Why didn't either of your parents call us?"

Angela rolled her lower lip beneath her top. For a second he wondered if she was going to answer.

"I don't know, to be honest. I guess they thought it was just Tina being Tina, you know? She'd turn up when she wanted to. She always did."

"But you know she went to the Crown that Friday night?"

"Yeah. I knew some of the regulars back then, and they saw her there during the evening. She was the life and soul apparently, same as always."

"Nothing struck you as unusual about what they said or how she behaved?"

Angela shook her head. "No one said so and, anyway, Tina was Tina."

"That's the second time you said that. How do you mean?"

"As lovely as she was ..." Angela tilted her head to one side thoughtfully. Tom read anguish in her expression, understanding why she looked far older than her years. "She was unpredictable. No one ever knew what was going on in Tina's head." She sighed then took a sip of tea. "Looking back, I've often thought that was just how she wanted it."

Tom allowed the silence to carry for a moment. A young family walked past heading towards the funfair. Two sisters were hand in hand, a couple of metres ahead of their parents who called them back, possibly fearful they'd run off into the funfair without them, fearful of losing them in the crowd.

"And your parents ... they left the area?" Tom asked once the family were out of earshot and they were alone again.

"Mum is still here. She has a place up at Redgates, on the far edge of town?" She looked at Tom to see if he knew where she meant and he nodded. "Dad lives down in Snettisham now, so he's not far." She drew breath, sitting forward and holding her cup in her lap with both hands. She stared at it as if it held answers. "It all got too much for them." She looked at Tom and then Eric, who avoided the eye contact. Angela Farrow was baring her innermost now. "The gossip. The finger pointing. This is a small town. Not much goes on around here ... and Tina disappearing the way she did left people with something to talk about. Not that anyone knew anything, not really. I mean," she turned to face Tom, "you lot looked into it, didn't find anything, did you?" Tom shook his head. There was an edge to her tone now, not accusatory but bitter. "Not that it stopped people making stuff up. Sometimes it would get back to me ... to us ... what people were saying." She looked skyward, her eye drawn by the gulls calling overhead. "It just got too much, that's all."

"Eric here," Tom said, gesturing towards him with his forefinger, "has a test kit back in the car. Would it be possible for you to give us a sample of your DNA? It is so we can compare it to ..." he stopped short as she looked up at him, her eyes full of hope and trepidation, "to the remains we have found."

She held his eye with her gaze, as if she were analysing him.

"You asked me before but do *you* really think it's her?"

He couldn't say with any certainty, although he was sure they'd know one way or another very soon.

"It is a distinct possibility but I wouldn't like to offer you false hope." She accepted the statement with a weak smile. "Could you walk back with Eric and he can take the sample? It won't take a minute to do."

Tom watched the departing forms of Eric and Angela as they walked away from him. He put his coffee down and rubbed at his eyes. There was something about Tina Farrow's story that resonated with him. They couldn't be sure until the DNA results came back but he had a hunch that they'd found a name for their victim, but he didn't feel any closer to understanding how she came to be in the ground. Making a mental note to speak directly with the investigating officer who originally looked into Tina's disappearance, he also found his curiosity piqued by the parents. His mobile rang; it was Alice.

"Hey. How're things?"

"Hi. Okay ... but don't expect me home any time soon."

"We'll eat without you. Will you be home before Saffy goes to bed?"

"Doubtful. Can you give her a hug from me and tell her I'll look in on her when I get in."

"Will do. Don't work too hard, okay? Love you."

Tom put the phone back into his pocket, his thoughts returning to the Farrow household. As much as Tina had form for pulling a regular disappearing act, he was certain, if it was his daughter, that he wouldn't wait five days before contacting the police and certainly wouldn't leave it to a sibling to do so. Furthermore, teenagers could play up, that was almost universal, but usually if someone's behaviour was that erratic then there would normally be a root cause. What else was going on in that household prior to Tina's disappearance?

CHAPTER SIX

TAMARA GREAVE KNOCKED on the door out of courtesy, but didn't wait to be bidden entry, holding it open for Tom following closely behind her. Dr Timothy Paxton was on the other side of the room, sitting at his desk. He glanced over his shoulder at the two detectives and smiled a greeting.

"You're keen. That didn't take you long."

"Detective Foresight here," she pointed to Tom, who smiled, "is inclined to believe we know who she is but without more detail to work with we're largely just shuffling old case files around," Tamara said, meeting Dr Paxton halfway as he directed them to the stainless-steel slab in the centre of the room. Although the interior climate was always maintained at room temperature, today it felt much cooler, probably down to the heat and humidity outside. A storm front was moving towards them and thunderstorms were forecast to increase in frequency in the coming days.

"Well, perhaps I can assist in some part. I worked through the night on her for you but we're going to have to wait on test results," Paxton said. "I'll come to that after I walk you through what we've been able to determine thus far."

Tom and Tamara came to stand beside the slab, facing Dr Paxton, both cast an eye over the skeletal remains painstakingly reconstructed since being unearthed the previous day. The doctor looked tired, unsurprisingly, but he remained bright-eyed and focussed.

"The first thoughts of Fiona's yesterday appear to have been borne out. We have a young woman, matured, but I would lean towards late teens or early twenties. I'll reaffirm that she hadn't given birth to a child. She was five-foot-four tall and I imagine her to be of slight build, judging by the tell-tale giveaways; wear on joints, the bone density and so forth."

Tamara visually recreated the figure in her mind. She was petite and with a slight build; would probably have weighed between six and seven stone, very little for a grown adult. "Any indication of the cause of death?"

"There are no obvious breaks or signs of blunt-force trauma to the bones, other than what we can judge to be resulting from the plough blades, however, yes, I can hazard a pretty good guess." Paxton drew their attention to the vertebrae of the spinal column where they met the base of the skull. Both Tamara and Tom leaned in to where he pointed with the tip of his pen. The two exchanged glances and the pathologist smiled. "Yes, it isn't obvious, even with me having cleaned away the soil. I only saw it myself with the help of the x-rays; hairline fractures to the vertebra."

"Caused by?"

"Not significant enough to be the result of an accident; being hit by a car for example." He looked at Tom who nodded. "In my opinion they were caused by a prolonged compression of the surrounding tissue—"

"Strangled?" Tamara asked.

"I believe so."

Tom sighed. "To break the neck would take some strength. It's one thing to choke someone to death restricting their oxygen flow but the neck muscles are strong."

"You're right," Paxton said. "The neck muscles push back. It takes time to manually strangle a person, sometimes anywhere from ten to fifteen minutes before the victim actually succumbs, passes out and expires. To cause fractures like this you would potentially be looking at a fall, not necessarily from height, or more likely, which is my personal opinion, she was strangled by way of an arm bracing her in a headlock." He demonstrated, placing his free hand in the crook of his arm and aggressively screwing his face up. "Choked the life out of the poor thing," he said, dropping his arms to his sides. "I know there *is* a great deal of damage to the top of the skull but, as I said, we can put that down to the ploughing. The damage is far too recent to have been done at the time of death. The same can be said with the damaged femur."

"And what can you tell us about the time of death?" Tamara asked. "How long was she in the ground?"

"Tough to say with any accuracy before we get the tests back." Paxton scanned the skeleton, thinking hard. "The fact that almost all of the organic tissue has gone is indicative of a minimum of fifteen years, possibly longer. We did find hair in the soil and we will look to match that to the skeleton with a DNA test just to be sure."

"Hair colour?" Tom asked.

"Brunette. Light brown to be clearer. The DNA sampling will be back tomorrow along with the comparison to the sample you provided last night. Does the description match your victim?"

"So far, yes," Tom said, frowning.

"What of the testing you mentioned before?" Tamara asked. "Is that just the DNA?"

Paxton shook his head. "The forensic team took samples of the soil with a view to helping establish an accurate date as to when she was buried." His expression became fixed, his eyes taking on a faraway look. "You'll recall Fiona was surprised not to find the girl's shoes." Tom nodded. "I'm also surprised not to find remnants of any other material. Natural fibres will degrade over time but I would still expect to find some trace of the victim's clothing in and around the remains, particularly with the preva-lence of man-made fabrics these days. Curious. It opens up other avenues for you I should imagine. Anyway, it was just a thought that you might be interested in."

"That's great, Doctor," Tom said. "Thank you."

They walked out and headed towards the car park, both deep in thought. The humidity struck them as they stepped outside: oppressive with almost no breeze to offer respite and it was still early. Tom blew out his cheeks.

"This storm front can't come soon enough," he said.

"True. A guy like you is always going to struggle in this."

He looked at her, unsure of her meaning. She smiled.

"You have a lot more frame to carry around than the rest of us," she said. "What do you make of the manner in which we found her? Lack of clothing and wounds, I mean."

"I don't think she was killed in that field, that's for sure."

Tamara agreed. If she had been the victim of an attack, even a surprise one in which she'd been unable to try and defend herself, there would be more to be found at the burial site. Had the assault offered a sexual element to it then they would also expect to find evidence; clothing perhaps, ripped or torn during the attack and then either discarded or ignored. Even if the attack was not sexual in nature, a premeditated murder with an, as yet unknown motive, or an opportunistic killer on the prowl, the lack of the basics, shoes or personal effects, was mystifying unless she was stripped of everything before burial. This was strongly indicative of her being moved to this location after the event.

"Stripped before disposal," she said unlocking the car. She hesitated, not wanting to get in straight away and opened the door wide to allow the heat to dissipate. The sun was hazy, behind thick cloud, only making the heat seem even more unfair. Tom did the same with his door, leaning against the car with his elbows on the roof. "Attacked in her home do you think?"

"That's what I was wondering. Summer's day." He looked around, indicating the surroundings with a nod. "If it was anything like today then she wouldn't be wearing much at home.

It would also explain the lack of personal effects and even the shoes."

"If it happened at home, then a burglary is possible but," she contemplated the theory, "it's more likely to be a close friend or a relative. If Dr Paxton is right and strength was required, then we're looking at the father or maybe a boyfriend."

"If it's Tina Farrow then there wasn't a boyfriend. No one regular anyway, according to the sister."

"I've seen the photos of Tina from back in the day," Tamara said with a sideways grin, "and if you're going to try and tell me she didn't generate interest from the men she came into contact with then I may as well turn in my warrant card now."

"*If* it's Tina Farrow," Tom said, raising his eyebrows. "Even if it isn't her, the facts are there. She was killed elsewhere, stripped of anything she was wearing or carrying and dumped in the corner of that field. Perhaps we're wrong in thinking she didn't put up a fight? Just because she didn't exhibit defensive wounds, she still could have fought back but it was too late. And we've no way of knowing if she was sexually assaulted."

Tamara thought about it. "A consensual encounter that took a turn for the worse?" Tom inclined his head to confirm that was his thinking too. "That's possible. A slight figure, already under the weight of someone much larger and stronger ... if it went bad, she wouldn't be able to do much about it."

"But there could have been superficial scratches, cuts, possibly even blood. Add that to any semen residue or sperm left on her clothing and there's a trail for us to follow *if* the body is discovered quickly. Perhaps the killer was forensically aware, which is why he stripped her and then chose his dump site well."

Tamara shook her head. "That's sinister. Have you ever heard of a newbie managing to minimise forensic trace evidence and pick an almost perfect drop location first time out?"

"Some people are lucky, but no, I've never come across one. Usually they're hopelessly inept, especially the ones who think they're really clever."

"Remind me," Tamara said, "what did scenes of crime make of the plastic found beneath the body?"

Tom shrugged. "Medium-grade plastic sheeting. That size is mainly used in agricultural settings. Nothing special about it. Why?"

"What's it doing there?"

"Well, it wasn't used to wrap the body which was my first thought; way too large and there was a lot of soil between it and the skeleton suggesting that they went into the ground at different times. Besides, the plastic sheet was a metre and a half below the surface but forensics think the body went into the ground curled up or, at least, dropped into a hole some distance above it, right?"

"Yes, which is why forensics don't see it as related to the murder. The grave wasn't exactly shallow but nowhere near as deep as the plastic. Natural movement of the earth shifted the location of the skeleton as the connective tissue decomposed which was why the skull and femur were able to come in contact with the plough whereas the remainder of the skeleton lay largely undisturbed."

She put her palms together and brought the tips of her fingers up to meet her lips. Shaking her head, she gestured for them to get in the car.

"Has to be a reason," she muttered.

Starting the car, she saw Tom glance across as she reached for the air con.

"I want to speak to the investigating officer who looked into Tina Farrow's disappearance," he said, staring at a nondescript point in the distance. "I've looked him up. He's still local."

She watched him with a quizzical expression as he turned to her. "You think he missed something?"

"Maybe," he said, looking away and shrugging. "Ah ... probably not but there's only so much you can get from a missing person report. He must have spoken to people, had a feeling about someone. We always do, right?"

"Okay. Do it. We'll know soon enough if your gut instinct that it's Tina is right. In the meantime, Cassie is still running down the other possibilities. Marta Kowalska's partner hasn't turned up yet despite several visits to his house and workplace. He called in sick according to his boss but he's not answering his door to us if he's there. I'm not doubting your male intuition, Tom, but I'll push that line just as hard. I'll also have Eric look at the dump site in greater detail. The killer could have buried her in any number of places; Norfolk is one big field for crying out loud, so why there?"

"What with all the strange goings-on in the area over the years that James Green spoke of, maybe it was Boudicca's ghost?" Tom said, smiling.

Tamara sighed, slapping him in the arm with the back of her hand. "I've enough to deal with as it is without investigating the spirit realm as well, thank you very much!"

CHAPTER SEVEN

Tom cast an eye down the length of the train: six carriages, all painted in the split crimson and cream of the early British Railways rolling stock. Passengers mingled around the doors, waiting patiently for their opportunity to board. A burst of steam was released from the engine as it idled, waiting for the off. Within moments the waiting passengers were on and the doors slammed shut. The guard whistled, signalling to the driver that everyone was safely aboard and the train could begin its journey along the coast to Holt via Weybourne.

Finding himself alone on the platform, he watched as the train departed. The Poppy Line, as it was known, the last surviving part of the former Melton Constable to Cromer Beach branch line was a private enterprise maintaining the age of steam in the modern age, a wonderful throwback to days past. It had been a while since he'd taken a trip and he couldn't think why. Saffy would love the round trip along the coast, and he was quite sure Alice wouldn't be opposed to a trip on one of the first-class dining carriages. Casually looking around for a timetable board, he was momentarily distracted and missed the approach of another man.

"Sorry to keep you waiting but I'm free for a bit now."

Tom waved away the apology, taking the measure of the man

standing before him in Victorian station master garb. John Drew was tall, not quite as tall as Tom himself but above average with a large frame, arguably more down to middle-aged spread than muscle.

"That's okay. Thanks for agreeing to speak to me on such short notice."

Now it was Drew who waved away the gratitude. He was no longer serving, having retired several years ago, but police officers could hand back their warrant cards, less so the mindset.

"Happy to. It's the least I can do." He smiled but it didn't seem overly warm. "You said on the phone you're following up a missing person's case. Which one?"

"Tina Farrow," Tom said. He raised an eyebrow. "You remember her?"

Drew exhaled. "Yes, of course. Blimey." He took his cap off and ran a hand through his sweaty, thinning grey hair, before replacing it. "That's going back some ... must be fifteen, twenty years."

"2001, yes."

Drew fixed Tom with a stern eye. "Has she turned up?" Tom looked away, screwing up his nose in a noncommittal expression. "You must think she has otherwise you wouldn't be asking."

"Maybe." It was the best answer he could give, and a truthful one.

"Maybe." Drew's gaze narrowed but he didn't press it. He sighed, gesturing with an open hand for them to take a walk along the platform. "Standing still in this weather isn't a lot of fun. I know it's voluntary but sometimes I wish the uniform wasn't black and made from this material." Tom smiled sympathetically. "What is it you want to know?"

"Background," Tom said, walking at a gentle pace alongside him. Drew seemed to have a slight limp. "What did you make of her disappearance?"

"You've read my report?"

Tom looked across at him and nodded. "Of course. But there's only so much you can draw from that. I'm interested in what you thought, not necessarily just what you wrote."

Drew nodded, grinning. "Old school, eh? I didn't think that was allowed anymore."

"Don't believe everything you hear," Tom said, returning the smile. The two of them resumed their stroll. "Tina?"

"Tina Farrow ... an interesting case but not on the surface."

"How so?"

"Sister reported her missing after almost a week, as I recall. Nice girl, Angela. Complete opposite to that tearaway of a sister of hers."

"You knew Tina?"

"Ah ... not in any real sense of *knowing her* as such. I knew of a lot of the kids back then. I grew up in the town and it's not that big, you know? Before CID I was a uniform in Hunstanton and during the winter months everything goes quiet; there isn't a lot to do." Tom nodded, remembering his own teenage years in Sheringham along the coast. "Even if they're not up to much you still find yourself in and around the local kids; residents complaining about them hanging around the pier and the promenade, making a nuisance of themselves ... drinking, having fun. Do you remember being young?"

"Not that young, no." Tom looked down the line, the track disappearing as it turned inland and away from the sea.

"Wait until you get to my age, lad. It'll feel like you're living in a foreign country."

"Anyway, Tina and her mates used to be a bit rowdy from time to time. I'd take booze off them – if they went too far – but on the whole, nothing major."

"I understand she was prone to running off."

Drew shrugged. "From time to time, yes, but that was never reported to us. I had a word with social services at the time when I was investigating and they had her on their books previously. Obviously, she was nineteen by then, so her case was no longer open—"

"And what was their interest – social services?"

"Truancy from school ... as I said, sometimes she ran away but it was only ever for a day or two. Most likely staying at a boyfriend's place, someone her folks wouldn't have approved of I expect. I think uniform picked her up once when she was fourteen or fifteen having skipped school and was heading somewhere with a bag of booze."

"Heading where?"

Drew turned the corners of his mouth down and shrugged. "As I said, boyfriend, I imagine."

"There's no mention of a boyfriend in your report."

"No. She didn't have one as far as I could ascertain. If anything, she probably had several."

"Several?"

"Yep. Popular girl. Good looking, extrovert. By all accounts, she was a flirtatious one. Everybody said so – sibling, friends, work colleagues – but no one could name anyone she was involved with."

"Maybe she was just that: flirtatious."

Drew snorted a laugh. It was no doubt involuntary but Tom found himself irritated by it, nonetheless. The retired detective noticed.

"Look, don't get me wrong, I had the impression she was a nice enough girl but you're a DI, you've done enough laps of the track to trust your instincts. If it walks like a duck, quacks like a duck ..." he raised both eyebrows in a telling gesture, "then it's probably a duck!"

"Meaning?"

"She wasn't into commitment, at least didn't appear to be, but she liked the attention and made sure she got it."

Tom thought back to what Angela Farrow had told him; about Tina being able to achieve anything she set her mind to. Although this wasn't what he'd had in mind when she told him that.

"You think she was promiscuous? Involved in multiple relationships?"

"Maybe. Maybe not." Drew shrugged again. His nonchalance was grating.

"Then what *can* you tell me?"

Drew hesitated, turning to face Tom and stopping them as they neared the end of the platform. "Look, I can see what you're thinking. I'm retired but I'm not daft."

"What's that?"

"That I did some half-arse job investigating her disappearance … and you're here now having to pick up the pieces twenty years on because I couldn't be bothered. Am I right?"

Tom smiled. "I wouldn't go that far, but you're not helping me much—"

"Hah! You guys have it easy nowadays. Think back for a second: 2001, mobile phones were around but not commonplace with everyone. As far as we could tell, Tina never had one. That means no GPS locators built in, no smartphones with an Internet search history. No call records, text messages or contacts list to work through. There was no computer in the home, so no email." He fixed Tom with an indignant look. "A nineteen-year-old girl who flits between casual jobs, probably cash-in-hand a lot of the time, so no records to help there either. A load of friends, but none of whom seemed to know if she was seeing anyone or not, so no one to confide in with her deepest, darkest secrets. Then you look at the parents: a controlling mother who seemed more put out at the inconvenience her daughter was causing rather than her actual disappearance and a … a father …"

"A father who? Go on."

"A father who didn't seem to give a toss either way!" Drew took a deep breath. "Angela was the only one who seemed genuinely bothered. I mean, yes, her friends did too but everyone …" He looked skyward, shaking his head, apparently reluctant to finish the comment. Tom waited, refusing to fill the silence in expectation of a conclusion. "Everyone seemed to think she'd just taken off. It was Tina being Tina."

"Yeah, I've heard that already."

Tom hadn't meant to come across as dismissive or judgemental but his approach obviously irritated Drew.

"Look, Detective Inspector, I went over her parents' house in as much detail as I could without having justification for a search warrant. There was no evidence of a struggle and no reports of domestic violence at the address. Tina wasn't one to keep a diary detailing her comings and goings. I had no witnesses report anything untoward at the time or in the run up to her disappearance. The father had been at work every day and none of his colleagues saw a change in his behaviour. That goes for the mother as well ... and the sister, too, while I'm at it."

Tom ran his tongue along the inside of his lower lip. He could sense the pent-up frustration Drew still carried from the case and, despite his best efforts to infer otherwise, Tom felt Drew knew there was more to the girl's disappearance but he'd been unable to follow it through at the time. Sometimes there was just the tiniest link that could unravel everything but if you couldn't find it then the case could easily drift away from you. He knew he was right when he saw the pained expression on Drew's face. The man wanted Tom's validation. The idea that something untoward had happened to her after all must have had his stomach turning. Unfortunately, there was little that could be said to ease his conscience.

Drew sank down on a bench alongside the station building, taking off his cap and holding it in his lap. Tom sat down along-side him, saying nothing.

"I knew it wasn't right." He turned to face Tom. "At the time. It didn't feel right. I don't know how you're fixed these days but back then we were under resourced ... the caseload was stacking up ..." He left the comment unfinished.

"You moved on?"

Drew nodded slowly, looking away. "At the end of the day, she was an adult. She could choose to go wherever she liked, when-ever she liked. With no evidence or motive for anything sinister, and a general impression that she'd turn up after a couple of weeks once the heat was off at home ... we put it down as her choice not to be found."

On the face of it that was reasonable but Tom still felt there were avenues left unexplored. "What about her bank account, credit cards. Did you look for any activity there?" He was careful to keep his tone neutral.

"Nah ... the decision had already been taken by then. I thought about it but there wasn't a lot of activity on that side of things ... like I said, Tina did a lot of cash-in-hand stuff working in hospitality, in bars, the holiday parks and so on. Most of her money never saw the inside of her bank account. *My* DI didn't see the point. And to be fair, it was a tough one to argue with." He took out a chrome double hunter pocket watch from his waistcoat, opening it and checking the time. "The next train is due," he said, hefting himself up and off the bench. He walked closer to the platform's edge, looking down the track and spoke over his shoulder. "I had a decent clear-up rate back in the day, Inspector. As much as I felt we let Tina's case go too early ... I stand by it that we didn't have anything more to work with." He turned back to Tom, meeting his eye. "Are you going to tell me I missed something?"

Tom raised his eyebrows. "If you did, then I haven't found it yet."

Drew visually deflated. "The *yet* in that answer is carrying rather a lot, isn't it? If it is Tina you've found. What happened to her?"

"We found the remains of a young woman. She fits the right age profile and time frame for Tina and her disappearance; we're just waiting on a DNA confirmation. Someone broke her neck and buried her in a field."

"Is that what you boys have been working on over at Brancaster?"

Tom nodded. "Most likely murdered elsewhere and dumped there."

"Then I did miss something."

"Not necessarily."

"That's kind of you to say but, let's be honest, if it's taken twenty years to realise a murder took place then I missed something."

Tom was keen not to dwell on potential mistakes. It wouldn't serve them well. "In your report you recorded Tina as last seen out drinking with friends?"

"Yes, she was at the Crown Inn, according to regulars. There was quite a party going on in there that night. There was a dig going on at the old Roman site of Branodunum, a lot of archaeologists and volunteers were staying in the area."

"So, lots of witnesses?"

"Yes and no." Drew frowned. "A lot of people remember seeing Tina there but no one recalls her spending time with anyone specific, when she left or who with, if anyone. You think someone there did it?"

"No idea but the pub isn't far from where she was found."

"That field you guys taped off is where the archaeologists were working that summer. They were finishing off around the time Tina went missing."

"Did you speak to any of them?"

"No, no. They were all packed up and long gone by the time Tina was reported missing. The landlord of the pub told us about it when we asked, that's all. Maybe we should have tracked them down; seen what they had to say. Maybe that was what I missed?"

Tom inclined his head. He didn't really have an answer.

"You'll let me know if it's her, if it's Tina?"

Drew was dejected. Tom figured he was in for a sleepless night tonight and not just because of the relentless humidity. The shrill whistle from a steam engine heralded the approach of the next train. Drew held Tom's gaze, unflinching.

"Yes, of course. I'll let you know as soon as I can."

CHAPTER EIGHT

Tom entered the ops room to find Tamara and Cassie waiting patiently as Eric beavered away at a white board. He appeared to be transcribing something in red marker onto the board from a sheet of paper held in his free hand. Tamara and Cassie glanced over their shoulders as he approached, greeting him with a smile. Eric continued beavering away.

"How did you get on with the old guard?" Tamara asked referring to John Drew.

"Yeah, okay. It was quite enlightening in a way but ..."

"But?"

"Not particularly helpful." Tom frowned, pulling out a chair and sitting down. "I think something about Tina Farrow's disappearance didn't sit well with him but there wasn't a lot for him to go on and he hit a wall and, under pressure from his DI, shelved it as a runaway."

Tamara's brow furrowed. "Do you think he dropped the ball?"

"No, I wouldn't go that far." Tom sat upright in his seat, scratching absently at his chin. "I don't think there were many lines of enquiry that he missed—"

"So, in your opinion, he did miss something then?"

"Ah ..." Tom was reluctant to speak of it until he'd had a

chance to flesh it out himself first. The number of people who were never traced who were present at the pub where Tina was last seen alive, unsettled him. Even if she had only been reported days later it would have been prudent to speak with these people even if there was no evidence of foul play. The failure to monitor the activity in her bank account was telling, almost as if the investigator was approaching this case as a runaway from the outset rather than considering it suspicious. Perhaps he would have done the same if he'd been in his place, perhaps not. It was easy to judge with the benefit of hindsight.

"What's all this about?" he said, gesturing to Eric's developing diagram. He could see now it was a rough layout of the Branodunum site, where the body was discovered. Eric had drawn the field's boundary in red and was now marking little rectangles of varying shapes and sizes in black, adding dimensions alongside, listing length, width and depth.

"Eric has been doing his homework," Cassie said. "Or should I say revisiting his homework from school."

Eric shot a snarky look over his shoulder at her, but otherwise carried on with what he was doing. However, he did answer Tom's question.

"The plastic sheeting was bothering the DCI and it set me thinking."

Tom looked at Tamara who nodded and indicated for him to hear Eric out before commenting, silently mouthing the words *he's got something* to him as she did so.

"I used to have a real interest in history," Eric said, looking at Tom with a big grin on his face. "Mum would always be on at me to turn off the telly because I was watching the Discovery and History channels pretty much on a loop. I used to be a bit of a nerd like that—"

"Used to be?" Cassie asked with weighted sarcasm. Tamara drew a hand back and clipped the DS around the back of the head. Eric continued unabated.

"Still do!" he said. "And the plastic got me thinking. When

archaeologists dig a site, if they find something that they are not intending to transport out to a museum, like an unbroken mosaic or something, and have to leave it in situ, they document everything they can, photograph it, map it out, and then they recover it, because that helps the preservation. But – and here's where it gets interesting – they will look to protect the find. Usually by covering the area with—"

"A sheet of thick plastic," Tom said. Eric beamed.

"Which would explain the size of it," Eric said. "So, I looked up the site's history: modern history." He held up the marker in his hand pointedly. "It's well known and has been thoroughly investigated over the years, twice in the last two decades. Curiously enough—"

"Here it comes," Cassie said, smiling playfully. This time Tamara merely frowned at her.

"Curiously enough, I was present the last time it was dug," Eric said triumphantly.

"How ... why?" Tom asked.

"I was at school, Fifth Form," Eric said. "There was a television show carrying out another dig at the site over a long weekend. They only had three days—"

"You were helping out?"

Eric nodded. "It was really exciting ... until we got there and were largely just shovelling soil around. They didn't let us near any of the really interesting stuff but it was still fun. So, anyway, I contacted the production company who made the television programme and had them send over a copy of it. I took a screenshot of the field with all the trenches and finds once they were all documented."

"And they were in the same area as we found the body?" Tom asked, sitting forward.

"No, sorry," Eric said, looking dejected. "We were in a completely different area of the site. They were digging on National Trust land whereas our grave site, if I can call it that, was just beyond the perimeter."

"That's a shame, Eric," Tom said. "And you're in your mid-twenties so that puts your Fifth Form excursion around ten or eleven years ago, right?" Eric confirmed the maths with a brief nod. "So that would rule out Tina Farrow—"

"Yes, if she had been found in and around that dig, but she wasn't. In the programme they talk at the beginning of a previous dig and which part of the site was dug. And that *does* cover where the remains were unearthed."

"Is that what you're mapping out?" Tom asked, standing and coming in front of the board.

"Yes. The previous dig was in 2001. The same summer Tina Farrow disappeared."

Tom wagged a finger at the board before turning to Tamara. "John Drew ..." Both Eric and Cassie offered blank expressions. "The investigating officer at the time, said that the Crown Inn was packed the night Tina was last seen alive, and that was a result of an archaeological dig going on nearby. It was finishing up that weekend and none of those present were questioned at the time as to whether they knew or had spoken to Tina before she went missing."

"Why not?" Tamara asked.

"Because they'd all packed up and left days before Tina was reported missing by her sister. It wasn't considered a proper use of resources to track them down at the time, not without any evidence that anything untoward had happened to her."

Tamara concentrated hard, focussing along with everyone else on the board and Eric's detailing of the dig locations. She came to stand alongside Tom, tapping the area where they found the skeleton. It was bang in the middle of a large trench the archaeological team had dug. Tom looked at the measurements. They'd dug down to a depth of one hundred and sixty centimetres.

"Do you know what they found in this particular trench?" Tom asked Eric.

He shook his head. "No. All I have is what came from the producers of the television show. However," he stepped back over to his desk, returning with another sheet of paper and offering it to Tom, "this is what I found regarding that particular dig."

Tom scanned the sheet. It was a confirmation that the dig in 2001 had been commissioned jointly by teams based at the University of East Anglia and Cambridge. He looked at Eric.

"We need to know who was in charge of the site and should arrange to speak to them—"

"Already have done," Eric said. "Well, the admin teams at any rate. Professor William Cannell and Alexander Hart were jointly registered as running the operation. Neither is still working at either university but I did a search through *Linkedin* and both of them came up."

"Local?" Tom asked.

"Cannell is working in the field of Archaeological Consultancy, here in Norfolk. He has an office in King's Lynn," Eric said, looking between Tom and Tamara. "Shall I give him a call and arrange a meeting?"

Tom nodded. "Yes, as soon as possible. What about the other one?"

"He's around too, but he's gone a different way. From looking at his connections, he is working in television production of sorts."

"Of sorts?"

"Logistics, facilities management and such … I'm not sure what exactly. His job titles have all been a little vague but he's definitely working in and around television documentaries. He's credited on programmes across Europe and North America but looking at the time frame they're listed in, on his profile, they are sporadic, nothing consistent."

"Excellent work, Eric," Tom said. He glanced at Cassie. "It's good that someone is able to make use of their school experiences rather than just offering up sarcastic criticism.

Cassie tilted her head towards one shoulder, placing an exaggerated hand movement to her chest. "Who, me?"

"Soil samples are back from forensics as well," Eric said. "The samples from in and around the remains."

"Any word on the DNA?" Eric shook his head. "I guess that would be too optimistic. Anything interesting from the soil analysis?" he asked.

"Yes and no."

Tom raised his eyebrows. "Which is it?"

"The dating was all over the place. Some of it returned dates from centuries back whereas other samples returned a date from a couple of years ago."

"It was all mixed or contaminated?"

"The lab team reckon it was because the site was unearthed during the dig and all the soil, once sifted for finds, ended up being bulldozed back into the trench and that's messed up the dating. Although," Eric said, scanning his notes, "they did come back with some interesting results regarding the other organic samples they took."

"Which was?"

"Seeds. They were in and around some of the apparently lesser-disturbed joints of the skeleton, so they thought they were worth dating. Testing dates them to around the turn of the millennium which puts them well in line with Tina Farrow's disappearance. But that's not the most interesting aspect of the testing. The seeds were *phragmites australis* which are—"

"Reeds," Tom said flatly, frowning. Eric agreed. "That's a bit odd."

"Why?" both Cassie and Tamara asked in unison.

"The location," Tom said. "There are several thousand hectares of open fenland in Norfolk and common reeds are not only farmed here but are also a natural defence against flooding. They thrive in marshy, flood conditions but the Branodunum site hasn't been close to the water for years."

Eric nodded enthusiastically. "When it was a Roman fort it was right on the sea, but if the seeds are dated to around the time of Tina's disappearance then I'd suggest they may have gone into the ground at the same time as she did. Maybe they were in her hair or something?"

"Couldn't they have just as easily been carried on the wind?" Tamara asked.

That was quite possible, Tom had to admit. He looked between Eric's drawing and a map of the local area pinned to another board nearby. "Or else we have an idea as to where Tina Farrow was murdered." He borrowed Eric's marker and crossed to the map. Locating the Crown Inn, he circled it and drew a line to the nearby water's edge roughly a quarter of a mile away and then another up to the Branodunum site. It wouldn't have taken more than a couple of minutes to drive the distance between the two points and a strong individual could carry someone the size and weight of Tina Farrow that far with relative ease, provided she was either incapacitated or deceased and they did so under the cover of darkness. "I wouldn't mind knowing exactly when that trench was refilled and by whom," he said, tapping the pen against the map. "Eric, get hold of William Cannell and, who was the other one, Alexander?"

"Hart," Eric said.

"Right. If anyone knows what was going on, on that site then it should be them."

CHAPTER NINE

TOM AND ERIC found the address on King Street, a stone's throw from the Custom House and Purfleet Quay. Following the one-way system, Tom parked the car on South Quay, alongside the magnificent Great Ouse where it passed out into the Wash. He hadn't been here in years. This part of King's Lynn must have been regenerated since his last visit; modern tidal flood defences were visible and in keeping alongside the Seventeenth Century homes and warehouses around them. Crossing through Purfleet Quay and passing the statue of Charles Vancouver, they returned to the offices on King Street where they were expected at the consultancy firm owned and run by Professor William Cannell. Unable to reach Alex Hart they spoke to the other, Cannell, who agreed to see them immediately.

The offices were set in an old timber-framed building that appeared to date to the late Tudor period, albeit with a stone façade added later, according to Eric, as they waited in reception.

"This part of town was built as the river shifted further to the west," Eric said, eyeing the period detail. He was clearly enjoying the visit to the old town. "I'm pretty sure the old land bank, protecting the town from flooding, used to run the length of King

Street. As the route of the river shifted and land became available, they built the warehouses behind us directly on the riverbank."

Tom smiled appreciatively, checking the time on his watch. The receptionist casually looked up at them above the rim of her glasses but returned to whatever she was working on. Eric continued.

"Did you know King's Lynn used to be one of the three biggest trading ports in England, only behind London and Southampton in importance?"

"No. I wasn't aware of that."

"If not for the Napoleonic Wars and then the collapse of coastal trading as a result of the advent of the railways, things could have been very different here."

"This is still a lovely town, Eric," Tom said.

"Oh yes, I know. It's just it used to be so—"

"Sorry to keep you!" They both turned to see a man leaning his back against a door in order to keep it open and beckoning them forward. Tom figured he was a similar age to himself, early to mid-forties, with the physique of a man who no longer laboured digging trenches in a field. He smiled warmly as they approached, offering Tom his hand. "William Cannell." He introduced himself. "Come on through."

They passed through the door which opened onto a small inner hallway with a line of windows overlooking a cobbled alleyway running the length of the building and into a courtyard to the rear. At the end of the short corridor, a staircase headed up but Cannell took them through a wide Georgian door, four panel, and judging by the strange shape of it had been adjusted to compensate for the movement of the building over the years, now sloping at an odd angle. Cannell held the door for them, ushering them through before closing it and offering them a seat.

The office was massive with panelled walls, heavily painted with what looked like multiple layers of gloss paint, the last now resembling an ageing, discoloured cream which had lost its sheen and was cracking and peeling in places. Their host noticed them looking around, Eric in particular.

"Please don't let the decor fool you."

Tom looked at him and raised his eyebrows.

"I know this place looks in quite a poor state but we haven't been here very long. We're looking forward to getting underway with a full set of restoration works. I've always wanted to be based out of this area and when *this particular* building came on the market it was too good an opportunity to pass up. It was previously owned by one of the foremost merchant families in King's Lynn, the Bells. Henry designed and oversaw the construction of the Custom House, among others. He was a contemporary of Sir Christopher Wren, you know?"

Eric's eyes lit up and he appeared ready to say something but he must have caught sight of Tom's expression because he thought better of it.

"Now, what brings you gentlemen to see me today? You said on the telephone it was something to do with a former dig site of mine; finding a body?"

"That's correct," Tom said.

"How odd. It's usually the archaeologists who dig up the bodies," Cannell said, chuckling at his own joke. Neither Tom nor Eric laughed and the smile faded rapidly. "So, what is it I can do for you?"

"You were in charge of a dig at the old Roman fort of Branodunum. Is that right?"

He sucked air through his teeth and nodded. "That's going back a bit. Early two thousands ... 2001, I think. Yes." He sat down in the chair behind his desk, resting an elbow on the arm and putting his fist beneath his chin. "Not one of the most successful of digs, that one, I must say."

"Why not?" Tom asked, sitting down. Eric did likewise, brandishing his notebook as he did so.

Cannell took a deep breath, glancing out of the window which overlooked the courtyard. There was a church visible beyond a six-foot high stone wall.

"It was a jointly funded dig, between ourselves at Cambridge and our counterparts in the faculty of the University of East Anglia. We were looking to determine the significance of the Roman presence in and around Brancaster. There was a question as to how large the garrison was and whether its size increased prior to, or after, the Celtic Iceni uprising of Boudicca in AD 60-61." He frowned, looking dejected. "I always had my doubts about the theory we were exploring ... but others pressed on, so I had to represent the university's interest."

Eric couldn't help himself, sitting forward eagerly. "Was it before or after?"

"I couldn't tell you. I'm afraid." He sat back, folding his arms together across his chest, his expression serious. "Not from our dig at any rate. Another group went back a decade later and found the answers we were hoping for—"

"I worked on that one," Eric said, beaming. The professor looked less than impressed. His gaze lingered on Eric for a few seconds before passing to Tom.

"What's all this about anyway?"

"We found human remains in the field where you were digging."

Cannell sat forward again, placing his hands flat on the desk in front of him. He was alert now. "I take it, because you're here, they aren't ... Roman?"

Tom shook his head.

"And so, what has this to do with the dig? Or me, come to think of it?"

"We have a plan of the site indicating your trench locations," Tom said, indicating to Eric who produced an A3-sized, folded sheet of paper. He stood up and the professor made space on his desk for Eric to lay it out. Cannell reached for a pair of glasses and examined the map, nodding slowly as he analysed each of the marked areas denoting the positioning of the trenches.

"Yes ... from memory they look about right." He looked up at Tom and then glanced past him towards a set of filing cabinets set against the far wall. "I dare say I probably have my old notes somewhere. I doubt they're here but ... I'm a terrible hoarder, Inspector, I hate throwing things away. Archaeologists have a love affair with old things, whether they're deemed useful or not. Very much *not* if you ask my wife!"

"The location of this last trench," Tom said, leaning over and pointing to where they found the remains, "is the one we are very interested in."

"Hm ... what would you like to know about it?"

"We understand that the dig concluded on the weekend of the 1st September."

Cannell's brow knitted in concentration. "Yes, I believe so. The first was the Saturday, I recall, and much of that day was spent closing off and backfilling those trenches. Those that hadn't already been seen to at any rate."

"You don't leave it all until you've completed the dig?"

He shook his head. "No, no, of course not. I mean, if it's quick and easy to do then you backfill it straight away but sometimes there are others you may leave until later. It all depends." He read Tom's passive expression as lack of comprehension but all Tom really wanted was to get him talking and recollecting details from almost two decades ago. "Excavation isn't much of a science, you know? At least not so much back then. Once you uncover your finds, that's when the really interesting work begins. Although, that being said, we were experimenting with the practicality of using LIDAR at the time, much more so now, but back then, although having been around for years, it was still in its infancy with us. It's hard to believe with the volume of work we do with it now."

"LIDAR?"

"Ground penetrating radar," Eric said, tipping his head in Tom's direction.

"Quite right," Cannell said flatly. He didn't appear to appreciate the contribution. "It can help map out the undulations of the ground and identify anomalies that could be worthy of investigation, invisible to the human eye and buried far under the ground: walls, foundations or even disturbances in the density of the soil. But, as useful as all of this is you still never really know until you open up a trench and get your hands dirty."

"So, you'll find some of the dig locations are not what you hoped for?"

"Exactly. And once you've realised it you don't want to waste any more time on those places, so you close them off and crack on elsewhere. Time is everything with these digs because resources are so tight, particularly on big sites such as that one."

"And that particular trench?"

Cannell returned to Eric's map, meticulously tracing the whole site with his fingertip. He lifted his glasses and rested them on top of his head. "I'm pretty certain that was the last one we closed off."

"Which would have been when?"

"Um ... on the Friday, I should imagine." He cast his eyes to the ceiling momentarily. "Yes, we called time on it late afternoon. The whole dig had pretty much been a bust by then and there wasn't a lot to be gained from persevering with it. Best thing for everyone was to throw in the towel and head to the pub!" He snorted a short laugh but gathered himself together quickly. "Sorry. But the best thing I remember from that whole experience was the local pub. A few sorrows were drowned in the bar I can tell you!" He sat back, grinning at the memory.

"And which pub was that?" Tom kept his tone casual.

"The Crown Inn. I remember it well. They had accommodation rooms there and some of us, who were lucky enough to get in first," he raised a pointed finger, angling it back to jab his own chest, "got to stay there."

"Many of you?"

"A few, yes. It was summer as you know and quite a few guests were tourists but we took as many of the rooms as possible. Like I said, it was a large dig." He seemed perturbed when he noted both Tom and Eric eyeing him. "Why? Is there something wrong with that?"

"Can you tell us who else stayed with you at the Crown Inn?"

Cannell looked to the ceiling once again, his lips moving silently as his brain ran through his memories. "Well, myself obviously. Then there was Alex—"

"Alexander Hart?" Tom asked. Cannell nodded.

"Yes, he managed the dig with me," raising a hand to his mouth, he lowered his voice to a conspiratorial whisper and spoke from behind the back of his hand, "it was really his site, you know? Because my university was putting up a lot of the funds they insisted on having a joint project coordinator and that *privilege* fell to me." Tom noted it and encouraged him to continue. "Then there was Julia." Tom looked up. "Julia Rose – Alex's partner at the time. Tim was also staying there, I believe. That's Tim Hendry. Together, we made up the senior team. Many of them were pretty green at the time, to be fair and that made them hard to manage. Alex was far too inexperienced for such a large dig, looking back. It was a shame."

"What was?"

"The failure of the project! That's the only way to sum it up really. I felt for him. It was his baby, as I said. It was the culmination of his doctoral thesis." Tom and Eric exchanged a look. Cannell spoke in a condescending tone. "He'd come up with this theory regarding Branodunum and lobbied for ages to obtain the funding and then ... well, it all sort of unravelled around him." Cannell sighed, running a hand through his hair and stopping to rub absently at the back of his neck, he shook his head slowly. "Never really recovered from that. Poor chap."

"Was it that bad?"

"Oh you had better believe it! Right from the off everything seemed to go against us. To start with it was a dreadful period of summer when we set up, lashing down with rain for days straight, which is unhelpful with a high-water table like we had there on site. Then the weather changed and we had a week of scorching heat which drove a lot of the volunteers away! No one planned for that."

"Who did you have working on site?"

He thought hard. "The teams from the two universities, obviously. The four of us were old compadres from back in our undergraduate days, so were fairly close. We had students," he cast a withering look at Eric, "who can be useful, some of the time, with the donkey work and the like. Then there were the volunteers who were largely made up of interested locals, amateur enthusiasts and registered archaeological groups. It was a real mishmash of people. Dreadful decision. Not mine, I should add. The calendar went against us too. We started later than planned because funding didn't come through as arranged, then the weather, and because it was getting close to September, the term was due to begin and we had to rush to finish before all the labour upped and deserted us. It's no wonder it all went wrong."

"And how many are we talking about?"

"Dozens. Some were there for the duration whereas others came and went during the dig. The prospect of digging a Roman site brought a lot of people out, it's an emotive period is Roman Britannia. Also, because it was in Norfolk, and not some windswept Hebridean beach, it was also seemingly quite a draw."

"And where did they all stay?"

"In and around … wherever we could obtain beds really. Accommodation was thin on the ground due to the time of year. Some stayed in hotels or bed and breakfasts. A number of the students brought tents and we had permission from the owner of the neighbouring field to use that, so many stayed virtually on site. A damn sight easier to get them up with hangovers when they're only a few feet away." Again, he snorted with laughter.

"And did you keep records of who attended the dig?"

"Not me, no. Personnel wasn't my remit. You should have a word with Julia. She organised and kept track of all of that."

"We found a layer of tarpaulin at the expected depth of the trench."

"Yes, that will have been us. Although the trench was at the outer edge of our scope, spanning boundaries between National Trust land, who own the Branodunum site, and the neighbouring landowner, we were pleased to find a ground mosaic where a building wasn't expected to be. It was rather large, so we documented what we could and covered it over for protection. Standard procedure."

"I'm sorry, I'm confused," Tom said. "I thought you said there was nothing to be gained from continuing the dig on the Friday afternoon?"

"That's true. The mosaic was uncovered," he scratched at his chin, concentrating, "late on the Wednesday, I recall. We uncovered all of it that was left intact on the Thursday but by midday on the Friday it was clear that we'd uncovered all that was present. The remainder was severely damaged and there was nothing left to uncover. It'd probably been desecrated by locals after the Roman army withdrew from Britain in the latter stages of the empire. We covered what was there to aid preservation and shut it down."

"Covered it with what?"

"With the plastic sheeting. After we catalogue a find the trench is refilled and the mosaic is protected for future generations. You can't take everything out of the ground, can you?"

"I suppose not," Tom said. "Let's go back to your accommodation. In the time you were staying at the pub do you recall getting to know any of the staff?"

The professor's brow wrinkled. "I remember the landlord was quite a garrulous sort of chap. And the serving staff were friendly enough but I was so busy I largely kept to myself apart from at mealtimes. My wife was at home with our little girl, she'd been born a month before, so I'd often retire to my room to speak with her in the evening. Children grow up so fast you miss out when you're working away as much as I was."

"Do you remember this girl?" Tom produced a photograph of Tina Farrow, taken from her missing person file. It was a shot of her standing against a wall with her arms folded across her chest a year before she went missing, aged eighteen. She was smiling. It was a sunny day. Cannell took the picture from Tom, lowering his glasses and holding it up in front of him. His gaze lingered on it. Both Tom and Eric watched intently for any flicker of recognition. Tom didn't see one. The professor passed it back, shaking his head.

"Sorry. Doesn't ring a bell. Who is she?"

"A young lady who worked at the pub you stayed in. She went missing around the same time as your dig finished."

"Oh I see." Cannell looked lost in thought and then his head snapped up, looking shocked. "Was she ... do you think she was the one you found buried in the trench?"

"That's still to be determined," Tom said.

"I don't see how." Cannell shook his head vigorously. "I mean ... there was no one in the trench when it was backfilled."

"You're sure?"

"Of course, I'm damn well sure!" He was indignant. "One of us would have bloody noticed if ... if ... a young woman was lying in it for crying out loud."

"You would expect so," Tom said. "One last thing. Would you consent to us taking a DNA sample from you today?"

Cannell baulked.

"You are quite within your rights to say no but it would help expedite the investigation if we could. DC Collet has a test kit in his bag and it won't take a moment."

The professor sat open mouthed for a few seconds before whispering his response. Tom couldn't make it out and asked him to repeat it.

"Yes. Certainly. If you ... erm ... think it will help."

CHAPTER TEN

TOM AND ERIC stepped out onto King Street and made the short walk back to the car.

"Make sure he comes through with those old records for the dig," Tom said to Eric as they crossed the road and passed by the Custom House again. Gulls cawed overhead and a breeze was coming from the Wash and gently buffeting them as they walked along the quayside. It was a pleasant feeling, even though the heat seemed to still be increasing.

"I will. He may have more useful information than he realises. Tell me, why did you want to take his DNA?" Tom met Eric's eye as they walked. "I mean, we don't have any trace evidence for a suspect that I am aware of—"

"No, quite right. I just wanted to see how he would react."

"And?"

"He reacted as one would expect him to."

The look on Eric's face told him he didn't understand the reply but he didn't press it. Whether the victim was Tina Farrow or not, she went into the ground around the time of that dig site shutting down. Those who knew the site, controlled it and had access to the victim couldn't number very many. Professor Cannell fitted the criteria but that didn't make him a killer. If there were dozens of people working there, any one of them could have killed Tina. Or the killer could be unconnected to the dig. But guilty men were often rattled by the suggestion of DNA and he wanted everyone they questioned to be rattled. One of them might just give something away.

Half an hour later Tom and Eric entered ops to find both Tamara and Cassie readying to leave. Tamara gave Cassie her car keys and told her they'd meet at the front of the station.

"DNA results came back," Tamara said to Tom. "Positively identified the remains as those of Tina Farrow. I've just spoken to Angela and we're heading out to meet her and her mother. How did you get on with Cannell?"

Tom loosened his tie and collar, feeling the warmth of being back indoors without the gentle breeze. "Swears blind the trench was empty when it was backfilled. I gather the dig wasn't a success and he pointed the finger largely at Alex Hart for that."

"Do you believe him?"

"About the trench? He seemed convincing enough, spoke openly but there's a lot left there still to unpick. I'm looking forward to speaking with the others on site. Hart was romantically involved with Julia Rose and she was responsible for coordinating the labour on site. If she was on top of it then it stands to reason she might know about the interactions between people."

"What next?"

"Cannell promised to send over the files he has from the time. Eric will track down the other leaders from the dig and, hopefully, get a lead on some more names who were around at the time and we can take it from there. Seeing as we have confirmation, I'll head over to where she was last seen and see if I can jog some memories with her old boss. You?"

"Appointment at the morgue, with the mother and sister," she said glumly. Tom nodded. It wouldn't be his first choice of duties either.

TAMARA AND CASSIE stood near to the chapel entrance, not wishing to intrude on a family's grief. The chapel adjoining the mortuary was compact and minimal; a representation of Christ hung on the wall behind a small altar with two rows of plastic chairs and a handful of bibles sitting on a table off to one side, should a visitor be in need of one. Angela Farrow and her mother, Patricia, stood silently side by side staring straight ahead. Not that there was much to look at; a small temporary casket, not of the ceremonial type used for a funeral service, but rather a functional container bereft of any reverence. Inside the box was a collection of bones bearing no resemblance to their loved one, merely an index number labelled on the exterior. The casket was draped in a white sheet; an attempt to tone down the sterile, austere presentation of an evidence box. It hadn't worked. This wasn't a fitting tribute to anyone but on short notice it was the best they could do. Patricia Farrow wanted to spend time with her daughter. Having lived with twenty years of not knowing what had become of her, it was understandable.

Patricia slowly reached out to her side with her hand, her fingers seeking out her living daughter's reassuring touch. Angela withdrew her hand upon contact. The movement didn't go unnoticed and Tamara exchanged a look with Cassie, who raised an eyebrow to indicate she'd seen it too. No words were spoken and the only sound came from Patricia, stepping forward and resting a palm on top of the casket, weeping softly as the raw emotion of the moment threatened to overwhelm her. Angela remained where she stood, impassive and unflinching.

There was never a *right* moment to call time on an occasion like this but eventually Angela looked over her shoulder at Tamara and smiled weakly. Tears were present in her eyes but she maintained her composure. Her mother's head hung low, she continued to cry. As Tamara came forward, Angela put a hand on the small of her mother's back. Patricia looked round but didn't speak. Her eyes furtively glanced at Tamara and without a word she allowed herself to be led from the room by her daughter.

The adjoining family room was bland and nondescript with white painted walls and a thin blue carpet that matched the cushioned chairs one commonly found in waiting rooms around the country. A low table was set centrally, the seating wrapping around it in a U shape. There was a gentle hum of passing cars. Angela helped her mother sit down, who looked unsteady on her feet. Tamara wondered if Patricia was experiencing the onset of shock. After two decades of not knowing her daughter's fate it would be impossible for her not to conceive of this day happening, no matter how much faith and hope she harboured. Inevitably, this day would be traumatic.

"I know this is hard for you, Mrs Farrow, but now that we have a positive identification, we need to ask more questions about the time of Tina's disappearance."

Patricia briefly met Tamara's eye with an anxious look before turning her gaze to her lap, constantly wringing her hands. "Y–yes, of course," she whispered, lifting her head. "We exchanged words that afternoon. Harsh words." Tears fell but she appeared not to notice, her expression stoic. "To think that was the last memory she had of me ... is heart-breaking."

Angela glanced at her mother but looked away, an unreadable expression on her face.

"What was the argument about?"

"Oh ... the same sort of thing we always argued about." Patricia wiped her face with the back of her hand, her composure returning. "How she lived her life. The lack of respect she had for anyone else. The usual. She stomped off as she was always prone to do."

"But you expected her to come home that night?"

She shrugged. "No, not really. I'd all but given up expecting anything where she was concerned." She read the look on Tamara's face and must have interpreted disapproval within it because she adopted a defensive stance. "I loved my daughter but mark my words she could be difficult. Couldn't she?" Patricia looked at

Angela who nodded almost imperceptibly. "It wasn't always that way."

"When did things change?"

Patricia breathed deeply, thinking. "Perhaps when she was nine or ten, maybe? Prior to that she was a lovely little girl; came at life with a broad smile and loved everyone. But ... then things changed, almost overnight. She became quieter, withdrawn. When she got into her teens she came out of herself again but she became argumentative, attention seeking. Her father said she was feisty ... and it ran in his side of the family I can assure you." Again, Angela looked away. Patricia shook her head. "I don't understand where we went wrong with her, I really don't."

"The impression we have from people who knew her," Tamara glanced at Angela, a look that passed unnoticed by her mother, "was of a popular, fun-loving young woman—"

"Oh she was certainly that all right," Patricia said dismissively. "Tina wanted the eyes of the world on her and made sure she got it, no matter the consequences."

"Mum!" Angela snapped.

"Well, it's true." Patricia was indignant.

"How do you mean?" Tamara asked. "When you say *no matter the consequences*?"

She shrugged, refusing to meet Tamara's gaze. "You couldn't trust her is all I mean. She'd say and do anything for attention. Even if she had to make stuff up. Is that all? I'd like to go home now." She stood up without waiting for an answer, looking down at her daughter. Angela remained where she was. "I'll call a cab and meet you outside ... if you want to share a ride back to town?"

She didn't wait for an answer and Angela didn't offer one. She was picking absently at the thumbnail of her left hand with her right forefinger. Once the door closed and they were alone, Tamara angled her head so as to be in Angela's peripheral line of sight, drawing her attention.

"That was tough to hear?"

Angela nodded briefly, sucking her lips inward, but didn't speak.

"Was it true, what your mum said about Tina?"

She sniffed. "Some of it, yes. Tina did crave attention."

"Why do you think that was?"

Angela turned her eyes to the ceiling, drawing breath. "I ... I ... don't know."

"What happened when she was nine or ten, do you think, that could lead to such a profound change in her? It sounded stark." Angela welled up; her teeth clenched. "I mean, people don't suffer dramatic changes to their personality without good cause. Not in my experience anyway."

"Can I go?"

Tamara was momentarily thrown. "Yes, of course you can."

She watched as Angela left the room without looking back. For a moment it seemed as if Angela was preparing to offer an alternative recollection of events but then thought better of it. Cassie exhaled with deliberate dramatic effect.

"What do you make of that?"

"Telling that the father isn't here. You'd think they'd be able to set aside their differences in order to grieve for a lost child, wouldn't you? Has anyone spoken to him yet?"

Cassie shook her head. "Not yet. Lives in Snettisham, Eric said."

"Before we speak to him, I want you to have a good look at his history."

"Doesn't have a record as far as I know."

"Double check. Look at any other family members as well while you're at it; uncles, grandparents, cousins, known acquaintances, if possible. Anyone who had access to those girls. Angela knows ... but I dare say she may well have experienced the same thing."

"A dark family secret?"

"I'd bet on it," Tamara said with a half-smile. "If I gambled, which I don't."

"I do."

Tamara raised her eyebrows, breaking her gaze from the form of Angela Farrow passing by the window outside and looking across at her. "Really? How do you get on?"

Cassie coughed. "Well, I can pay rent this month … but I'm not sure about next."

"And that's why I don't gamble."

CHAPTER ELEVEN

THE CROWN INN was located on the main thoroughfare through the village. A traditional pub, it was a local landmark and drew people in from the surrounding villages even when the tourists were scarce in the off season. Tom pulled his car around to the rear, wheels crunching the gravel beneath them. The car park was half full and he cast an eye towards the building, seeing people moving about inside through the windows. The staff would no doubt be clearing away from the lunchtime covers and preparing for the evening meals as the guests returned and locals came out for a drink. The original entrance was off the road at the front but the main route in and out of the building could now be found at the rear. The reception desk was unattended and he waited patiently for someone to appear, hearing sounds of people in the bar and also through a nearby door with a sign indicating it should be accessed by staff only.

He didn't have long to wait before a man rounded the corner. He was in his early sixties, around five-foot six tall and carrying a little extra weight. His expression was fixed in concentration but upon seeing Tom, his face split into a broad, welcoming grin.

"Sorry to keep you."

"No problem," Tom said, brandishing his warrant card. "DI Janssen. Could I speak with the landlord please?"

"That's me. Paul Tennant." The grin faded, turning serious. "Is there a problem?"

"We're investigating the disappearance of Tina Farrow. Do you recall her? I understand she used to work for you here."

"Yes, yes I do. Tina did work here as it happens. Not always but certainly when it was busy, we threw the odd shift her way. Nice girl, Tina. Shame what happened."

"What did happen?"

Tennant started. "Well, going missing and so on, you know. We half expected her to walk into the bar one night and crack a smile, bow low and tell us it was all an elaborate wind up! She was that sort."

"I don't understand."

His demeanour changed as he anxiously looked around, seemingly uncomfortable at the scrutiny. "Just ... she was up for a laugh, you know?"

"She was here on the night she went missing, wasn't she?"

Tennant pursed his lips. "That's what people said after the event but ... I have to admit I didn't recall seeing her at the time. You have to understand it was summer and the place was packed out, the bar and the beer garden." He indicated behind them to the rear with a thumb over his shoulder. "All our rooms upstairs were let, as were the old stables."

Tom looked towards the door, trying to see beyond it. The landlord followed his gaze.

"We converted the old stables into extra letting rooms ... and we had the bunkhouse as well at the time."

"Fully booked?"

He nodded enthusiastically. "Pretty much peak season for us, or at least the tail end of it, and the people from the dig were here then, too. Boosted the coffers, I must say. Could do with a few more periods like that."

"Aside from Tina going missing."

Tennant rowed back swiftly. "Yes, of course. Goes without saying obviously."

"What did you make of Tina?"

A party of guests appeared from the bar and Tennant smiled politely as they passed, wishing them a good day. There were six of them; they appeared dressed for a walk.

"The bus stop is along to the right, ladies and gents." He glanced at his watch. "You'd best get a move on, it's due any minute. Several members of the party hustled the others out of the door and one tipped his hat towards both of them. Tom smiled and nodded. Once the door closed, Tennant's smile evaporated and he turned back to Tom. "Where was I? Tina. Yes, as I said, she was a nice girl, popular with both staff and regulars. Always on time, polite. Exactly what you want in a member of staff. She just got on with things."

"Why was she only casual if she was so good?"

He blew out his cheeks. "More her than us, to be fair. I don't think she liked responsibility much; happier to come and go. If we had shifts and she was around then she'd take them on but if not then she'd go elsewhere."

A woman came out from the nearest door, the kitchen seemed to be beyond it. She stopped, looking between them. Tennant half smiled and Tom sensed his reluctance to introduce them. She was a similar age to the landlord and had an air of authority associated with her apparent confidence. She waited for an introduction, her eyes darting between them but when it didn't come quickly enough, she took it upon herself.

"Louisa Tennant." She smiled warmly but it seemed well practised. She tilted her head to one side. "And you are?"

"This is Detective Inspector Janssen," Tennant said. "He's from the police."

His wife shot him an exasperated look as he stated the obvious, before turning to Tom. "I didn't think you were a guest somehow. What can we do for you?"

"He's asking after—"

"I think the delightful inspector is more than capable of answering for himself," she said.

"I'm investigating the murder of Tina Farrow—"

"Murder!" Tennant blurted out, drawing a sharp note of disapproval from his wife. He lowered his voice, looking around to make sure no one was within earshot. "You didn't say it was murder."

Tom was about to respond but Louisa got in first.

"Perhaps we shouldn't stand here talking." She looked around. "Come through to the bar. It's quiet at the moment, people find it too warm inside." She put a hand on Tom's upper arm and guided him through the opening and into the bar. Aside from an elderly couple sitting in the far corner, and a young woman attending to the bar, it was empty. Ushering Tom to a table away from anyone else, she pulled out a chair for him and looked over to the bar, drawing the woman's attention. "Magdalena, could you bring us a pot of tea?" Tom was about to decline but the order was taken. The three of them sat down and Paul Tennant looked tense, his wife less so.

"What's this about murder?" he asked, sitting forward and keeping his voice low.

"Tina's remains were found at the weekend—"

"Is that what's going on, on the edge of the village?" Louisa asked. Tom nodded and she sank back in her seat. "I didn't know what to think with all the police cars."

"Odd goings-on over that way, always have been—"

"Oh for heaven's sake, Paul. Your imagination does run away with you at times!"

"It's not just me. Other people see things too."

"Ridiculous!" Louisa dismissed him and her husband visibly shrank before her. "Poor Tina ... and Angela. Is she okay? Have you spoken to her?"

"We have. Did Angela work for you too?"

"Sometimes," Louisa said. "But not front of house. She didn't have the same personality type as her sister. Much quieter, more suited to the housekeeping side of things."

"Unreliable too," Paul said. His wife agreed. "We had to let her go in the end." He spread his hands wide in a placatory gesture. "Some guests reported items going astray." He didn't elaborate further.

"Cast your mind back, if you can, I know it's a long time ago. What do you recall from the night Tina went missing?"

Louisa sat forward, splaying her hands wide. "That's easy, not a lot! I wasn't here. I travelled to the south coast to stay with my sister the week before. She lived in Newhaven at the time; moved on to Lyme Regis now—"

"I don't think he needs the family memoirs, darling—"

"I'm just saying I wasn't here."

"You never are when it's really busy!" She glared at him and he looked away, as if her irritation wouldn't be real if he failed to acknowledge it. Tennant focussed on Tom instead. "Like I said, it was really busy. You'd expect that archaeology lot to be studious and a bit geeky but believe me they went at it like a bunch of teenagers! Apparently, Tina was here that night but I don't recall seeing her."

Tom glanced around. "Is there anyone here now who was working for you at the time who might?"

Paul shook his head, turning the corners of his mouth down. "Sorry, but our staff turnover is quite high. It's not the most invigorating work and people come and go."

"Yes," Louisa said, "we used to have locals who worked with us for years but they moved on and youngsters tend to be drawn into London these days. Norfolk is too quiet for them. We find people coming to us from further afield these days."

"Was Tina close to anyone who worked here?"

"No, sorry. Couldn't say," Paul said.

"What about Sally?"

Paul looked at his wife, his face dropping momentarily. Then, when he caught Tom looking at him, he lightened his expression, smiling awkwardly and nodding. "Yes, Sally. I forgot." He looked at Tom. "You could try speaking to Sally, Sally Webber. She worked here at the same time as Tina. They were friendly but I've no idea where she is now."

"Nonsense!" Louisa said firmly. "She lives in Wells now. She's working for Terry and Anna. You remember?" She elbowed her husband in the ribs and he grimaced.

"Oh, yes. I forgot. Terry and Anna own the Ship in Wells. We saw Sally there the last time we had dinner with them. But you can forgive me, it was six months ago."

"Thick as thieves those two," Louisa said. "If anyone knows what Tina was up to then it would be Sally. I could give them a call and ask if she's there, if you'd like?"

"I'm quite sure the inspector is capable of doing his own job without your help," Paul Tennant said, placing a restraining hand on his wife's forearm as she made to stand. Tom thanked them, making a note. Sally Webber wasn't a name that had come up previously, to his knowledge, although she might have been mentioned in the original case file and he'd missed it. The investigating officer, John Drew, said he'd spoken to Tina's work colleagues at the time. If she was as close to Tina as Louisa Tennant believed then why hadn't she come forward and shed light on her disappearance before? It was quite possible she had kept her counsel two decades ago out of a sense of misguided loyalty to her friend. Perhaps the discovery of Tina's remains would change that. It was worth the drive over to Wells.

"Do you still have records from 2001 detailing who stayed here?"

"I'm afraid not, Inspector. We keep six years of information but that's all," Paul said, shaking his head.

"Okay. You said Tina was popular but did she ever fall out with anyone; staff members or patrons?"

The couple exchanged glances and shook their heads in unison.

"She was popular," Louisa said. "Often ... I don't wish to speak ill of the dead ... but often she was perhaps too friendly with some of the regulars."

Paul looked uncomfortable, glancing away and pursing his lips once more.

"Can you define *too friendly* for me please?"

"Overly friendly might be a better description, to be fair," Louisa said. "It wasn't a massive issue but once or twice her attention was ... misinterpreted ... and that led to a misunderstanding regarding her actual intentions."

"I see," Tom thought hard. "And this led to difficulties?"

Paul dismissed the question with a flick of his hand but his wife seemed less inclined to do so.

"I had to speak to her about it," Louisa said. Her husband eyelids fluttered and he turned his gaze away from her towards the window. Was it surprise or annoyance, Tom couldn't tell? Louisa caught her husband's eye. "Well, you were never going to say anything." She turned to Tom with a disparaging look. "Utterly useless when it comes to reading people, worse when confronting them." Paul bristled but said nothing further. "Anyway, I had to speak to her about her behaviour and point out that not everyone is capable of recognising when an attractive young woman is merely seeking a little pick me up, as opposed to making a play for them."

"How did she take it?"

Louisa seemed surprised by the question. Magdalena appeared at their side, placing a tray on the table with a teapot and three cups. Tom thanked her as she made to leave but neither of the Tennants acknowledged her. Louisa looked over her shoulder at the departing Magdalena and once she was out of earshot she spoke.

"A young girl like that; feisty, opinionated, unused to being told what's what. She didn't like to hear it but it needed saying. If her parents couldn't set her straight then it had to come down to someone else."

Paul eyed his wife warily. "And that *had* to be you."

It was a statement and not a question. He shook his head and, internally, Tom smiled.

"Why didn't you report all of this after Tina went missing?" Tom asked Louisa.

She appeared confused by the question. "Why would I? How would I know it was even relevant? And, besides, I was away at my sister's for a further fortnight and Tina being casual staff, we didn't miss her." Tom focussed his eye on her after that comment and she back-pedalled. "I only meant that she wasn't scheduled to work for us, so her disappearance didn't inconvenience our business."

CHAPTER TWELVE

TOM GOT into his car and immediately switched the engine on so he could get the air conditioning going as quickly as possible. There was little sun today, instead the clouds were heavy and the light breeze of the morning had disappeared leaving a stifling heat. If they didn't have a thunderstorm later that evening he would be surprised and they'd be in for a sticky, uncomfortable night. Picking up a bottle of water from where it lay on the passenger seat, he used the voice activation controls to call Eric. Sipping at the water, now disappointingly warm from resting inside the car, he waited for the call to be answered.

"Hi Tom." Eric's upbeat voice was always welcome. "How did you get on with the former employers?"

At that moment Paul Tennant emerged from the pub into the beer garden, roped off from the car park. Louisa followed and appeared to be remonstrating with her husband. Tom watched, unable to make out what was being said but Paul seemed more than a little irritated, his cheeks flushing. For her part, Louisa looked confused. He couldn't help but wonder if this was largely how their relationship played out on a routine daily basis or whether his visit had brought it out of one or both of them. He adjusted the volume on the steering wheel, conscious that these calls could often be louder outside the cabin than you may realise. He continued to watch them argue as Paul made a decent fist of clearing the tables of empty glasses, stacking them in a carrier ready for transporting back to the bar.

"Interesting couple," he said quietly. They hadn't noticed he was still there, his car parked among several others. "How have you got on with tracing the other archaeologists?"

"Pretty well. Tim Hendry is a lecturer at the University of East Anglia. I've spoken with him on the telephone and he's happy to meet up tomorrow. He lives in Lower Gresham, so it would probably be easier to catch him at home. I've not been as lucky with Dr Rose. You recall, she was Alex Hart's partner at the time of the Branodunum dig? Well, she is based at Cambridge but is currently on a dig site abroad and I haven't been able to get contact details for her as yet. I could fire across an email through her *Linkedin* profile in the meantime, until the university admin gets back to me. What do you reckon?"

"Yes, do it. There's no harm." Tom saw Louisa Tennant turn her back on Paul and stalk back inside. Paul continued the clear-up, evidently muttering something to himself. "What about Alex Hart himself?"

"I found him, although it wasn't easy. He lives over in West Runton. I tried his number but there was no answer. I'll keep trying and it's not far from here so I could always drive round to his place and knock on the door."

"Hart might be out at work. Cassie and I can swing by his place tomorrow after we have a chat with Hendry. We'll need to speak to all of them at some point anyway, so it's not urgent." Tom heard a discernible sigh. "Eric, is something wrong?"

"No, not really."

Tom knew there was. "What is it?"

"Well ... it's just that after looking up Tim Hendry, I realised ... you see, he did this series about Roman Britain. I watched all of them—"

"You want to meet him, don't you?"

Eric hesitated. "Um ... yeah, I really do."

"All right," Tom said, smiling to himself, "you and I will go and see Tim Hendry at his home tomorrow." He could picture the width of Eric's grin as he said the words, he'd no doubt be punching the air. "But one thing, Eric."

"Yes?"

"If you ask him for an autograph you'll be walking back to the station."

"Understood!"

"Can you do me a favour and look through Tina Farrow's file and find me her father's whereabouts, please? Angela said he lived in Snettisham." He heard the thud of the receiver being put down on the desk and Eric began riffling some papers. He was back soon enough.

"One second," Eric said. "Right, here we are – Conrad Farrow. Do you want his home or work?"

Tom glanced at his watch. It wasn't yet one o'clock. "Better give me his work."

"He works for a construction firm, Amplefield Homes, as a site foreman."

"Better give me their head office number if he's likely to be out on site somewhere."

Passing through Hunstanton, he drove out of the town on the Heacham side and followed the road to the outer boundary. The site was easy to find. There had been extensive building works at both ends of the town, catering for the increased demand as the north Norfolk coast was seeing a resurgence in popularity as a place to live rather than just a holiday destination. He wasn't sure what was driving the demand, perhaps the modern broadband age made it possible for people to base themselves almost anywhere provided they had a decent wireless connection. Parking the car near to the site entrance, he got out and looked around for the office. The most visible was the sales cabin, situated alongside what appeared to be the show house.

A number of houses were already complete and with cars on the driveways were already inhabited. In other places the site was in various stages of construction from those barely out of the ground to others wind and watertight. He was grateful for the period of hot and dry weather because without it, much of the site would have quickly become a quagmire judging by the heavy plant vehicles traversing the roads in front of him.

Entering the sales office, a lady turned to greet him with a well-practised and seemingly genuine smile. Many years ago, Tom dated someone who worked on sites like this. Often estate agents placed their most experienced sales negotiators in these roles as they needed to close deals sooner rather than later; the pressure from developers to generate returns was high and it was his understanding that the negotiators were well recompensed for signing people up.

"Hello. You're a new face. Welcome to Amplefield's New Redcar site. My name is Wendy."

Tom smiled warmly, taking out his warrant card. "Hello Wendy. Unfortunately, I'm not looking to buy a new house."

"Shame. We have some great deals available."

Tom knew she was only half-joking. "I need to speak with your site foreman, Conrad Farrow. Do you know where I can find him?"

Five minutes later, a short, stocky man huffed and puffed his way into the office, peeling off a hard hat and running his hand through a mass of black, sweaty hair shot through with grey. He nodded a greeting to Wendy, who offered yet another polished smile, and indicated to Tom waiting patiently in the clients' seating area, next to a pedestal fan. Conrad Farrow was much as Tom expected; middle-aged and with a face that was well worn. He ambled over to Tom, giving him a half-smile as Tom rose to meet him.

"Conrad Farrow?"

"Yeah. What's this about?" The question wasn't laced with hostility, but he did seem apprehensive. "You were lucky to catch me as I'm about to clock off and send the lads home." Tom showed him his warrant card and introduced himself before indicating towards the door.

"Care to take a walk with me?"

Conrad shrugged and set off for the outside. The sound of heavy plant was louder as vehicles criss-crossed the site as they walked, like a mechanised anthill with everyone knowing their roles. Tom was surprised that this was the first the man had heard about developments in his daughter's case. He stopped, turning to Tom, a pained look in his eyes.

"So, you found her." There were no tears, no emotional outburst. If anything, Conrad Farrow appeared relieved at the news.

"Yes. I'm sorry for your loss."

Conrad bit his lower lip, shaking his head. "I knew," he whispered. Tom's eyes narrowed. "I guessed; I should say before you get any ideas. After a couple of months and we'd heard nothing from her, I just knew she wouldn't be coming back."

"Why didn't you report her missing?" Tom asked, watching him closely as they resumed their walk. Here, they were closer to the coast with no barrier to the gentle breeze coming in off the sea. It was a relief. "Why leave it to Angela?"

"Ah ... should have done, you're right," he said, dabbing at his brow with a far from clean handkerchief he had stashed in his filthy trouser pocket. "What is it with this weather. I swear I've lost twenty pounds since I started on this site." He glanced sideways at Tom, who was still waiting for him to elaborate on his answer. "Hindsight's a wonderful thing, Inspector. But from what you're telling me, it wouldn't have made much of a difference."

"May have given us a greater chance of catching her killer."

Conrad inclined his head at the logic. "Yeah," he said softly, "you're probably right." He sniffed then, reaching up and covering his mouth with the palm of his hand. He turned away from Tom and a few moments passed before Tom realised he was crying. Allowing him a little time, Tom glanced around the site. It was quite a substantial building programme they were undertaking, possibly the largest the town had experienced for decades. A dumper approached, its driver bouncing around in the seat on the uneven ground. He slowed as he drew alongside.

"Where do you want this, gaffer?"

Conrad wiped the tears from his eyes and absently waved towards a general point off to their left. It seemed like a vague instruction to Tom but the driver didn't query it, engaging a gear and the roar of the engine picked up as he reversed, accompanied by the automated beeping before heading off as instructed.

"You've got your work cut out here," Tom said.

"Yeah, I do." He looked at Tom, smiling briefly. Tom figured it was out of gratitude for allowing him a personal moment. "But I'll never complain. Not again."

There was something in those words, resentment maybe?

"Why do you say that?"

Conrad exhaled heavily. "You've no idea." Tom offered an open expression, encouraging him to explain further. "After Tina went missing ... most people were very supportive, people at my work and Pat's. Everyone we knew was either dropping cards through the door or stopping us in the street to ask if there was any news." He met Tom's eye. "You know, that type of thing. But as the days became weeks and then weeks became months things began to change. The sympathy dries up ... the finger pointing starts. From sympathy and compassion to blame, all in the space of a season. That's the thing with a small town; small minds. It doesn't need any evidence or facts to support the rumour." His tone shifted to bitter and resentful.

"In the absence of answers some people will fill in the gaps with their imagination," Tom said.

"*Some* people!" He turned on Tom and pointed a finger at him accusingly. "You know, six months after our Tina went missing my contract expired and despite years of decent service, rolling contracts, I was suddenly no longer required."

"And you think—"

"I don't think it, I know it! You know I couldn't get work for two years after that. Two years! You think about what that feels like when you've been employed since you were sixteen years of age. Nowhere. No one local would take me on. You explain that to me."

Tom couldn't.

"Do you know of any relationships Tina was in at the time of her disappearance or anyone who had a grudge against her?"

He scoffed. "Other than my missus?" Tom tilted his head to one side. "No. None that I'm aware of. Tina was full of fun. She didn't seem to do relationships."

"Strange, for a nineteen-year-old. Usually, they've had at least *one love of their life* by that point."

"Not my Tina." He shook his head.

"Why do you think your ex-wife or daughter haven't been in touch? We've seen both, taken DNA from Angela to help us with the case."

He stared straight at Tom, his face a picture of controlled anger and frustration.

"We don't talk any more. Haven't done for years. Not since the divorce."

"Even Angela?"

"Even her," he said aggressively. "She didn't just take her mother's side when our marriage broke down ... I think she blamed me for Tina's disappearance. Same as her mother did."

"Were you to blame?"

He spun on Tom, the movement catching him off guard, stepping into him and snarling. "I had years of people laying it at my door!" he barked, furiously wagging a pointed finger in Tom's face. "What happened to my girl had nothing ... *nothing* to do with me. Do you hear?"

Tom maintained an impassive expression, allowing him to vent until his anger subsided.

"Nothing at all," Conrad said quietly, removing his hat and slumping against a shrink-wrapped pallet of block pavers, positioned at the end of a partially laid driveway. He looked up at Tom, squinting as the sun momentarily broke through the clouds. "I made mistakes, Inspector Janssen, both as a husband and a father, but I didn't hurt my little girl. I loved her."

"Her home life appears to have been fractious at best."

"Between her and her mum, yes," he said, drawing breath and exhaling heavily. His shoulders sagged. "I should have been around more. I was always working; figured that was my role, you know? But maybe if I'd been around more ..." He shook his head.

"That's hindsight again for you," Tom said. "We all do what we think is for the best."

"Ah yes, we do, that's true."

"I can arrange for you to spend some time with her, if you'd like? We did it for her mother and sister."

He looked at Tom with an unreadable expression as the words sunk in. Then he shook his head. "When we're allowed to bury her, I'll have a place to make my peace but not now." He looked out over the sea. "I'm not ready."

CHAPTER THIRTEEN

THE HOUSE WAS SET back from the road, a brick-built house with impressive bay windows that somehow appeared lost within the size of the grounds despite being quite imposing up close. How far the boundary stretched to each side was unclear as there didn't appear to be any fencing or natural boundary in the form of a tree line or hedgerow. Presumably everyone knew the extent of their landholding and respected it. The lawn encircling the property was well tended with Yew trees strategically placed to break up the space. These were also well maintained having been trimmed into different shapes, their growth controlled.

A dog barked as they approached the front of the building. By the time Tom switched off the engine, a golden retriever was waiting for them at the corner of the house, watching them, its tongue lolling to one side trying to keep cool in the heat. A figure appeared from behind the dog, smiling in greeting, as Eric came alongside Tom and they walked to meet him.

"Mr Hendry?" Tom asked.

"The very same. You must be Inspector Janssen."

He offered his hand and they shook; his grip was strong and confident. He did likewise with Eric who returned a broad smile of his own. Tim Hendry was a slim man but not unhealthy with it.

He had the build of a fell runner; very little excess body fat and toned muscle, and he moved with agility, stooping easily to pick up a ball and launching it some distance for his dog to chase.

"You said on the phone this was regarding the dig over at Branodunum?" Hendry asked, indicating for them to join him and he led them around the house to the rear. The dog returned offering him the ball and he took it, throwing it once more only this time it bounced and disappeared from view with the dog in pursuit. Hendry gestured for them to take one of the chairs set out beneath a pergola to offer some shade, despite the thick cloud cover making that unnecessary. However, should the sun break through that would change. Running water could be heard and when the dog reappeared its bottom half was wet through. There must be a stream cutting through the back garden not quite visible from where they were sitting. "Would you like a drink?" Set out on the table between the chairs was a jug of either iced water or lemonade, it was unclear which. Not waiting for an answer, he poured two extra glasses and set them in front of each of them. Eric thanked him and eagerly sipped from his.

"We found human remains at the dig site, in the same proximity as one of your trenches; a young woman who disappeared the same weekend your dig concluded."

Hendry was surprised.

"That's … rather disconcerting. You say in proximity to or do you mean actually in—"

"In the trench, yes. We believe she was murdered."

"Good Lord!" He sat back in his chair, open mouthed and ran a hand through his brown hair. "How terrible. Do you know who she was?"

"A local girl, Tina Farrow. Do you know her?"

Hendry concentrated hard. "Not by name, no. Do you have a photograph by any chance?" Eric produced a photo and passed it over to him. Hendry's brow furrowed as he concentrated on it, holding the photo in one hand, his thumb and forefinger of the other resting across his mouth and chin. "She does look familiar.

It's the smile ... but I can't place her." He looked at both of them in turn lowering his hand from his face. "Should I? Was she a helper at the dig?"

"She worked at the Crown Inn, in Brancaster—"

"Where we were staying? Right, that'll be it then," he said sitting back and nodding. "Can't recall her specifically but that must be it. What do you think happened to her?"

"We believe she was attacked on the Friday, the 31st August, possibly murdered that night before being buried in the last trench to be backfilled on your site."

Hendry's eyes widened and he blew out his cheeks slowly. "That's ... truly awful. Are you certain about that, the timings I mean?"

"Why do you ask?"

Tom knew they had no idea as to exactly how and when Tina wound up where they found her as it was impossible to say for sure.

"The poor girl couldn't have been in the trench when it was backfilled, I'm sure." Tom raised his eyebrows in query. "Someone would have seen her, obviously."

Eric put his glass down on the table, it was now almost empty. "Unless the person backfilling the trench was also the killer?"

Hendry shook his head. "Even so, he wouldn't have been alone. There's no way the driver of the digger would have been left to do it without supervision. We have a contractual agreement to leave the ground as close to the way we found it." He shrugged. "That isn't always possible but we try our best. There's no way that only one person would be there, I'm certain."

"Who did close off the last trench?" Tom asked, indicating for Eric to produce the map of the site which he duly did, passing it over to Hendry who took it and examined it carefully.

"This one here?" he pointed with his finger. Tom nodded. "That was definitely the last trench to be closed. It was also the only one to produce significant finds. I mean, we found some footings in one and a small waste pile in another which was truly exciting as we saw what was cast aside by the inhabitants. Sorry, I digress," he said, reading Tom's impassive expression. Eric, however, was hanging on his every word with a curious smile on his face.

"The closure of the trench?" Tom repeated.

"I'm sorry, I couldn't say." Hendry placed the map on the table and sat back. "I'm afraid I wasn't there on the last day. That was Saturday, I believe. The 1st of September. The dig overran and I had a weekend seminar scheduled for the Saturday morning that I was unable to move – not that I wanted to."

"Why not?"

He frowned. "The whole experience was utterly shambolic, to be honest. It started well enough but when we didn't find what we were expecting to it all went sideways on us. Poor Alex," he said, shaking his head.

"Poor Alex?" Tom asked, pretending to be ignorant.

"Yes, Alex Hart. The dig was his path to a doctorate, which never came to pass I'm afraid." He sighed. "Didn't take it well. It was a crying shame, not nice to see a friend go through that at all. Anyway, I was happy to get away. If it wasn't for personal loyalty to him, I think I would have left much earlier. As I said, I had a seminar in London that Saturday morning, so I left on the Friday but I'd already rescheduled a number of things in my calendar, in order to stay on and support him."

"Do you know who would have been on site that Saturday to oversee the closure of the trench?"

The dog came over to Hendry dropping the ball at his feet and resting its head in his lap, eyes looking up longingly at him. Hendry ruffled the dog's fur to begin with and then affectionately stroked its head. "Alex, obviously. His partner, Julie. Have you spoken with her yet?"

Tom shook his head. "Not yet but we intend to."

Hendry nodded. "And Billy of course." He saw Eric twitch at the name and then smiled. Drawing himself fully upright, he affected a mock upper-class accent. "Professor William J. Cannell," he said, the smile broadening into a grin before he returned to his usual voice, "as he prefers to be known these days. Back then, before carving out a wonderful career in academia he was plain old Billy Cannell." Hendry chuckled, shaking his head. "I'd bet he wouldn't answer if you called him Billy now."

"Anyone else?"

"We hired a driver to operate the digger, so he would have been present. We all had a go with the machinery. We were like children playing in a giant sand pit ... but you need to know what you're doing, so we had the driver present as well. There were numerous others but I don't have any names for you, sorry."

"You work in academia yourself, don't you?" Tom asked.

"Yes, for the UEA here in Norfolk. I lecture at the university, have done for the last few years."

"And do you still see the others? We understand the four of you were undergraduates together, as well as close friends."

"Oh best of friends, yes, that's true," Hendry said, pouring Eric a top-up of the lemonade, which Tom figured had to be home-made. Eric was grateful. "Not that we see much of each other. Billy, sorry, William I don't see at all. He largely cut ties with the rest of us. That was soon after the Branodunum shambles come to think of it."

"Why?"

Hendry tutted, his face wrinkling. "*On paper* he was jointly in charge of the dig. He didn't take the lack of success well and it caused ructions in the camp. He blamed Alex ... and for his part, Alex didn't really stand up for himself. That fell to me and Julie, his other half. He could have done. I mean, it wasn't all his fault. We were all there interpreting the data and forming a cohesive plan for the dig, so it fell on all of us really, but William doesn't accept failure very well; always worried about other people's perception of him. I doubt much has changed in that regard."

"The others, Alex and Julie?"

Hendry raised his own glass and drained the contents. Swallowing hard and licking his lips, he placed the glass back on the table, the remaining ice cubes clinking against the sides. It looked to Tom as if he were hesitant. "I still speak with Julie from time to time and I see Alex a fair bit. He lives over at West Runton, not far from Sheringham." The dog lowered its head, retrieving the ball and dropping it into his lap, stepping back and waiting expectantly. Hendry did as he was bid and threw the ball. The dog set off to give chase. Hendry shook his head. "I love dogs but sometimes they are a bit daft. Why he wants to run around in weather like this, I'll never understand?" He indicated Tom's glass. "You should drink that before it gets warm."

Tom smiled, lifting the glass out of politeness and sipping it. The lemonade was crisp and sweet. Putting the glass down he thanked him, then looked to Eric.

"Tell me, do you have anything from that dig site; photographs, diaries, anything that might detail comings and goings or help identify people who were there?"

"Oh yes. I'm sure I'll have something. Not diaries, I'm afraid I'm not much of a writer beyond lectures and essays but I like to document what I do. What I have will be easy to find and there are plenty of shots with the volunteers in and so on. Bear with me and I'll gather it together before you go if you like?"

"Perfect, thank you. If we need anything further we'll get in touch."

"Any time, Inspector," Hendry said, smiling warmly. "Nasty business. If I can help in any way, I'll be happy to do so."

"Come to think of it," Tom said, turning to Eric, "it would be helpful if we could take a sample of your DNA to compare with evidence found at the grave site." He kept his tone light and casual. "Would you mind?"

"Not at all. Happy to oblige if it helps," Hendry said confidently. "Should I come the station or—"

"Not necessary. DC Collet has a sample kit in the car."

Tom dispatched Eric to fetch the kit, the DC catching Tom's eye as he passed. Hendry was genuinely happy to assist. While they waited for him to return, Hendry looked at Tom, once again appearing hesitant. Tom held the man's gaze, silently encouraging him to reveal what was on his mind.

"I take it you haven't spoken to Alex yet?" Tom didn't answer, merely inclined his head. "I figure you haven't because otherwise I'm sure you'd be asking more questions."

"Really? What sort of questions would I be asking?" Tom was intrigued.

"About Alex ... and his past." Hendry chewed nervously on his lower lip. The dog returned but this time he shooed it away. Indignantly, the dog loped off and sank down under the over-hanging branches of a large willow tree located next to the stream, the only reason it could have held onto its leaves in this dry spell. "Please go easy on him."

Tom's curiosity was piqued. "Go easy?"

"That's the wrong phrase, I'm sorry. It's just that Alex has a ... fragile constitution. He struggles with the world sometimes, that's all."

"He doesn't work in the field of archaeology anymore, does he?"

Hendry shook his head, pursing his lips. "He didn't manage to complete his PhD. There isn't much of a future in the field without one, I'm afraid. It's not impossible but archaeology is one area where you need the credentials in order to thrive. The whole process left Alex a little sore to say the least and, well, his life spiralled out of control from there on in." Hendry was glum. "He found his way back, with a little help from his friends of course."

"Are Alex and Julie still—"

"No, no, no," he said, shaking his head emphatically. "I'm afraid it all got on top of him and their relationship ... reached its conclusion shortly after the Branodunum fiasco; perhaps the following year but I can't say for sure. I understand they're still close, though."

Eric returned, placing the test kit on the table and donning a pair of nitrile gloves. Tom took the time to evaluate Tim Hendry, walking a short distance away from them. He saw the dog lift its head, watching him on the off chance that Tom might be up for a game of fetch. Disheartened, it set its head back down on to its paws. Tom took out his mobile as Eric swabbed the inside of Hendry's mouth. Tom called Cassie.

"Can you do me a favour? Look up Alexander Hart and find out everything you can about him, please."

"What am I looking for?"

"We have the obvious, home address and so forth." He looked back at Hendry. "I've just got a hunch there's something to find in his past that might prove useful. The dig was a total failure and largely ruined Hart's academic career, not to mention his relationship fell apart soon after. It's a curious coincidence."

"I'll see what I can do."

CHAPTER FOURTEEN

THE HOUSE WAS DETACHED, traditional Norfolk brick and flint, and overlooked the Church of the Holy Trinity, an impressive twelfth century Anglo-Catholic church. There was no driveway to the house, it was positioned almost on the roadside and appeared to be one of the oldest properties around, probably constructed several hundred years previously.

"Is this the place?" Tom asked. Eric craned his neck from left to right and nodded.

"Yes, I think so."

They approached the front door but there was no visible sign that anyone was home. Tom rapped the knocker repeatedly and they waited. With still no sign of movement, Tom stepped to one side and attempted to peer through the window to his right. The interior was shrouded from view by thick net curtains, ornate and patterned. He gestured for Eric to head around to the rear. The passage running down the side of the house was screened by a gate taller than Eric. It was secured by a sliding bolt.

Tom joined him and, being comfortably over six feet tall, almost a foot taller than Eric, he was able to reach over and slide it away. The gate swung open and they passed through to the rear. The neighbouring property was built close to the boundary and

Alex Hart's house had creepers climbing along the length of the wall and, what with it being summer, they were overgrown, flowering and hanging down to thwart progress. Tom was forced repeatedly to duck and move them aside with one arm, handing them off to Eric as he passed underneath.

At the rear they found a small courtyard garden with a gated access big enough to bring a car through. An old Ford Focus was parked there. It looked neglected with green algae growing across the bonnet, wheel arches and along the rubber seals at the base of the windows, much as you find with a vehicle frequently left under dense foliage. Tom caught Eric's attention and indicated towards the car with his eyes.

"Run the plates on this, would you?"

Eric nodded and took out his mobile phone, walking around to the front of the car to read the registration plate. Tom walked over to the kitchen window and looked through. Here, there were also net curtains but they only ran up the first third of the window, the rest was unobstructed. The kitchen was untidy, dirty crockery stacked up alongside the sink which itself could have done with a thorough going over. However, the place looked tired above all else with kitchen cabinets dating to the seventies or eighties. The latch on the rear gate clicked and the hinges groaned as they took the weight.

The newcomer was startled to see Eric move into view from the front of the car, then his eyes darted anxiously to Tom.

"Alexander Hart?" Tom asked. The man fixed his gaze on Tom with an accompanying, almost imperceptible, nod. Tom took out his ID and held up his warrant card. "DI Janssen," he said, inclining his head towards Eric, "and DC Collet from Norfolk police. We would like a word."

"What's this about?"

Hart wasn't quite what Tom was expecting. He was barely a couple of years older than Tom but the man standing in front of him, clutching a newspaper in one hand and a small white carrier bag in the other, looked to be in his mid to late fifties. He was

balding and what little sandy-brown hair he had was either thinning or speckled with flecks of grey or white. His eyes were
sunken, suggesting he regularly didn't sleep well, and he stood
with an exaggerated stoop which probably added to the impression of him being older than his years. Strangely, he was not only
wearing a long-sleeved white shirt and trousers but also a sleeve-
less burgundy jumper. It appeared to be thin, possibly lambswool,
but in this heat it was rather odd.

"The car's registered to an Alan Hart," Eric said.

"That's my father. What of it?"

Tom glanced back towards the house. "Do you live here with
your father?"

"No, not anymore. He died last year."

"I'm sorry to hear that."

"What's this about?" Hart asked again, only this time without
the nervousness and instead seemed irritated.

"We would like to speak to you about the archaeological dig
you managed at Branodunum back in 2001."

Hart snorted, his face breaking into a broad grin. "I know it
didn't go well," he said, stepping forward and taking his house
keys from his pocket. Moving past Tom, he glanced over his
shoulder at him as he slid the key into the lock of the back door.
"But I didn't think it was a crime. A crime against archaeology
perhaps." He pushed the door open, looked at Tom and Eric in
turn and tilted his head towards the interior. "You'd best come
inside then."

There was an odd smell in the kitchen. Tom couldn't put his
finger on what was causing it. It was a curious mix of a waste
bin that desperately needed emptying on a hot day crossed with
the type of smell you found in care homes or outpatient clinics
or dental surgeries. Maybe it was a mix of cleaning products
and rotting food, either way it left a pungent aroma drifting
through the house. Alex Hart put his carrier bag on the work
surface and opened the fridge, transplanting the contents from
one to the other. By the look of it he'd been to a local conve-

nience shop, returning with a pound of sausages, some milk, cheese and a half loaf of bread. Hart noted Tom eyeing his shopping.

"Is my lunch a matter of interest to Norfolk Constabulary these days or something?"

Tom looked at Eric who was hovering at the rear door, thankfully keeping it open. He obviously didn't like the smell either. Once Hart was done, he turned and headed into the adjoining sitting room. The detectives followed. It was evident that this was Hart's parents' house. The wall was decorated with wallpaper with a distinct floral pattern. There was a sideboard set underneath the window overlooking the front, a piece made in the sixties, dark wood, highly polished with spindly legs. Hart sat down on the sofa, large cushions with yet another floral print pattern which clashed with the walls. A clock hung on the wall, its ticking overly loud. Both Tom and Eric sat down.

"You want to know about Branodunum? Why?"

"Have you heard that the body of a young woman was found on the site over the weekend?"

"No! I hadn't. That's awful."

"She was murdered." Tom watched for a reaction. There wasn't one. Hart waited patiently, his eyes fixed on Tom's. He splayed his hands wide.

"And? What does that have to do with me?"

"We believe she was murdered around the time of your dig and was buried in one of your trenches. And that she may have been buried there the same weekend you closed down the site."

Hart sat there with a vacant expression, open mouthed and unblinking.

"Do you understand what I'm saying?" Tom asked. It was as if he'd zoned out. Tom waited patiently. Hart blinked.

"She wasn't there when we left on the Saturday. We would have seen her."

"We?"

His brow wrinkled and he looked to the floor. "Me, Julia ...

Billy. Not to mention the other helpers we had floating around. There must have been eight to ten of us on site that day."

"You were there when the trench was closed?" Tom asked. Hart appeared uncertain, eventually nodding briefly. "You're sure?"

"Um ..." Hart looked up at the ceiling, his eyes drifting around the room, past Eric and back to Tom. He nodded again. "Yeah. I think so. But, hey, it was a long time ago."

"Of course," Tom said, reaching into his pocket and bringing out the photograph of Tina Farrow. He passed it across to Hart who took it and examined the picture. "Do you recognise her?" Hart's gaze lingered on the image, his expression unreadable. Tom waited but Hart continued to stare. "Do you recognise her?" he asked again.

Hart snapped out of his trance-like state, shaking his head vigorously. "No, no I don't."

"Are you sure because it looked like she was familiar—"

"I *said* I don't, all right!" He thrust the picture back into Tom's hand. His tone and expression had changed, no longer distant and vague but turning mildly aggressive and looking more than a touch fearful.

"You stayed at the Crown in Brancaster for the duration of the dig, didn't you?"

Hart had his hands in his lap now, fingers interlocked but moving. He was agitated. He nodded curtly. "Yes. We stayed in the old stables out the back."

"With Julia Rose?"

Again, he nodded, silently mouthing the word 'yes'.

"This girl, Tina Farrow," Tom said, holding up the picture to him again. "She often worked at the Crown and was there on the last Friday night before you completed your excavations. We believe it was this night when she went missing. Do you recall seeing her at the pub?" Hart stared straight ahead, not looking at the picture. "Mr Hart, please could you look at the picture."

"I didn't bloody know her!" He glared fiercely at Tom, his eyes flitting between him and the image of Tina. His expression softened, as did his tone. "I ... told you already. I don't know her. If she was there, then I don't recall her. Okay?"

"Okay," Tom said, turning the picture of Tina towards him and glancing at it before putting it away. "We also understand that the entire dig was quite stressful for you personally."

"What has that got to do with anything?"

Tom shrugged. Hart took a deep breath, lifting himself upright and exhaling slowly.

"You're right," he said, sounding deflated. "It was tough. Things didn't work out." Tom waited for more but he didn't look like adding to the comment.

"You no longer work in the field?" Tom asked.

"No. Well, peripherally." He sat forward, resting his elbows on his knees and looking infinitely more comfortable discussing this than Tina. "I get some work in television from time to time. Not in front of the camera, obviously, but behind the scenes helping with logistics and so on. I know some people. It helps, you know?"

Tom cast an eye around the room. The pictures adorning the walls looked like they belonged to a different generation with frames to match. His eyes lowered to the mantelpiece above the open fire where photographs were neatly set out. Tom stood up and crossed over to them. Hart was in all of them, apparently taken at various archaeological dig locations. In his youth he wore his hair long to the collar. In some of them the people present were heavily wrapped up against the elements, in others the weather was far better. One of them might have been taken in the desert because of the arid backdrop. The people in it seemed to be shielding their eyes from the glare of the sun. He pointed at it.

"May I?" he asked. Hart sucked his lips inward, nodding. Tom lifted the picture, examining it before angling it towards Hart. "Egypt?"

He shook his head. "The Atacama Desert, Chile."

"Looks like many of the same people in each of these." A youthful Hart was easily recognisable standing with his arm around a young woman, presumably Julia Rose. He wasn't sure but the man on the far left could be Tim Hendry who also wore his hair long in a similar style.

"The four amigos," Hart said softly, smiling wistfully. "At university we made a pact to take part in digs on all six continents before we died."

"Six?" Eric asked, his eyebrows meeting.

"Not many digs going on in Antarctica that I'm aware of," Hart said, cutting a wry smile in Eric's direction. "Unless you're a conspiracy whacko and looking for a secret alien base underneath thousands of years of ice!"

"Of course," Eric said, his face flushing.

Tom smiled, careful not to let either man see. He put the picture frame back and cast an eye across the others. There was one that stood out, taken on an overcast, wet day with a stunning backdrop of steep mountains descending into water. There were only two people in it, and Tom thought this might be a holiday snap of Alex and Julia rather than one of work but he quickly realised his mistake. It was Tim Hendry alongside Julia. He pointed to it. "Did you take this one?"

Hart stood up and came over, picking it up, his brow furrowing as he spoke. "No. Julia sent this one to me while I was in hospital recuperating from an operation. That was taken a few months before we broke up." He sounded melancholy, slowly putting the picture back and neatly lining it up alongside the others. He looked at Tom, meeting his eye. "Is there anything else?"

"We would like to take a DNA sample from you, if you have no objections?"

Hart was taken aback. He looked over at Eric and then back at Tom. "Why ... why would you need to do that?"

"To compare with trace evidence samples found among the human remains. It will help us rule suspects in or out."

"But ... but I told you I don't know her."

"It's not a prerequisite for a killer to know their victim, Mr Hart." Tom stared hard at him, not offering him any opportunity for an easy get-out. "Will you willingly provide a sample?"

Hart held Tom's gaze for a few seconds then looked at his feet. He nodded slowly.

"Good. DC Collet will take it from you now, it won't take a moment." Tom looked at Eric who set off to retrieve the kit from the car. Alex Hart sank back onto the sofa, rubbing at his chin and avoiding Tom's gaze. "How did you get on with the pact?" he asked while waiting for Eric to return.

"Sorry, what?" Hart said, looking up, eyes wide.

"*The four amigos.*"

"Oh yes ... we managed three before ... well, we managed three," he said glumly, drawing breath. "Europe, an easy one. North Africa and Chile."

"Just the three left to go then."

"Yeah. Just the three." Hart nodded, sniffing loudly and looking away, evidently not keen to continue the conversation.

CHAPTER FIFTEEN

WALKING INTO OPS, Tom found Cassie still at her desk with a telephone clamped to her ear. It was approaching seven o'clock in the evening and he half expected Tamara to have sent Cassie home for the day by now. She angled the mouthpiece away from her face and turned her chair towards him.

"I'm on hold, trying to get a call through a satellite link to Dr Julia Rose. She replied to the message we left for her yesterday and sent me a Zoom link from where she was staying but the connection kept dropping and we gave up. I told Tamara I'd speak to her and then head home." She glanced at the clock on the wall, her face dropping. "That was an hour ago. How did you get on with Hart and Hendry, were they happy to provide DNA?"

"Hendry was happy to. No problem."

"Hart was less than forthcoming?"

"Less keen but didn't put up too much of an argument. Where is Dr Rose?"

"*Svelgen*, Norway. She's part of a team from the Norwegian Institute for Cultural Heritage who have uncovered a Viking longboat buried near to the mouth of the *Svelgselva* river. Apparently, it has the bodies of four warriors inside." She yawned, talking through it. "It's quite a big deal as these finds are rare but don't mention it to Eric whatever you do, I can't be doing with the questions."

Tom laughed. "He likes his history."

"Yeah, well, I've spent a bit of time with Becca and she's more of a Netflix girl, so he'd better shape up or she'll trade him in for someone who acts like they're in their twenties and not twice their age!" She turned back to her call. "Yes, I'm still waiting. Okay, can you ask her to call me back at the mobile number I gave you? Where is Eric anyway?"

Cassie put the phone down, abandoning the effort to speak to Julia Rose.

"I told him to head off once he'd filed the DNA samples. I doubt they'll be useful beyond shaking up our potential suspects but we may as well put them in the database. What did you make of her, Dr Rose?" Tom asked.

She shrugged. "Surprised to hear from us, from what I could tell, but the connection was so bad the video was unwatchable and the sound not much better. She sounded keen to help, though. When she calls back, hopefully, she'll be back in the town. The site is fairly remote, hence the satellite comms."

A uniformed constable poked his head around the corner from the corridor, his eyes searching the room and settling on Tom.

"Someone in reception to see you, sir."

"Who is it?"

"A lady called Sally Webber," he said, but evidently he had no further details to offer. Tom nodded and said he'd be right there and the officer disappeared from view. Cassie looked up at Tom.

"Who's Sally Webber?"

"A former work colleague and friend of Tina Farrow's," he said, concentrating. Cassie shook her head, glancing at the information boards but Webber didn't feature. "No, I only heard the name myself today when I spoke to Paul and Louisa Tennant."

"The owners of the Crown?"

"Yes, Sally worked for them at the same time as Tina, lives over in Wells now. They said she was close to Tina but why she's in reception I've no idea. I figured I'd call in on her tomorrow."

"Word travels fast," Cassie said, looking at the clock again. "Do you want me to come with you?"

Tom waved the offer away. "You get yourself off home and I'll see you in the morning."

"Thanks. Lauren was hoping we'd be able to eat together tonight, but I guess I can grab a takeaway on the way home."

"I expect Becca will say the same about Eric. We need to speak with Julia Rose and then get together and have a recap as to where we are. How did you get on digging into Alex Hart for me by the way?"

Cassie was shutting down her computer as she spoke over her shoulder. "Interesting. He's got some medical history that might be useful, but I need a magistrate to grant us a warrant to release his files to us. Purely a bureaucratic delay – should come through first thing tomorrow. Anything else before I go?"

Tom shook his head and she collected her car keys. She set off and he agreed to walk out with her. Buzzing themselves through the secure door and into reception, Cassie bid Tom goodnight as he smiled to the woman waiting for him. She was sitting at reception, hands in her lap and her legs together, as if she were in a dental surgery waiting for a root canal. She rose as he approached and introduced himself. She looked nervous.

"Is it true, that you've found Tina?"

He nodded, glancing over his shoulder at the member of the public standing at the desk speaking to the desk clerk.

"It's a little stuffy in here. Would you like to take a walk?" he asked. She nodded and they left together, Tom holding the door open for her, allowing her to pass through before following. The breeze was picking up now, which was a relief, and he thought he could hear the low rumble of thunder in the distance off the coast. Perhaps the weather was going to break earlier than forecast.

"What brings you to see me, Sally?" Tom asked as they walked. He glanced sideways at her. She was in her late thirties with sandy-brown hair hanging to her shoulders. She brushed the fringe away from her eyes with one hand, tucking it behind her ear. She met Tom's gaze, smiling awkwardly.

"Louisa." The smile faded as she looked away. Tom considered that Mrs Tennant must be quite the gossip to have spread the story to Sally's ears already. "She's good friends with my current employer, although I don't know why. Louisa's dreadful."

Tom smiled. "In what way?"

"You never wanted to be the first person to leave the room, I'll say that much." This pretty much confirmed his first thought. "She drove over this afternoon. I could tell she was talking about me, the snide way she looks at you, you know?" Tom inclined his head. "So, you want to speak to me about Tina?"

"Yes. I had planned to come by and see you tomorrow. You were friends?"

"Good friends, yes. Although Tina was two or three years older than me when we worked together, so she was often behind the bar or waiting tables at dinner service and I was clearing up back of house."

"Do you remember seeing her that Friday night, the last time she was seen alive?"

She nodded curtly, turning to face him. "Yeah, I saw her, didn't speak to her though. It was crazy busy," she said, sweeping the hair from her face once more. She looked out over the sea. "She was up for it that night. Really, really up for it."

"In what way?"

"Tina's way," she said, laughing. "She was on the wind up. She'd do it to some extent every time she was in, working or social, but that night she was spreading it around. Those archaeologist guys were hitting it pretty hard as I remember."

"Yes, the dig didn't go well, so were probably drowning their sorrows—"

"Well, that excuses one night but how about all of the others?" Tom looked at her quizzically. She grinned. "I figured they'd all be proper geeks ... reading books in the bar, in bed by nine o'clock, that type of thing but believe me, they were anything but! I'd never seen the Crown jumping so much before or since. I guess I should've known having watched Indiana Jones."

Tom smiled warmly and they set off again. "You said Tina was *up for it*. What do you mean by that?"

She laughed again dryly, shaking her head and looking at the ground as she walked. "Tina was such a wind-up merchant. Virtually every bloke she came in contact with was utterly enthralled by her; she was gifted. I mean, she was attractive which gave her a head start on most. Have you seen pictures?" He nodded. "Well, then you'll know why she could draw them in but it was more than that. She ... she seemed to feed off their attention and she played up to it." She saw Tom watching her intently. "Don't get the wrong idea, she wasn't a slapper or anything. She didn't go with a lot of guys, at least not as far as I know, but she definitely got off on hooking them and reeling them in. It was like she couldn't stop. I always imagined she'd pop up on one of these daytime TV shows talking about her insecurities or sex addiction ... something like that."

"You think it was compulsive behaviour?"

Sally snorted a laugh. "No idea but it was something. Whether it was a power game or a desire for affection, I've no idea. She didn't do it for bragging rights or anything. I mean, she never boasted about it; not to me. It didn't make her popular with the others though."

"I thought she was popular. That's what the Tennants said."

"Yes and no. The other girls didn't care for her flirting, even if they knew she wasn't taking it further. And she certainly wasn't with Louisa. She used to ride Tina pretty hard when she was around. Jealous, I thought." Tom asked her to elaborate. She hesitated.

"There's no reason why anything you say about her should come back to you. Even if Louisa Tennant is friends with your boss."

She relaxed a little. "Tina had an effect on women too, you

know. The men followed her around with their tongues hanging out and the women ... they were jealous, I imagine. That includes Louisa."

"Not you?"

She laughed with genuine humour at the question. "I was sixteen, Inspector, and as green as grass. Tina was a legend to me! I figured if I could have half the effect on boys that she had then I'd have been winning. Not that I ever would have had the confidence to do the stuff she did."

"Such as?"

She shrugged. "The accidental touches, flashes of a sultry smile in passing. The kind of thing that made any guy think he was the one; he was the one who she'd chosen." She shook her head again. "Even if they were the second or third person she'd done it to that evening, they'd all think they were special. *This time* they would be the one that it'd be different for. She really had a talent for making guys feel special. Men are so pathetic." She shot him an apologetic look, fearing she'd overstepped the mark. He smiled and waved it away.

"Many of us are suckers for a pretty face, it's true."

"Especially if you think you're in," she said, smiling a knowing smile.

"What about that night then, the Friday? Who was Tina ... how would you put it—"

"Flirting with?" she asked. Tom nodded. She concentrated hard, trying to remember. "Pretty much the whole bar at points, as far as I could tell. The archaeologists were wrapping things up the next day, so they were off. They were hell bent on having a blow-out to finish off on, and I reckon a couple of them thought they'd have a last crack at Tina. I don't remember their names but there was a group who I think were in charge; one guy in particular quite fancied himself, always flirting with the girls, especially Tina. I think he was married. At least, someone shouted at him across the bar that his wife wouldn't be happy if he didn't calm down. I saw him with his arms around Tina at one point."

"How so?" She looked at him, puzzled. "Aggressively, friendly, warmly appreciated or was she pushing him away?"

"Oh, it was in the main bar in front of everyone. Music was playing and he wanted her to dance with him. He was absolutely hammered. She looked to have him under control. She was flirting a lot with one of the others too. Now he was interesting." She smiled at the memory.

"Interesting how?"

"Because he hadn't shown much interest in her before. Tina said so. I think she saw him as a challenge; said she was going to have a go at *breaking him in*. I thought she was half joking, but maybe not."

"Was he immune to her charms or merely not interested?"

"More likely he didn't want to do anything in front of his girl-friend! They were staying together in the stables," she said, smil-ing. "I know she didn't appreciate Tina's attempts at flirting with her other half." Tom figured she could only be referring to Julia Rose and Alex Hart.

"Do you know if she had success with him?"

Sally shrugged. "Not as far as I know but I saw the couple having a proper ding-dong in the rear reception. He was stum-bling around half cut and I think she'd had a few as well. I was in the kitchen, just the other side of the door but could see and hear everything; it was a really unpleasant exchange."

"And what time was this?"

Her brow wrinkled in concentration as she thought about it. Tom felt the first few spots of rain on his face. He hoped for more. "It was a long time ago … maybe around nine to nine-thirty? I can't be certain but I know I should have left earlier when my shift finished at nine after evening service in the restaurant. Paul offered me twenty quid to stay on to help clear the glasses from the bar. Like I said, it was manic. Come to think of it, he was often one to have wandering hands himself."

"Paul Tennant?" Tom couldn't mask the surprise in his tone.

"Yeah, why do you think Louisa gave Tina such a hard time?

She was well aware that her husband could get a bit gropey – those of us working at the Crown called him *Paulie the Octopus*. And Louisa was away that weekend, too, so he was worse than normal. That's one reason why I stopped working there! I wouldn't have been surprised, what with Louisa being away, if Tina thought she'd wind him right up."

"Dangerous game," Tom said. She agreed.

"Danger can be thrilling though, can't it? Tina could wind Paul up ... then drop him like a hot rock. She said he deserved it but he *always* came back for more."

"Thinking he could be the one," Tom said quietly.

"Like I said, they all thought they were but—" She ran a hand through her hair, looking dejected. "None of them would ever be the one."

"Why do you think that?" He was curious. This woman was potentially one of the few who had any real insights into the personality that was apparently kept so well hidden from everyone around her.

She was reluctant to answer but he encouraged her. Eventually her expression softened, her demeanour lightening as she spoke, "I don't think Tina knew what she was looking for," she met his eye, "so how on earth could anyone else expect to?"

CHAPTER SIXTEEN

THE TEAM WERE GATHERING, Tamara waved a greeting to him through the window as she entered, Eric and Cassie were both going through their notes. Tom finished typing out the text message reply and tapped send. By the time he got home the previous night, Saffy was already sound asleep, Alice alongside her in the little girl's bed. Neither of them stirred when he'd slipped into the room, loosening the covers and pushing the window further open as both were sweating. Saffy had been struggling to get off to sleep for some time now, the after-effects of losing her father, and even when she did, she'd become prone to night terrors. More often than not Alice wound up sleeping in with her, or Saffy would pad into their room in the early hours and climb into their bed.

Arriving home late, and an early start today, saw him leave the house before either of them woke up. In his haste to get to the station he hadn't left a note or anything but he did set out the breakfast table for them just to make Alice's life a little easier. She'd appreciated it, sending him a lovely message. Rising from behind his desk, he slipped the mobile into his pocket and gathered his own notes, picked up his cup of coffee and joined the others in the ops room.

Following his conversation with Sally Webber the previous evening, they'd agreed to carry out a detailed check on the three archaeologists and Paul Tennant. None of them appeared willing to offer an accurate account of that particular Friday night, the night of Tina's disappearance, with all having potentially self-incriminating reasons not to do so. Perhaps there were patterns in their lives prior to, or since, Tina's murder. Tom pulled up a chair and Tamara looked over at Eric.

"Eric, you kick us off with what you know about Professor Cannell, please."

Eric cleared his throat, glancing down at his notes. The detective constable looked tired to Tom as if he hadn't been sleeping well.

"Following on from what Sally Webber told Tom last night, I checked and Cannell was the only one of the leadership team who was married at the time." He glanced down, double checking the dates once more. "He married his wife, Susan, in 1999. They were both students at Cambridge during their undergraduate years, marrying a year after graduating and both embarked on their post docs. Stands to reason as if he were the one Webber referred to as – how do I put it, harassing … Tina?"

"Sounds apt," Tamara said. "What else?"

"Achieved his doctorate in 2003 … highly regarded within academic circles. He specialised in the Romano-British and early medieval periods, taking up a position within Cambridge University's Archaeology Faculty. While he was there he pioneered a broad outreach programme designed to raise the profile and aspirations of young people within the field, spearheading a resurgence in excavations." Eric took a breath, glancing around to ensure everyone was still attentive. They were. "He left his role after a decade to set up his own consultancy which is thriving. His resumé is impressive, noting his leading of successful dig locations in Southern and Eastern Europe along with former Roman colonies of North Africa. He is cited as the foremost knowledge as to how extensive the Romans were in their movement east beyond the Rhine, proving settlements went further than previously thought."

"That's an impressive professional list, Eric," Tom said. "How about in his personal life. Is he known to us?"

Eric shook his head. "Not so much as a speeding ticket, although," he raised his eyes from his notes, tilting his head to one side, "it is purely hearsay, but I spoke to someone still working at the faculty and there was a suggestion of impropriety with one of his students."

"Prior to him leaving?" Tamara asked.

"Yes, that's my understanding. Whether that hastened his departure I'm not sure but there was something fishy about the timings; there was no indication of his departure prior to doing so."

"Was there an official allegation made?"

"No. At least, there was nothing on record but what was said behind closed doors, I couldn't say." Tom was about to ask a question but Eric read his mind. "And I'm still trying to find out the name of the student in question, so I can ask her. When I showed interest my source clammed up, probably for the same reasons as the whole thing was kept quiet in the first place."

"Good work, Eric," Tamara said, looking at Cassie. "Who did you have, Cass?"

"Tim Hendry," she said, putting aside the notes she'd taken from Eric's briefing. "His career hasn't been as prolific as his friend's, although he's considered an expert on the Middle Ages and alongside his academic work – presently at the University of East Anglia – he has also carved out a career in front of the camera, capitalising on certain peoples'," she looked directly at Eric and smiled, "interest in studying archaeology from the comfort of their armchairs."

"Cheap shot," Eric muttered under his breath but his half-smile demonstrated that he clearly saw the funny side.

"And he seems to be in great demand with it, too," Cassie said, flicking through her notes. "He's featured on television programmes for National Geographic and Discovery, to name a couple as well as our domestic channels here including the Beeb. All of which have taken him on excavations across Europe, notably Central and Eastern Europe," she read from her notes *"charting the movements and developments of peoples in those areas ...* blah, blah, blah." Looking up, she met Tamara's gaze. "Interestingly, on the personal front, he was arrested and interviewed following a domestic incident during what was an acrimonious divorce case from his first wife. He escaped prosecution after his estranged wife expressed discomfort at the prospect of speaking in court. As a result, Hendry accepted a caution. He married again two years later, and they are still together with no record of any similar occurrences."

"What was the nature of the dispute?" Tom asked. "How serious did the attending officers think it was?"

"A visit to Accident and Emergency for his wife, but no broken bones. Soft tissue injuries, primarily to the face and upper body. Hendry cited work stress alongside the breakdown of the marriage; an account accepted by the investigating officers by the look of it. It didn't seem to do his television career any harm."

"When was this?"

"Um ..." She checked her notes. "2007. Maybe it would have been different these days with the explosion of social media," Cassie said with a shrug. "He doesn't sound like the type of guy to get on the wrong side of to me."

"But we don't have any witnesses linking Hendry to Tina Farrow that night," Tom said, nodding his thanks to Cassie as he picked up his notes relating to Alexander Hart. "We already know the Branodunum dig was categorised as an abject failure by everyone present. From what Cannell and Hendry told us and we've no reason to doubt them, it was this dig that culminated in the end of Hart's academic career which to the lay man seems a little harsh. Thanks to Eric's perseverance," he nodded in Eric's direction, "we've been able to obtain Hart's medical file. He has been sectioned under the Mental Health Act for his own safety on two occasions, once in 2002 and again five years ago. On the first occasion he experienced an episode, alleging he was being followed by a woman and subsequently confronting her in a supermarket. On the second, he was found wandering along a rural street semi-naked with no recollection of how he came to be there. On both occasions he spent a short period of time under evaluation before being discharged and treated as an outpatient."

"Treated for what?" Tamara asked.

"His diagnoses have shifted but he is listed as having a *suspicious personality disorder*; in this case a *Schizotypal Personality Disorder* which can manifest in ways that see the sufferer experiencing distorted thoughts or perceptions. Unlike with schizophrenia it doesn't lead to psychosis but the person can think and express themselves in ways that others find odd or unusual, often making the formation of close relationships difficult. They can also experience extreme anxiety or paranoia in social situations and in some circumstances, they believe they have special abilities—"

Eric wrinkled his nose. "What sort of special abilities?"

"Belief in a sixth sense, that type of thing," Tom said.

"You said the diagnoses had shifted?" Tamara asked. "Was there a different conclusion reached before or after that one?"

"The first evaluation leaned towards an *Antisocial Personality Disorder* – probably due to the aggression and impulsive attack on the woman he thought was following him. A look into his teenage years at school saw him in frequent trouble for his behaviour. Academically he was considered highly intelligent but interpersonally he got bored easily, acted impulsively and was quick to anger." Tom reread his notes. "His Head of Year wrote in an end of term report that *Alexander appears to have little or no empathy for his fellow classmates and acts for his own indulgence, irrespective of the effect on those around him.*"

Tamara raised her eyebrows at the statement. "Sounds like a guy who thinks about himself first and no one else after."

"This specific disorder can lead to someone getting into

dangerous or risky situations without adequately assessing the consequences." Tom put his notes down on the desk beside him. "They'll often struggle to maintain concentration making it difficult to hold down a job."

"Hart fits that bill, doesn't he?" Tamara asked. Tom couldn't disagree. Alex Hart had flitted between jobs in and around the television industry for years but such work would be irregular, bearing in mind the nature of the industry. However, it didn't necessarily scan well with him.

"The initial diagnosis could point us towards what happened to Tina, impulsive, quick to anger but ... he had been able to hold down close relationships with friends and notably with Julia Rose, so I think it's too early to reach for that in my opinion." Tom looked at Eric. "How did you get on with *Paulie the Octopus*?"

"Prior to their taking on the Crown Inn, Paul and Louisa Tennant ran a small boutique hotel down in Suffolk, close to Ipswich. They sold up three months after Paul successfully defended a sexual harassment case brought against him by an employee. The member of staff was an eighteen-year-old migrant worker, recently arrived to take up a place at a local college and looking to make some money before her course started. The Tennants claimed she'd attempted to blackmail them with malicious gossip prior to going to the police and subsequently suing. She alleged Paul Tennant assaulted her on three separate occasions but Louisa testified he was with her on at least one of those times, offering her husband an alibi. The Crown Prosecution Service didn't proceed with the case and the civil case ruled in Paul's favour."

"Sounds like quite a charmer nonetheless," Cassie said. She looked at Tom. "What did you make of him? Did he come across as a sex pest?"

"Can't say he did but then again, if they were easy to spot, they wouldn't get away with it. He struck me as a man dominated by his wife and it wouldn't be too much of a stretch to see him abuse his position of authority in that way in order to compensate. Sally

Webber stated it was public knowledge." He looked at Tamara. "How do you want to proceed?"

"What about the father, Conrad? You were thinking there was more going on behind closed doors?"

"I still do," Tom said, casting an eye over the white board with Conrad Farrow's picture on it. He pursed his lips. "But the friction within the house seems largely to be between Tina and her mother. No one has Tina returning home after her night out and no one puts Conrad anywhere near her that night, let alone on the Friday at all. It seems to me that local gossip and innuendo pushed him to the front of the queue rather than the evidence. I just don't see it at the moment – I think we have stronger suspects."

"Well, we've been polite so far but, seeing as our archaeologists' recollections have been rather economical with reality when it comes to both Tina and that particular Friday night, I think we should speak to them again. Only this time we'll squeeze them a little more."

CHAPTER SEVENTEEN

ERIC SLOWED the car down as they entered Roydon, a small village to the east of King's Lynn. William Cannell wasn't in his office when they called. The lady on the reception desk stated he'd called in sick that morning and would be working from home.

"Just past the *Three Horseshoes* on the right, didn't she say?" Tom asked, raising a pointed finger as the pub came into view. "Should be the next right."

There was a cut through lane to Chequers Road and Eric navigated past several parked vehicles and came to a stop at the junction. Tom looked left and right, trying to match the description they'd been given to what was in front of them. He indicated for Eric to turn right and he did so. The next house along was Cannell's. It was a period farmhouse, set back in substantial grounds. As the car wound its way up the drive Tom caught sight of an outdoor pool to the rear. The gravel crunched under the tyres, heralding their approach. A woman stepped out from inside a cart shed being used as a garage and eyed their approach.

She smiled in greeting as they got out but was clearly puzzled as to who they were. Tom guessed she was Cannell's wife. She was dressed in loose fitting riding gear and was loading equipment into the rear of her Discovery.

"Mrs Cannell?" Tom asked, taking out his warrant card. "DI Janssen. I'm looking to speak to your husband again."

"Again? What about?"

"He hasn't mentioned our visit to you?"

Her expression of surprise switched to fearful as she shook her head. "No. Why, what's going on?"

"We just have some follow-up questions to ask him. Is he around?" Tom turned to look at the house, seeing no movement.

"Yes, of course."

She closed the door to the car and gestured for them to join her and they walked together across to the main house and around to the rear.

"Will this take long?" she asked, opening the door to a boot room adjoining the kitchen.

"We'll be as quick as we can, Mrs Cannell." Tom had to duck as he entered.

"Charlotte, please," she said, smiling, although she was clearly perturbed by their presence.

"Is your husband very unwell?"

"Unwell? No. Why do you ask?"

Tom shook off the comment, making eye contact with Eric as Charlotte turned her back on them and led the way through to the kitchen. Eric evidently thought the same as he did; William Cannell was comfortable misleading almost anyone in his life. Passing from the kitchen and into an open hallway they found William in the living room, sipping a cup of freshly brewed coffee, judging from the aroma in the air. He looked up as they entered, frowning at his wife.

"I thought you were off to the stables—" seeing detectives behind her, his frown dissipated to be replaced by open-mouthed shock as he put the cup down on a small table beside his seat. "Inspector Janssen ... I–I wasn't expecting to see you so soon."

"And when were you going to mention this to me?" Charlotte said pointedly folding her arms across her chest. Her husband spread his hands wide in a placatory gesture.

"I didn't see any reason to, darling."

Any further conversation between the two of them was cut short by Tom.

"Professor Cannell. We've now positively identified the body as that of Tina Farrow and we have a few more questions regarding your relationship with—"

"What body? And what relationship for that matter?" Charlotte said, glaring at her husband but turning her attention to Tom. "What is all this about?"

"It's nothing, love, honestly," Cannell said, lurching up from the sofa and placing a reassuring hand on her forearm, strategically placing himself between his wife and them; a rather obvious attempt to gain control of the situation. "I'll tell you all about it later. It was all a long, long time ago. Why don't you get off to the stables—"

"Just who the hell is this Tina," she looked at Tom, "what did you say her last name was?"

"Farrow," Eric said, much to Cannell's irritation. He flashed a dark look at Eric who didn't register it with a response.

"Honestly, it's nothing to be concerned about." Cannell looked at his watch. "Seriously, you'd best get yourself off or you'll be late for Harriet's riding lesson."

Charlotte's gaze lingered on him for a few moments as he ushered her away from Tom and Eric. Reluctantly she allowed him to do so, walking through into the hall and placing a hand on the balustrade. She glanced at Tom before looking up the stairs. "Harriet, darling! It's time for us to go." The sound of heavy footfalls from upstairs as their daughter descended making far too much noise for one so slight. Tom figured she was twelve or thirteen.

"Who are they?" the girl asked, looking past her mother, as she reached the foot of the stairs. Charlotte shooed her off, only glancing back over her shoulder with an anxious expression once and then, with the sound of a latch dropping into place behind them, they were gone. Cannell turned on Tom, his face reddening. Any embarrassment or awkwardness was gone to be replaced by a flash of anger.

"Just what the hell are you playing at walking in here announcing all manner of—"

"This is a murder investigation, Professor Cannell," Tom said flatly. "And we're not playing at anything." He cast an eye up and down the man. "You seem to have recovered from whatever ailment stopped you from going to work today."

Cannell reddened further, only this time with embarrassment. He shrugged. "I needed some time at home."

"To rethink your story?"

He glared at Tom, his expression darkening. "What are you talking about?"

"Tina Farrow," Tom said, producing the same picture he'd shown him the day before yesterday and holding it aloft in Cannell's face.

"I told you, I barely knew her—"

"No. You told us you didn't know her at all." Cannell's face dropped, he turned away averting his eyes from Tom's gaze. "So, which is it today, barely or not at all?"

He didn't respond.

"Or is there another option you've not yet used that's still on your short list?" Eric asked. Cannell looked up, eyeing both of them in turn.

"I didn't know her very well, that's the truth."

Tom raised his eyebrows. "But you did know her." Cannell nodded silently. "And what are the odds of us finding your DNA among her remains do you think?"

"Don't be absurd," Cannell retorted, "it will have degraded by now—"

"Will it?" Tom asked. Cannell, realising his mistake, sighed and chewed on his lower lip. "There's no need to deny it further, we have witnesses who put you and Tina together on the night she disappeared and – how can I put this politely – you were all over her!"

"That doesn't mean I bloody killed her, though, does it?" he said with a flash of accompanying anger.

"Leaves us with plenty to discuss at the station though."

Tom stepped to one side, leaving Cannell standing in between the two of them, gesturing for him to follow Eric. Cannell closed his eyes, took a deep breath and followed Eric out of the room.

———

SEATED IN AN INTERVIEW ROOM, William Cannell cut a dejected figure. Sally Webber had described him as being the one who *really fancied himself*. Tom thought he held himself in high regard, certainly, but whether that extended to his perception of his appeal to women was another matter altogether. He'd lied several times and seemed comfortable doing so but as he rightly stated – that didn't make him a murderer. Tom entered, Eric was already sitting there and Tamara was watching via a video link from another room. Tom put a cup of coffee down in front of Cannell who smiled appreciatively, reaching for it. Tom reread the caution and Cannell waved away the offer of representation. He stared at Tom, ensuring he had his attention as he sat down.

"I don't need a solicitor because I have nothing to hide," Cannell said firmly but keeping his tone measured. "I'd like it on record that I am willing to participate in this interview in order to set things straight but I emphatically deny having any involvement in the disappearance of that young woman."

"Duly noted," Tom said, opening the folder in front of him and taking out the picture of Tina. He laid it gently on the table, turned it to face Cannell and slid it across in front of him. "Tina Farrow. Tell us about that Friday night."

Cannell's eyes shifted to the picture and away again. He sniffed, brushing the tip of his nose with the back of his hand. "Fun girl. We liked her."

"We?"

"The team. All of us who were staying there during the dig."
He shrugged. "She wasn't around much ... but made her presence
known when she was." Tom offered him an enquiring look,
encouraging him to continue. "Flirtatious. *Very flirtatious*. Like I
say, a fun girl."

"And that Friday night?" Tom put his hands together, interlocking his fingers. Eric maintained a focussed gaze on the
interviewee.

"Erm ... what's to say really?" Cannell raised his eyebrows and
then he cast his eyes around the room. "The dig was wrapping
up." He opened his hands, palms wide. "It had been an abject
failure and we were drowning our sorrows in the bar and trying
to make the most of what was a piss-poor experience."

"Again."

"Excuse me?" Cannell met Tom's eye, his gaze lingering as if he
was trying to ascertain what he knew.

"You were drinking again. Apparently your team partied
pretty hard during that dig, contributing massively to the
Tennants' takings that summer."

Cannell rolled his eyes. "Tennant. Yes, that was him." He half
smiled. "Paul Tennant, now there's a guy you should look at. He
was always squeezing past the young women behind the bar, little
touches here and there. They didn't like it. You could see it in their
faces when he wasn't looking. Slimy man."

"A witness states you had your hands all over Tina—"

"I'd had a skin full, Inspector!"

"Which makes it okay?"

Cannell waved away the remark, picking up his cup and
sipping at the contents. Wiping his mouth with the back of his
hand, he sat forward resting his elbows on the table. "I ... may
have got a little overly friendly, I'll admit." He held an apologetic
hand up before him as he spoke. "But she'd been flirting with me
... and not just that night but also several others. And she didn't
exactly push me away, you know? I thought she was up for it."

"Up for what?"

He shrugged. "You know … a bit of fun."

"Would your wife see it that way?" Eric asked.

"None of her business," Cannell shot back. "Then or now." Eric turned the corners of his mouth down, glancing at his notes, but made no further comment. Cannell appeared to have a need to explain himself, or at least to offer mitigation. "Look, it was a stressful dig and I was away from home a lot. I was missing my wife and our daughter, our first daughter – you saw Harriet, our second, earlier – and things can happen, can't they?" He held up both hands, indicating the two of them. "You're both men. You know how it is, right?"

Both Tom and Eric ignored the question.

"Describe the sexual contact you had with Tina?"

"Now look, there was no sexual contact!" He glared at Tom. "I'll admit there was an encounter … of sorts, but it wasn't sexual contact."

"But you did leave your DNA on her person, you as good as said so—"

"Yes, yes, yes," Cannell said. "I know what I said earlier. We had a *brief* moment in the rear lobby if I remember right. We'd been flirting with each other for much of the evening and I followed her out," he coughed nervously, "when she went to the ladies. I met her in the lobby and she dragged me into a small office in the rear that she had a key to and—" He shifted awkwardly in his seat, taking a deep breath. "And that's where it happened. But it was brief, like I said, over in minutes."

"What was?" Cannell cleared his throat, although Tom doubted there was any obstruction. His neckline and cheeks were reddening. "We're waiting, Professor."

He took a deep breath. "We kissed. It was consensual, no doubt about that." He raised a pointed finger as if to emphasise it. "And she … um … she undid my trousers … and um … took my trousers and pants down." He was speaking barely above a whisper now. Tom glanced at Eric who raised a single eyebrow in response but Cannell didn't notice, he was staring at the table in front of him, gripping his polystyrene coffee cup with both hands as if it was the only thing anchoring him to this world.

"And?"

"She walked out."

Tom exchanged a glance with Eric who appeared to be on the verge of grinning but managed to stifle it under Tom's scrutiny.

"She walked out?"

Cannell nodded, his face flushing. "Walked out and left me standing in the middle of the office with my trousers around my ankles."

"Where did she go?"

He shrugged. "How would I know? The cheeky cow had it all planned, I bet. I've been embarrassed before but that," he shook his head, "was a humiliation like no other."

Tom rolled his tongue against the inside of his cheek. "That must have made you angry, furious even?"

"Quite the opposite! It sobered me up. I realised I was making an idiot of myself and I went back to my room – alone – to sleep it off."

"Anyone see you go?"

He shook his head. "Not as far as I know. I didn't really want to see anyone. I figured she'd gone back into the bar and had a good old laugh about me with everyone. I couldn't face it. As it happens, no one mentioned it the next day, so I guess she didn't."

"And what time did you go to your room?"

He thought about it, eyes wide and eyebrows raised. "Ten-ish, maybe. Hard to say. All in all, I was pleased to put Branodunum behind me and move on."

"What else can you tell us about that night, seeing as your memory has miraculously returned?"

"Look, I'm telling you the truth! You can understand why I didn't mention it, surely? But I had nothing to do with that girl's death. You should be speaking to ..." His head dropped and he began chewing on his lower lip.

"We should speak to who?"

Cannell looked up and met his eye. "Oh, it doesn't matter now, I'm sure. I doubt it'll make a difference. She – Tina – was making eyes at Alex. It was really annoying Julia and Tim was stoking it up that evening, pointing it out to Jules."

"Tim Hendry?" Tom asked, curious. Cannell bobbed his head. "Why would he do that?"

Cannell shrugged in response. "For fun, maybe. The drink was flowing and everyone had the hump with the dig. Maybe he was doing it for a laugh."

"I thought you were all friends?"

"We are. Well, we were back then. Even so, there was a bit of jealousy between those three." Tom sat forward, fixing him with a stare. "Between the three of them, Alex, Jules and Tim; a proper three-way relationship."

"They were all in a relation—"

"No, no, no," Cannell said, grinning. "I don't mean it that way. Alex and Jules were an item but I reckon Tim held a torch for Jules. I mean, Tim would never admit it but I'm telling you it was obvious, if you knew them. As plain as the nose on your face. I know they were friends and all, but should they have ever split then I'm certain Tim would've made a move on her. Absolutely certain of it."

"Are you suggesting one of those three may have killed—"

"I'm not suggesting anything of the sort," Cannell said, splaying his arms wide. "But if you're looking at me because I kept things secret, then I'm just saying you can find secrets elsewhere just as easily! Now, I think you will agree that I have been more than forthcoming with you today." He fixed Tom with a direct stare. "And as I understand it, I am not under arrest."

"No, you're not."

"In which case I would like to leave now, unless there is something else you wish to ask me?"

Tom picked up the photograph of Tina, replacing it in the folder under Cannell's watchful eye. He closed the flap and took a breath. "You're free to go." Cannell slapped his palms gently on the table, smiled, and pushed his chair back as he stood. Tom caught his attention. "For now." The smile faded. "DC Collet will show you out."

CHAPTER EIGHTEEN

EMERGING FROM THE INTERVIEW ROOM, Tom watched the retreating forms of William Cannell and Eric as the latter escorted him along the corridor away from the custody suite and towards the front office. Cannell shot a nervous glance towards him, over his shoulder, as Eric indicated for him to turn left at the end. Tamara emerged from the third door along, coming to stand next to Tom.

"What do you make of that?"

Tom inhaled through gritted teeth, wrinkling his nose.

"I take it you are not entirely convinced by his explanation," she said.

"It's not that," he said, frowning.

"Then what?"

"Cannell just offered up another motive, unwittingly I should add."

"One for himself and another for Alex Hart—"

"And Dr Julia Rose, too, while he was at it." Tamara glanced at him, inclining her head to one side. "If what he described actually happened – embarrassed, humiliated even, and full of drink, there's no reason not to think someone in that scenario might react very badly. We need to find someone who saw Tina alive after the time he stipulated, ten-ish, to try and back up his timeline."

"If he was telling the truth about that?" She touched his forearm, gesturing for them to head back to ops. "He doesn't strike me as a man who can tell the truth under any circumstances. How can we trust anything that he says?"

"Do you think he's smart enough to keep one step ahead of the investigation, especially after all this time? He would need to remember an incredible amount of detail in order not to trip himself up."

They entered ops, Tamara deep in thought. He went straight to the coffee machine, picking up a cup and angling it towards her. She nodded and he set about making both of them a cup. The machine was a fine decision on his part and all of them chipped in with the pods. There was only so much vending machine or recycled brewing in the canteen that a person could handle.

"If he is drip feeding us information," Tamara said, coming alongside him and leaning against the desk, folding her arms across her chest, "as and when he thinks it necessary to direct us away from him as a suspect, he's certainly intelligent enough to do so, don't you think?"

Tom had to agree but there was something troubling him and it was focussed on the location of the burial. The machine hissed and gurgled as Tamara's espresso pumped through. He handed it to her and walked over to the white board detailing where they found Tina Farrow's remains. Tamara glanced at him and then the machine. She crossed the room to join him, both palms encircling the cup in her hand.

"What are you thinking about?"

He was so focussed he almost didn't hear her. He looked sideways at her and she raised her eyebrows. "Tom?"

He shook his head. "Sorry. I was just thinking – the dump site, burial place, whatever you want to call it – it's an odd choice ... for a killer, I mean."

"Remote, not overlooked, easy access from the highway. What's not to like?"

He looked at her, assuming she was playing devil's advocate

because he could see in her eyes that she was thinking similarly. As a dump site, it was good for the reasons she stated but it was also an extremely poor choice for a host of others and it didn't make a lot of sense. He pointed to the trench where Tina was found.

"It is reasonable to assume that they are telling the truth when it comes to Tina not being laid there prior to the trench being backfilled, unless we are going down the road of arguing Cannell, Hart, Julia Rose and the digger driver were all participants in either the murder or the cover-up."

"Agreed," Tamara said, sipping at her coffee. "That would be absurd but look at where we found the remains, in the trench at the outer edge of the field. Do we have any pictures showing how the field boundary was delineated back then? If there was a hedgerow then there's every possibility her body could have been stashed behind it and slid into place on the Saturday."

"Too risky, surely?" Tom said, picking up a marker pen and tapping the board with the lid. "Even if the killer was able to operate the digger themselves, enough to shovel a couple of scoops onto the body to conceal it, they would still be taking a *massive* risk of being seen." He shook his head. "There were still a number of bodies on site, I just don't see it. It would have taken a boldness that these guys just wouldn't have."

"Probably right." Tamara's gaze narrowed. "Then we have to conclude that Tina was either held somewhere from, potentially, late on the Friday night until she was killed and deposited in the ground sometime late Saturday after everyone left or perhaps even Sunday."

"That's a lot of time to keep someone captive, particularly if the killer is one of the dig team—"

"Maybe she wasn't captive," Tamara said. "Maybe she didn't go home but got an offer she liked, only it ended up killing her soon after? Perhaps it was a day or two later?"

"In which case we might be well wide of the mark in looking at the archaeologists," Tom said. "It's a damn shame we have no idea of Tina's movements after nine-thirty, unless we trust Cannell's description of events."

"I'm loathe to do that."

"Me too. It sounds like Tina gave him what he deserved."

Tamara smiled. "I think I would have liked her; you know?"

"Remind me not to get on the wrong side of you," Tom said. Tamara smiled as she drank her coffee. "Still, though ..." Tom looked back at the board. "That dump site is bugging me. There must be a significance."

"Does there have to be? Could it not just be a place that was convenient?" Tamara said.

"Yes, of course but if convenience is what you're looking for then surely you'd just dump her in the marshes ... or behind a hedgerow. There are any number of winding lanes and farm tracks around these parts where you could dispose of a body without being seen—"

"But," Tamara wagged a finger at him pointedly, "she would be found sooner or later, probably within a couple of days."

"And that's another thing about the choice of location; she would be found eventually. It was a known archaeological site. It was excavated again in 2012, so there was every possibility that the body would be uncovered, so why choose it?"

Tamara's expression took on a look of consternation. "That's true. Not thinking ahead?"

"Which would go against our assumption of intelligence and planning."

She shrugged. "Maybe it is our assumption that's wrong? If Tina was killed soon after leaving the Crown Inn, then her body could have been stashed somewhere and presumably the killer returned the following day and buried her on the Saturday. Otherwise, in the heat of summer, she would have started to make her presence known." She pinched the end of her nose with thumb and forefinger for dramatic effect. Tom nodded. "Which brings the archaeologists back into it because they were set to leave on the Saturday."

Tom stepped back, running a hand casually across his chin. "Follows Tina from the Crown, kills her and stashes the body out of sight. The next day they close off the dig and everyone departs—"

"But the killer stays back and retrieves the body, burying her in the field." Tamara rolled her lower lip beneath the upper.

"What?" Tom asked, trying to read her expression.

"How long do you think it takes to dig a grave?" She looked at him quizzically. "I mean, not a shallow one or even a proper one, not six feet, but one to the depth to which forensics reckon Tina was buried in?"

"Three hours," Eric said, walking into ops in the background. Both of them looked round at him.

"That was said with confidence, Eric," Tamara said, smiling.

"A new hobby of yours?" Tom asked.

Eric grinned. "I've been looking it up. If you were to dig a grave for an adult person to the depth of six feet, it would probably take the average person at least ten hours. A professional, used to that level of labour and physically fit could arguably halve that. Then factor in the reduced depth that we found the majority of Tina's remains at and you get three hours," he looked at them in turn, "give or take. The soil would be easier to turn over as well." Tom and Tamara exchanged a look. "The soil was freshly dug, broken up mechanically as well. It would be far easier to dig in one of the trenches than to scoop out virgin ground, so to speak."

Tom was impressed. That was simple logic and added weight to the convenience theory. "So, it would be quicker to hide the body—"

"And less likely to be discovered for years," Tamara said, finishing for him. "Eric, you're a genius!"

The constable flushed red at the praise. Cassie entered the room, gawping at Eric's expression.

"What have I missed?"

"Eric's genius," Tamara repeated.

"Really?" Cassie said, looking sideways at Eric. "Will there be another one along in a minute?"

Eric side-swiped her across the upper arm, smiling.

Tom returned to the coffee machine, loading it with another capsule. "I still think there's more to the choice of burial location, although I don't doubt Eric's genius at all." Eric seemed uncomfortable with the third reference in quick succession, taking his seat at his desk. "If it is someone tied to the dig then it's clever but hints at experience to me. It's what we talked about the other day, about killers getting lucky first time out. This guy killed someone without leaving a trace, disposed of the body in such a way that we didn't find it for decades—"

"And did so only through good fortune, we should also add," Tamara said. "You think this isn't his first kill? That's a stretch, isn't it?"

"Ask yourself, could a murder committed in a drunken rage as an act of revenge or one carried out by someone suffering a mental episode really be done so well as to remain uncovered for this long? Something doesn't add up."

"Fair point. What do you want to do?"

Tom thought about it for a moment, glancing across the room to where Cassie and Eric were busy at their desks. "Cassie, what have you got on at the moment?"

She spun her chair round to face them. "I'm running through witness statements from 2001, trying to cross reference a timeline from then to what we know now."

"Okay, brief Eric on what you have so far and then I want you to start looking through missing persons' reports."

"I thought we'd already done that—"

"When trying to identify Tina, yes, I know. But I want you to look at William Cannell and Alex Hart, log where they've been working during their careers and then cross reference that with missing persons' cases in those areas around the same time."

"Right," Cassie said, making a note. She hesitated; her pen poised above her notebook. She looked up at him. "They've been working in and around dig sites for the better part of twenty-five years, not to mention they're not necessarily UK based."

"I know. Have you got somewhere you need to be?"

Cassie exhaled slowly. "No, of course not." She tapped her pen against the pad and turned around. Tom could picture the expression on her face. He saw Eric lean in towards her and almost thought he heard him whisper something about a genius. She flicked out with her right hand but Eric was too quick for her, recoiling, and all she found was fresh air.

Tom picked up his coffee cup. Now he felt better.

"Shall we pay Alex Hart another visit?" Tamara asked.

He nodded. "Next on the list."

CHAPTER NINETEEN

Tom drove past Alex Hart's house, the curtains were closed much the same as before, pointing it out to Tamara and took the next right turn. A narrow lane led to the rear offering access to the back gardens of several properties. The gates were closed and Tom pictured the rotting car on the other side of them, imagining those gates hadn't been opened for quite some time. Two other cars were parked up, one in front of the other, and he recognised the nearest. Gesturing, he drew Tamara's attention to it.

"It looks as if Hart has a visitor. I'm pretty sure that's Tim Hendry's car."

Tamara glanced at it and followed Tom to the pedestrian side gate nearby. It wasn't locked and they entered the garden to find Alex Hart standing at the entrance to the kitchen speaking with Tim Hendry, who looked like he was readying himself to leave; he had his hand resting on Alex Hart's sagging shoulders in a supportive demonstration of camaraderie. They both looked round at the sound of the gate opening. Hart's eyes widened when he recognised Tom, looking anxiously to his friend who maintained the supportive grip for a second longer. Hendry nodded at Alex and said something Tom couldn't make out but he thought he saw Hendry smile. Was it encouragement, he couldn't tell? It was Hendry who addressed them, releasing his friendly grip on Hart and turning fully to face them, positioning himself, Tom thought deliberately, between them and Hart.

"Back so soon, Inspector?" He looked at Tom and then to Tamara. "We haven't met."

"DCI Greave," Tamara said. Hendry smiled and offered her his hand.

"Tim Hendry. Bringing out the big guns, are you?"

Tom eyed him quizzically.

"The higher rank." Hendry glanced around at Hart whose anxiety was visibly growing, Tom wondered if he was on the verge of tears. "Must be important."

"We're still building a case, Mr Hendry, speaking with people as and when more evidence comes to light."

"What is it that brings you here then?"

It was Tamara who spoke, her eyes trained on Hart behind him. He was shifting his weight between his feet. "I think that's for Mr Hart to hear first."

"Yes, yes, of course. As it should be," Hendry said apologetically. He looked between the two of them and back at his friend once more. "Right, well, I was just off." He turned to Hart, offering him a quick pat on the upper arm. "Chin up, mate." Hart smiled but it was clearly forced. "And if you need me, just give me a call, okay?"

"I'd like a quick word, if I may?" Tom asked Hendry as he made to walk past them towards the rear gate where his car was parked. Alex Hart's head snapped up towards them but he averted his eyes when Tom looked at him. "If you have a moment?"

Hendry nodded and Tamara acknowledged Tom's silent request to leave them to it. She walked up to Alex Hart who backed away into his kitchen.

"May I come in?" she asked him and Hart, appearing nervous, nodded curtly without a word and beckoned her in. Tom waited until she pushed the door closed and he saw the two of them move past the window and out of view.

"What can I do for you, Inspector?"

"What prompted your visit here today?" he asked.

Hendry shrugged. "Isn't it obvious? You're investigating a murder and speaking to all of us." He looked back at the house. "I was worried about Alex." His expression was serious. "After what I learnt from your visit to see me, I called Alex to check on him, make sure he was okay. He ... wasn't great on the telephone, so I thought I ought to pop across to see him."

"Why the need?"

Hendry hesitated. "I called him repeatedly last night. He wasn't answering and I only got through to him very late on." His eyes came up to meet Tom's and away again. "I was worried. I'm sure, by now, you're aware of Alex's history." Tom inclined his head but said nothing. Hendry sucked air through his teeth. "I'm not surprised. You wouldn't be much of a detective if you didn't." He smiled but one without genuine humour. It dissipated as quickly as it had come. "Look," he sought to choose his words carefully, "Alex has made real progress in recent years. I mean, *real* progress. There were times I thought he wouldn't make it, you know?"

He fell silent, frowning.

"What is it you're concerned about?" Tom asked.

"That this," he said, swirling his hand around in front of him, "will all set him back, and none of us want that."

"We will treat him fairly, Mr Hendry," Tom said.

Hendry nodded. "Good, good. I never doubted it ... but please do try to understand ..."

"How much do you know about his condition?"

"Oh ... probably more than anyone else, aside from his late father." Hendry scratched at his chin, glancing towards the house. "Alex moved back here a few years ago, when living on his own was deemed ..." He looked at Tom and swiftly away again. "It was best for all concerned. After his last stay in the unit, it was considered best for everyone if he didn't live alone. Now his father has passed ..."

"And the nature of his condition?"

Hendry stared at Tom. "Manageable. As long as he sticks to his meds and continues attending his psychiatric appointments then I'm sure he will be fine. It doesn't hurt for his friends to help him along though."

"And looking back, do you ever recall Alex having any outbursts; fits of pique, that kind of thing?"

Hendry shook his head, almost too quickly for Tom's liking. "No, nothing like that." Then his brow wrinkled. "You don't mean around 2001?" Tom maintained an impassive gaze. "No. Absolutely not," Hendry said, shaking his head. "Alex is a gentle soul. No. No sign of that at all. Why on earth would you—"

"A witness saw Alex on the night of Tina's disappearance; he was drunk and very aggressive, by all accounts."

Hendry thought on it. "Now ... the dig hadn't gone well and there were a number of people upset about it, me included," he said quietly. "As I recall a lot of people were either giving the dig a proper send off in the bar or drowning their sorrows. Alcohol can magnify emotions, as I'm sure you know, and maybe he was blowing off a little steam? Don't we all sometimes? But *murder*? I think you're barking up the wrong tree, Inspector, I really do."

"What was described to us wasn't *blowing off steam*."

Hendry pursed his lips, avoiding Tom's scrutiny by glancing back at the house. "I wasn't there. What can I say apart from it just doesn't ring true?"

"And Tina Farrow – do you remember her ever flirting with Alex?"

He scoffed. "Is that what your witness said?"

"Did she?"

Hendry shook his head, slightly bewildered. "Quite frankly, until you showed me the picture I didn't even remember the girl, so I've no idea about whether she flirted with Alex ... or anyone else for that matter. But, if you're asking me my opinion, no, I doubt Alex would have been involved with her even if she had tried to initiate it."

"Why not?"

"A *waitress* in a pub!" He shook his head forcefully. "Not Alex. She wouldn't be his type, at all."

"What about your type?"

"This Farrow girl? No, not mine either."

"What is your type?" Tom asked, curious.

"I've never really thought about it." He hesitated. "I've never been one to focus on physicality or looks necessarily ... shared interests maybe? Intelligent, articulate ... educated ..."

"Someone like Julia Rose?"

Hendry met Tom's gaze sucking on his lower lip, looking nonplussed. "Can I infer from your question that someone's been talking?" Tom didn't answer and waited for a response. Hendry inhaled deeply through his nose, his expression stern. "And I can hazard a guess as to who, but he's talking out of his backside, Inspector. I should imagine you are well trained in sifting through speculative gossip and rumour, in order to get to the truth?"

"The truth is all I'm looking for," Tom said. "Are you saying there was never anything between you and Dr Julia Rose?" He cast a sideways glance at the house. "At the time of the Branodunum dig, before or since?"

Hendry slowly closed his eyes, letting out a sigh and visibly deflating. He followed Tom's eye line to the house, running a hand through his hair and looking furtively around the garden at anything but Tom. "We were close – all of us – and it stands to reason when you love the same things, a love of archaeology I mean, and spend so much time in each other's company ... that feelings develop. It's totally natural."

He was avoiding answering the question, attempting to mitigate his actions first.

"Was there anything between you and Julia?" Tom asked.

"Once, yes." Hendry exhaled, shaking his head. "But it didn't go anywhere, not really. We realised very quickly our mistake ... and set everything straight."

"And when was this?"

"Oh, I don't know exactly; years ago," he said, dismissively waving it away. "And not at the Branodunum dig, either, just for clarification. It was much later!"

"Before or after her split with your friend Alex?"

Hendry's expression darkened and he chose not to answer. That told Tom all he needed to know.

"You'll not mention this," Hendry chewed on his lower lip, "to Alex? It would devastate him, even after all this time. What with his paranoia, he barely trusts anyone anymore. I dread to think what will become of him if he isolates himself further."

"I'll not mention it as long as it doesn't become relevant—"

"Why the hell would it *become* relevant?"

"Then you have no need to worry," Tom said. "But you may have been in a position to take advantage of Julia's unhappiness if she were to find out Alex was involving himself with a *waitress*, wouldn't you say?"

Hendry picked up on the intonation, immediately seeking to row back on his previous comment. "I didn't mean anything by that ..." He looked up at the sky briefly before lowering his gaze back to Tom. "I would never intentionally look to hurt my friends, Inspector, and certainly not in order to ... to gratify myself."

"And you wouldn't turn an opportunity to your advantage?"

The question irritated him; it was obvious. His expression clouded once again and his tone took on a degree of measured defiance. "I'm not a saint, Inspector, and I'd challenge you to find an honest man who claims to be one. But, in this instance, no, I most certainly did not. Is that all or would you like to assassinate my character any further?" Tom shook his head. Hendry made to walk off, hesitating at the last second and turning back to him. "Please bear in mind what I said about Alex." His eyes darted to the house. "I am genuinely concerned for his wellbeing."

CHAPTER TWENTY

TAMARA FOUND Alex Hart an odd character. He was polite and well mannered but his anxiety, clearly visible upon their arrival, only seemed to increase when he was left alone with her as Tom stayed outside to speak with Hendry. At first she thought it was merely what many people experienced when the police called, more so on this occasion due to the case they were investigating, but it was more than that. She couldn't help the nagging feeling that he was uncomfortable with her for some reason.

The sitting room was in almost complete darkness despite it being early afternoon; the heavy curtains offering almost blackout conditions. The air indoors was stale, unsurprising with the windows closed, and the humidity was brutally amplified indoors. Hart may well have been comfortable sitting in the dark with the only natural light spilling in from the adjoining kitchen but Tamara found it more than a little strange and crossed to draw back the curtains, without asking, as quickly as possible. Alex Hart, perched on the edge of the sofa with his hands clasped together in his lap, cut a weary figure. His skin was pale, which was quite some achievement following the recent spell of hot summer weather. His eyes were sunken with dark patches hanging beneath them and his cheekbones were pronounced, the result of his skeletally thin frame. He obviously hadn't shaved for several days and Tamara was sure a notable factor in the pungent, unpleasant smell permeating through the room originated from him.

Hart offered only monosyllabic responses to any attempt at conversation she made, and all without making eye contact. Deciding to wait for Tom, she cast her eye around the interior. Eric had been right in his description; this house was like a mausoleum for Hart's deceased father. Very little of a younger man's personality had been embedded in the furnishings or the decor, as far as she could tell. The pictures above the fireplace were the only personal effects he seemed to have added unless he'd done so in other rooms in the house. Without wishing to be too obvious, she assessed Alex Hart as he sat there, gently rocking backwards and forwards almost imperceptibly as would a sapling in a stiff breeze. He was agitated, nervous, but more so than one might expect. Judging on his medical history, they would have to tread lightly.

The kitchen door opened; Tom would be joining them. He entered the room and she smiled.

"Sorry," he said, "I just needed to clarify a couple of things."

"Anything interesting?"

"A few things to talk about, yes."

She was intrigued. He was playing it down, obviously due to Hart's presence, and she was keen to see what had transpired between the two of them. She was sure Tom was just as surprised to find Tim Hendry here, no one had the impression from talking to them that they were particularly close, so Hendry's immediate visit was interesting. Hart looked up at Tom and then at her, wringing his hands.

"Why have you come back? I told you everything you needed to know yesterday."

"That suggests there were things you didn't tell my officers yesterday that you thought they didn't need to know."

Hart's eyebrows knitted briefly, his mouth open. Then he shook his head. "No, no ... that's not what I meant at all."

"Okay," Tamara said, indicating to an armchair next to the window adjacent to the sofa. "May I?" He nodded and she sat down, sitting forward and focussing on him until he slowly met her gaze. "We understand that on the Friday night, the night we believe Tina Farrow went missing, you were in the Crown Inn. That's right, isn't it?" He bobbed his head, holding her gaze. "How were you and your partner, Julia, getting on that night?"

He shook his head, turning the corners of his mouth down. "Okay, I guess. Why do you ask?"

"We have a witness who says you and Julia were having an argument. Do you remember that?"

His right leg began to twitch, apparently an involuntary movement because he made no attempt to stop it. He looked away, staring at the wall above the fireplace.

"Mr Hart, do you remember?" Tamara repeated. No answer. "Mr Hart!"

"Yes ... no, I mean ... maybe," he said, shaking his head emphatically. She exchanged a glance with Tom, Hart noticed. He glanced furtively between them. "Yes. We had words but I don't see what that has to do with anything."

"That rather depends on what the argument was about, doesn't it?"

"I don't recall—"

"Really?"

"Yes, really," he said, shooting her a fierce look. His expression softened but only a little. "I'd had a few. We both had to be honest. It was a tough time."

"Why?"

He blew out his cheeks, his lips rattling as he exhaled, his eyes scanning the room. "Lots of things going on." His brow wrinkled and he clamped his eyes shut. "You wouldn't understand."

"Could it have been something to do with Tina?" Tom asked. Hart shot daggers at him.

"I told you, I didn't know her."

"Forgive us, Alex," Tamara leaned forward and drew his eye to her, looking almost apologetic, "but you were staying at the Crown for a number of weeks and she worked there, socialised there and two witnesses," she said, holding up two fingers for emphasis, "*two witnesses* have put you together and one stated that she was flirting with you on a consistent basis—"

"No." He shook his head, clasping his palms together in front of his face and touching his fingers to the tip of his nose.

"So, Tina wasn't flirting with you?"

"No!" he said, pushing his hands over his cheeks and up the side of his head where they met at the crown, interlocking his fingers. "I don't remember. Not my fault," he whispered, the rocking movements were more pronounced and Tamara looked at Tom, unsure if it was deliberate. Tom met her gaze but watched on with an unreadable expression.

"Alex," Tamara said, softening her tone and trying to get his attention but he remained focussed, staring straight ahead, his lips moving but no words emanating. "Alex, do you remember Tina?"

He shook his head, hands still locked in place and pressing his elbows in to shield his face from her stern gaze.

"I don't remember," he said again.

"We're not saying you did anything, Alex. We just want to know—"

He spun on her, eyes wide, with such speed that it startled her. He threw his arms down to either side of him, palms flat, slamming them hard against the sofa in frustration. Tom instinctively took a step forward but checked himself as Tamara raised a hand to stop him.

"I don't remember!" Hart barked at her. The flash of anger subsided. "It's not my fault," he said quietly, turning away from her. He didn't seem to be speaking to either of them directly, merely talking to the room.

"What's not your fault?" she asked.

"Any of it!" He glared at her. "I don't remember her ... that night ... any of it! And what happened to her isn't my fault, okay? I just want to be left alone. Why can't anyone understand that. It's not my fault."

"Maybe we should have a cup of tea or something?" Tamara suggested, the intensity of the moment needed calming. Hart slowly turned to her with a blank expression and nodded. She looked over at Tom and he appeared ready to object but she pointedly met his eye and he glanced towards the kitchen.

"I'll make it," Hart said, following her gaze to Tom and standing up slowly. He moved like a man many years his senior, carrying the weight of the world. "You don't know where everything is anyway."

"May I use your bathroom?" Tamara asked and Hart looked over his shoulder, smiling weakly and pointing to a door in the corner of the room.

She thanked him and casually left the sitting room. The door opened into an inner lobby, barely a metre square. Besides the front door, there was another leading into a reception room and stairs to the first floor. She poked her head into the second reception room which housed a grand dining table and six chairs. The table was covered in a patterned lace tablecloth and the room didn't appear to have been used recently. It was decorated with a similar floral print wallpaper to the sitting room. She closed the door quietly and made her way upstairs. There were three bedrooms and a bathroom off a tight landing, two of the bedrooms were neat and tidy, beds made with pastel throws and surrounded by aged furniture. The floorboards squeaked underfoot and she tried to tread lightly so as not to give away her movements.

The third bedroom she concluded must be Hart's. The curtains were still drawn, much as every other room in the house, and the bed was unmade with the smell of stale body odour hanging in the air. Clothes lay strewn around the room and it was impossible to tell what was clean and what was dirty. Retreating, she went into the bathroom pulling the door closed behind her. She wasn't shocked to find the bathroom was in need of a thorough clean. Putting that aside, there was a build-up of calcium on the ends of all the taps, several of which were also dripping indicating the washers needed replacing. Thick lime scale deposits lined the water's path to the drain. It was reminiscent of what she'd found when she'd bought her own house, although she was well into the process of fixing hers.

Opening the small mirror-faced cabinet above the basin, she casually inspected the contents of the two shelves. Much of it was what everyone kept in their bathrooms: basic medicines, plasters and, curiously, a small glass containing a dental plate housing two teeth. She wondered if this also belonged to Hart's late father. She spotted some flecks of mould growing on the plate, it must have been there for some time. In amongst two half-empty bottles of mouthwash were three brown plastic bottles, prescription issue judging by the printed labels from a local pharmacy. She turned them all to face her; all three were in Alex's name. Tamara took out her mobile phone and photographed them in situ. She thought she'd heard of one of the drugs, used to treat depression if she remembered correctly, but the other two were new names to her and she resolved to look them up later. Hearing footsteps on the stairs, she hurriedly put her mobile away and closed the cabinet, the click as the catch locked into place sounding ominously loud in the tiled room. She reached over and depressed the flush on the toilet and turned one of the taps on in the basin.

Someone was on the landing and turning off the tap she opened the door to find both Alex Hart and Tom on the landing. Tom was at the top of the stairs and Hart was barely three feet from the bathroom. He cast a suspicious eye over her, then looked to his right and the bedrooms.

"I told you she was okay," Tom said, smiling. She recognised the *telephone voice* edge to his voice.

"All okay?" she asked lightly.

"I thought you'd got lost or something," Hart said. His tone was neither menacing nor accusatory, but deadpan. She looked past him to Tom who offered her a raised eyebrow.

"No, not at all."

"We've made coffee," Tom said.

"I haven't got any milk, though," Hart said, not taking his eye from her. "Is that okay?"

"That's fine with me. I don't take milk anyway."

Hart nodded, turning away and walking slowly back to the stairs. Tom made way and allowed him to pass and descend first. Unbeknown to Hart, Tom looked at Tamara and silently made an O shape with his mouth. She knew she had pushed it and had almost been rumbled. She couldn't help thinking it was worth it.

CHAPTER TWENTY-ONE

"WHAT WAS THAT YOU JUST SAID?" Tamara asked. Eric stopped. He'd been in full flow running through his findings. He looked at her quizzically. "Something about impulsive behaviours?"

Eric scanned back through his notes, focussing on the previous paragraph. "*Aripiprazole*, a powerful anti-psychotic that can lead to side effects including impulsive behaviours which may lead the subject to unusual actions out of the ordinary; notably an increased sex drive, a preponderance to sexual thoughts or feelings, excessive eating or spending habits—"

"And the last one?"

"Addictive behaviours," Eric said, looking up. She nodded. "Gambling for instance. What was his dosage?"

"Thirty milligrams, according to the label."

"Highest dose available," Eric said. "Is it safe to infer from that that Alex Hart has an acute condition?"

"It would be good to get a medical opinion on that," Tamara said. "Maybe you could give Fiona Williams a call and ask. She will be discreet. I don't want anything slipping out from this investigation to the media. The interest in this case is gathering pace and I don't want us to be the ones to destroy someone's career or reputation unnecessarily." She leaned around and picked up her cup of coffee. It had gone cold but she would drink it anyway. Turning her attention to the information board, her gaze drifted over their list of suspects and the lines drawn between them and the victim, noting their interactions and possible motives. She was an instinctive detective and every time she scanned the list a different name leapt out at her. "Any word on Julia Rose?"

Cassie shook her head. "Mobile cuts to voicemail every time I call. The hotel she's lodging at in Svelgen say she hasn't returned there since she left yesterday morning."

"Did you make it clear we are investigating a murder here?"

Cassie spread her hands wide. "Absolutely. The line was bad but she knew what we were talking about, seemed shocked. I sent her an in-call chat and followed it up with an email. There's no way she doesn't know."

"Okay," Tamara said, putting her cup down on the desk and folding her arms across her chest. "Keep trying. She's the last of the senior team we need to speak to and, incidentally, the one person who can clarify what was going on that night between her and Alex Hart." She caught sight of Tom in the corner of her eye, his expression fixed and apparently deep in thought. "What are you thinking, Tom?"

Without taking his eyes from the boards, he frowned. "I think we're still missing something."

"One more reason to speak with Julia."

"I don't disagree, but we're putting a lot of energy into Alex Hart and it's not sitting well with me."

She angled her head to one side. "You think we are prejudiced against him because of his state of mind?"

He waved away the comment. "No, that's not what I mean. I agree that Hart seems unstable, perhaps he could be dangerous under the right set of conditions that might trigger him. We have the assault on the woman in the supermarket but that happened a long time after Tina Farrow's death. If we're looking at her murder as a result of a mental condition then it's unlikely to have been premeditated. An impulsive assault doesn't fit well with the clear-up; the hiding of the body until it could be disposed of on the Saturday, if we're right in thinking that Tina died that night, not to mention the burial itself. To go about it like that ..." He slowly shook his head. "That's a calmness that doesn't fit with someone acting on impulse. Those murders are quick, brutal and then the body is cast aside and the killer puts as much distance between themselves and it as possible because when the body is found, and it almost always is, then every person between them and the victim becomes a suspect before they do." He ran his tongue along his bottom lip, coming to stand in front of the board. "Does that really sound like Alex Hart? I'm not so sure."

"But you said his diagnosis changed. Perhaps in 2001 it was different again?"

Tom exhaled, raising his eyebrows at the plausibility of her suggestion. But he was also correct. There wasn't any evidence to put him top of their list of suspects aside from the future incidents already noted.

"You're right," she said, casting an eye over the boards and then looking at Eric. "I want you to find Tim Hendry's first wife and speak to her about the incident that saw him cautioned. She withdrew her complaint against him but that was years ago. Maybe a bit of time and distance between them will make her more agreeable to talk about it now." Eric made a note.

Tom's brow creased. "Hendry was on his way to London for the Saturday morning seminar, remember?"

She nodded. "Yes, I remember but did anyone see him leave and besides, you can do Brancaster to London in ... what would you say, two to three hours by train or road?"

"Longer I expect, but eminently doable."

"We think the body was possibly buried after the excavation officially closed. Hendry could have come back on the following day. He knew the site and there would be fewer eyes on him then. I don't see any reason to dismiss him as a possibility, not when he has form for violence against women."

"*A* woman," Tom said. "And one rooted in a marital dispute, which obviously doesn't get him a pass but it is different. Worth checking all the same."

"Cassie," Tamara continued, "how have you got on with Tom's theory about other missing women in locations close to our archaeologist's movements?"

She grimaced. "Nothing yet, but we're talking about three very active archaeologists. Not so much with Alex Hart but I've been searching the locations where he was filming as well and nothing yet."

"Good, keep going. I also want you to recheck the movements of Tina's father, Conrad Farrow, as well as Paul Tennant as far as we know them, see if there are any opportunities for us to investigate further. We have what CID didn't twenty years ago and that's a timeline to follow, even if there are some pretty big gaps in it. Let's not get bogged down in focussing just on the archaeology leadership team; there are any number of helpers on site and I'm well aware it could just as easily be one of those as well, but let's work with what we have for now. Also, no more messing around, let's get hold of Dr Rose, enlist the help of our Norwegian colleagues if necessary. This is a murder investigation and I don't care how important this discovery of a longboat is—"

"Excuse me, ma'am." They all turned towards the entrance where a uniformed constable waited. "I'm sorry to butt in."

"What is it?" Tamara asked, irritated by the interruption. The constable looked at Cassie apologetically.

"There's someone in the lobby asking to speak with DS Knight and she's quite insistent."

Cassie glanced between him and Tamara, shooting him an enquiring look. "Who is it?"

"A lady by the name of Dr Julia Rose, but she won't say what it's regarding."

Tamara exchanged a look with Tom. "Well, well, well," she said quietly.

CHAPTER TWENTY-TWO

Dr Julia Rose sat in the canteen with her hands wrapped around a cup of coffee. She looked like she hadn't slept a wink in days. Not only did she appear fatigued, she was agitated, struggling to get comfortable. As she sat there, her shoulders would flinch and she would absently adjust her clothing, but no amount of loosening of clothing or repositioning of how she was sitting appeared to resolve the issue. Her eyes came up to see Tamara observing her. She smiled and Dr Rose returned it, although hers seemed artificial.

"When was the last time you slept?" Tamara asked.

She shook her head, moving aside the long dark hair from her eyes with her right hand. She glanced over at Tom who was sitting to her right on the next table, allowing her some personal space.

"I don't know, thirty-six hours, maybe?" She shuddered and lifted the material of her blouse off her shoulder. "I can't get the travel off me ... Do you know what I mean?"

Tamara smiled warmly. "It sort of sticks to you, doesn't it? Where are you staying?"

Dr Rose lifted her head from staring at the cup in front of her with a blank expression. "I don't know. I didn't think."

"I'm sure we can help find you somewhere," Tamara said, reassuring her with a friendly touch to the back of her hand. She smiled gratefully. "How long was the trip?"

"Svelgen is an hour by plane to Oslo," she said, lifting her coffee and sipping from it. "I was lucky to get a seat and then I was on standby in Oslo for the first available flight back to England. I landed in Manchester early this morning and drove down."

Tamara glanced at Tom and he raised his eyebrows. That was quite a journey. Dr Rose noticed the shared look and nodded.

"I could never sleep in airports or on planes." She chuckled humourlessly. "You'd think I'd manage it better what with all the travelling I do with my work."

"Where does it take you?"

"I'm predominantly based in Europe these days, Scandinavia in particular." She scratched an itch on the side of her neck, pausing to apply pressure as she inclined her head towards that side and stretched, grimacing momentarily. "The post-Roman kingdoms of Northern Europe are my specialist field. That's why I'm in Svelgen—"

"The longboat?"

Her expression briefly split into a broad grin. "One of only four complete boats that have been uncovered in the last three decades. To find it with the bodies of two noblemen and one woman inside is really quite something." She looked at Tamara, pride in her eyes.

"And yet you are here?" Tamara said softly. Rose's eyes drifted to hers and she pursed her lips, nodding slightly. "We were happy to speak with you on the phone. Why did you come all this way?"

She took a deep breath, lifting her gaze to the ceiling. Two uniformed constables entered at the other end of the room, sharing a joke. Upon seeing the three of them, they lowered their voices and hovered around the vending machines selecting their snacks for their refreshments.

"Why did you come?" Tamara asked again.

"I had to. When your sergeant called – DS Knight – she said you'd found the body of a young woman on the Branodunum site ..." She shook her head. "I–I knew you'd be speaking to all of us, to Alex and ... I just knew I had to come." She sighed, sitting forward and cupping her drink again. "That bloody dig was cursed from the outset! But I must admit, when we shut the dig down I always expected there to be some fallout from it – it will always happen if you allocate that level of resource and get almost sod all in return."

"It was Alex's site, wasn't it? The failure came down on him—"

"Yes, they certainly made sure that it did!"

Tamara was taken aback but didn't let it show. "How do you mean?"

"It was a joint venture. Alex was only responsible for half of it. He was desperate to prove his theory. He'd spent years working towards it and this was the culmination of so many months ... years even, of energy and effort. But it didn't pan out and someone had to carry the can, so to speak."

"It fell on Alex?"

She nodded furiously, sniffing hard and rifling through her pockets looking for a tissue. Tom rose from his seat and returned with a box of tissues, placing them alongside her. She thanked him, plucking one from the box and wiping her nose.

"It shouldn't have been that way. There were those of us who joined the call for the excavation; me, Tim ... and Billy." She looked between them, wondering if they knew who she was referring to. Tamara signalled that she did. "Good old Billy. He made damn sure he didn't shoulder any of the responsibility. If anyone was as accountable as Alex then it was him, but nothing stuck." She looked dejected. "Tim tried to speak up for Alex at the review. I couldn't, the two of us being in a relationship skewed my perspective in the mind of the review body's Chairman. As I say, Tim tried but Billy was *so* keen to tie it around Alex's neck and watch him sink."

"I thought they were friends?" Tom asked.

"They were, great friends," she said, smiling weakly and then shrugging. "But Billy was the one making great strides in his career and Alex was the closest to him in that respect. They both shared a competitive streak and there was a fellowship on the horizon for Billy, and all of us thought if Alex proved his thesis then he would be the one who garnered the limelight. Billy ... he's not keen on sharing the platform, you know?"

"To such an extent that he'd throw his best friend under the bus for the sake of his own career?" Tamara asked.

Rose closed her eyes, shaking her head. "They were friends, close friends even, but you also have to appreciate the dynamic between them." Tamara sat forward, eagerly waiting for the explanation. "Although Billy was the one making great strides in building his reputation, it was Alex who our peers admired the most." She smiled, fondly recalling her memories. "Alex was quite the personality. When he walked into a room everyone turned towards him. Have you ever met someone like that? Someone who almost attracts you whether it be consciously or not. He was rather dashing, charming, quick with a smile and people hung on his every word."

Tamara found it difficult to reconcile this image of the man with the wreck of an individual whom she met. Julia Rose must have read her mind because she found her watching her intently as she processed the information.

"Have you seen him recently?" Rose asked tentatively, chewing her lower lip. "Alex?"

"Yes, we've spoken to him," Tamara replied, her eyes moving to Tom. Rose followed her gaze.

"How is he?"

Tamara ducked the question for now, keen not to get side-tracked. "When was the last time you spoke to him?"

Rose thought about it, her eyelids fluttering and her expression turned vacant. Tamara noticed her hands shaking.

"When did you last eat something?" she asked. Rose shook her head to say she didn't know. Tom got up and went over to the vending machines. The serving staff from the kitchen had cleared away from lunch and there was no hot food available. Tom returned to the table with a few biscuits on a side plate and a cheese roll wrapped in cellophane. He set them down in front of Rose who smiled appreciatively. Reaching for one of the biscuits, she broke off the end and put it in her mouth, sweeping away the crumbs that fell onto the table in front of her. Picking up her coffee cup, she sipped from it.

"I've not spoken to Alex for over a year, not seen him for even longer." She swallowed hard. "It's difficult when … when you have such a shared history."

"Didn't you break up eighteen years ago?" Tamara asked.

"Longer, I think," Rose said, her eyes lingering on the roll. Tamara gestured for her to help herself and Rose didn't need to hear the offer twice and set about unwrapping it. "But I still care for him very deeply." She lifted the roll to her mouth, hesitating. "We just couldn't stay together anymore."

"Why not?"

Rose chewed on her food slowly, Tamara waiting patiently.

"Alex was – is – a troubled soul. It just got too difficult to manage." She tilted her head to one side thoughtfully. "He was always difficult to manage. There was so much going on behind the smile."

"We understand that the failure of the Branodunum dig dealt him quite a blow, career wise?"

"That was a catalyst, certainly," Rose said, setting her roll down on the side plate. "But he was struggling for years before that." Her eyes reflected an unspoken pain. "He hid it well. I helped him. Together we kept it from the others. From the outside looking in, Alex was everything we all aspired to be but it wasn't the reality. Many nights, even when we were undergrads, I would find him curled up in his room, in tears. He was prone to drinking binges, often leading to blackouts where he'd disappear for a couple of days and have very little recollection as to where he was, who he was with or what he got up to. Or that's what he'd tell me."

"You didn't believe him?" Tamara asked.

She smiled weakly and rolled her eyes, indicating to Tamara that she just didn't know. "I wanted to. Sometimes he would self-harm ... the pain he suffered and the pressure he would put himself under in order to maintain his success was immense. It was impossible really. Don't get me wrong, he was brilliant, truly brilliant in the field. His career was only on an upward trajectory and was going to be anything he chose it to be, that's how impressive he was!"

"It didn't go that way though."

Rose pursed her lips, offering a curt shake of the head. "If only he could have got control of his demons then it all would have panned out differently."

"You say he self-harmed but did Alex," Tamara paused, searching for the right words, " ever hurt you or anyone else?"

Rose fixed Tamara with a hard stare. "Emotionally? All the time. He didn't mean to, I'm certain, but he would spiral into these depths of depression and if we couldn't catch it early enough then he was prone to draw in those closest to him. It was a devastatingly destructive cycle. That's why I had to leave in the end; I couldn't bear seeing him that way and I felt myself slipping into it as well."

Tamara solemnly bobbed her head. "And what about any physical manifestations?"

"Against me?" she asked, averting her eyes from Tamara's watchful gaze. She looked awkward now, uncomfortable with the question. Tamara sensed her reticence.

"Julia, was Alex ever physical with you?"

CHAPTER TWENTY-THREE

"ONE TIME, YES," Rose whispered. Then she looked straight at Tamara. "But it was *one* time and I know he didn't mean it. He was just lashing out and I happened to be the one to be there."

"They never mean it," Tamara said quietly. Rose bristled. "Can you describe it? When did it happen?"

Rose closed her eyes, her fingertips gently drumming on the table in front of her. "That night; the last Friday at Branodunum." Tamara saw Tom edge forward in his seat. "He'd been drinking. We'd all been drinking. There were some heated words spoken that night, accusations flying around in all directions; about the dig … and … other things." Rose, wringing her hands, was on edge.

"Tina Farrow?" Tamara asked. The hand wringing stopped and a dark veil descended across Rose's face. "You remember Tina?"

"Yes, Tina. Who could forget her?" she said, dismissively.

"Is that what you and Alex were arguing about?"

Rose was surprised, drawing herself upright.

"A witness reported seeing the two of you in a heated discussion. She said it was unpleasant to watch—"

"It was a damn sight more unpleasant to be a part of, I can assure you! Yes, it was outside the Crown. We argued in the rear lobby and it spilled outside. He tried to walk away and I pulled him back." She shuddered. "I should have let him go but ... I was furious with him." Rose took a deep breath, rubbing at her cheeks and then pressing her fingertips into her eyes. Slowly drawing her hands from her face, she sighed, looking like she was carrying the weight of the world. "It wasn't about Tina, not really. It was no secret she'd taken a shine to Alex. She wasn't the first and wouldn't be the last either."

"How did that feel, having Tina flirting with *your* partner so brazenly? Because it was brazen wasn't it, flaunting it in front of you?"

"Yes, it was," Rose said, exhaling heavily. "I didn't care for it, that's for sure. Fair enough though, isn't it, to be annoyed? I mean, I barely knew her. The guys on the other hand ... they lapped up the attention."

"An attractive girl."

Rose nodded. "Yes, and she made sure they all saw it. I've come across the likes of her before ..."

"How do you mean?"

She shrugged. "Low self-worth, lack of confidence despite outward projections to the contrary ... she was quite typical, really. A very damaged young woman."

"Is that what you thought at the time?"

"No, of course not. At the time I wanted to ..."

"You wanted to do *what to her*?"

Her shoulders sagged and her eyes looked up at Tamara and away again. "Honestly? I wanted to smash her teeth in."

Tamara raised her eyebrows at the venom behind the words.

"I'm just being honest," Rose replied with a shrug. "I couldn't stand her. She barely spoke to any of the girls on the dig. Even her colleagues didn't like her, you could see it in the way they interacted. Looking back now, I can see how damaged she was, how vulnerable and I can only wonder what made her behave that way."

"And Alex, how did he respond to her attention?"

Rose scoffed. "Alex was hanging on by his fingernails at that point. I think he only noticed because it bothered me so much – and it did bother me – because she was attractive and adept at turning a guy's attention to her. They were all enthralled by her, Billy, Tim … her boss, practically anyone who moved in her sphere."

"Did you challenge her on her behaviour?" Tom asked. She shook her head.

"I didn't have the nerve to. I've never been good at dealing with confrontation. With Alex it was different, I could have a go at him quite happily." She smiled weakly, nursing her cup. It must have gone cold by now but she didn't say anything and drank it anyway. "Especially with a couple of gin and tonics inside me."

"So that evening you had a row with Alex?"

"Yes," she said flatly, her eyes looking up as she thought through the detail. "There was quite a party going on in the bar, with a lot of people there celebrating the end of the excavation. They don't always go well but you can be sure of a decent send off. Anyway, what with the stress of it all, the last few days were catching up on us; not enough sleep, the upcoming evaluations, hell, the absolute failure of it all, and it all came to a head. We'd been sniping at each other for a couple of days—"

"You and Alex?"

"No, the whole senior team. It was clear that the scrutiny was coming and I guess everyone was trying to get their heads around it. We agreed not to discuss it anymore that evening and we would just join the team in blowing off a little steam. These things happen after all. So we scheduled a discussion for the following day to run through it, to get all our ducks in a row before heading home."

"A meeting with all of you present?"

She nodded.

"But none of us could set things aside and after a few drinks the finger pointing started again. Billy was constantly digging at Alex, bringing up every decision Alex had made during the excavation and in the months leading up to it as if it was all his fault. Usually I would step in and help but," she sighed," I was so annoyed with him. Tina was flitting around them all, more so than usual with a few drinks under her belt as well, so I left him to it which only exacerbated the situation. Tim wasn't himself either."

"Tell us about Tim," Tamara said. There must have been something in her tone because Rose's demeanour shifted slightly, eyeing Tamara warily.

"You've spoken to Tim already, haven't you?"

"Yes. He was quite forthcoming."

Rose sank forward, head in hands. It was a few seconds before she lifted it again, taking a breath.

"It wasn't planned, at least not on my part. Alex and I fell out and he'd stormed off. I was going back to our room, fully intending to pack my things and leave." She laughed dryly. "Not that I could go anywhere. I was half cut, it was around ten o'clock at night and Alex was driving us! But I bumped into Tim."

"On your way back to your room?"

"No. I went out for some fresh air. It was a clear night, warm and I needed to clear my head. I met Tim outside. He saw I was upset and tried to do what any friend would do and calm me down, make sure I was all right." She hesitated, interlocking her fingers before her and staring at them. "It shouldn't have happened but," she said drawing a deep breath, "he was drunk as well and I guess ultimately, I allowed it to. I was so damn angry with Alex!"

"What happened exactly?"

Her brow wrinkled and she pursed her lips, trying to recall the events of that night. "It was so long ago."

"Please try."

"Okay ... I don't remember who initiated it. It could just as easily have been me but I don't remember. I knew Tim fancied me. He wasn't overt with it but," she looked at Tamara, "a woman just knows, doesn't she?"

"Did you spend the night with Tim Hendry?"

"No, no I didn't. Whether it was the sea air sobering me up or the realisation of what we were doing, I don't know, but I came to my senses and pulled away from him."

"And?"

She shrugged. "And nothing. I went back to my room. Tim tried to follow, pull me back but I shook him off and ran away from him."

"Was he angry with you?"

"No, nothing like that. I think he was frightened I'd say something to Alex I expect."

"Did you?"

She shook her head. "He wasn't there when I got back to our room. I crept in in case he was asleep but the bed was empty and hadn't been slept in. He didn't come back that night. I didn't set eyes on him until I got to the site the next day."

"Where did he stay, did he tell you?"

"No and I didn't ask. There was so much about that night that I wanted to forget ever happened." She picked up the remainder of her cheese roll and inspected it. It was only half eaten and she put it back down, pushing the plate to one side.

"But you and Tim did have a relationship though, correct?" Tom asked. Rose looked at him glumly and nodded.

"Some time later, after Alex and I split. It was over in a couple of months though."

"Why, if you don't mind me asking?"

"Not at all, no." She shrugged. "By then I was spending much of my time in Scandinavia, Sweden mostly at that time. Tim was carving out a career for himself in Southern Europe and the whole television documentary circuit had earmarked him as a fresh talent. Have you seen his shows?"

"No, but," Tamara said, thinking of Eric, "but I know someone who probably has."

"Anyway, it's hard to maintain a relationship at that distance. Besides, I don't think I was as interesting to him as he first thought." She met Tamara's enquiring look and smiled. "I think after years of silent pursuit, Tim found the fantasy was more exciting than the reality. In any event, he married soon after and that was that."

"Can we revisit the final day, the Saturday," Tamara said, thinking. "Who do you remember was present on the site to close things down?"

"That's easy: me, Alex and Billy plus a handful of others to help clear up any mess, pack up the tents and whatnot. Any finds we'd dug up were already catalogued and boxed ready for shipping. Not that there was a lot. Most people had been sent home already."

"Tim Hendry?"

She chewed on her lower lip. "No, he wasn't there. He had something on in London on the Saturday morning."

"And have you any idea when he left for London?"

"No, sorry. Why?"

Tamara ignored the question.

"And following your argument with Alex, did you see Tina Farrow again?"

"No, I didn't. Why do you ask?" She looked puzzled.

"Because it was the remains of Tina Farrow that were found at Branodunum."

Rose gasped, raising a hand to her mouth.

"You didn't know?"

"I–I... no, I didn't."

Tamara glanced at Tom, checking if he'd heard enough and he offered a slight wave of the hand to indicate he had no further questions.

"We'll get you another cup of coffee," Tamara said, slowly rising and inclining her head for Tom to join her. "Then we'll arrange somewhere for you to stay. You must be exhausted." They walked over to the other side of the room to where the vending machines stood. Tamara dropped some coins into the machine and selected a white coffee, looking back at Julia Rose sitting in her seat, staring straight ahead with a vacant expression. She dipped her head in Rose's direction. "Is it possible she really didn't know?"

Tom frowned. "If she's been travelling since early yesterday and – Svelgen being so remote – I'm not sure news of our local crimes necessarily travels there very quickly. Tina's name has been out in the public domain for less than forty-eight hours, so I guess it's possible."

"And Hendry has been withholding information; didn't he say he'd left Brancaster for London on Friday evening?"

"Yes, although his leaving out the part of the evening where he hit on his best mate's girlfriend is something we shouldn't be surprised about."

"Speaking from experience?"

Tom smiled ruefully.

"Not to mention he would most likely have been well over the limit to drive, if she's right," Tamara gestured in Rose's direction, "and he was as drunk as she says."

"Maybe the fresh air sobered him up too?"

"Or the rejection saw him lash out at another woman, much like when his first wife left him?"

Tom grimaced. "Yeah ... I'll give you that as a possibility. Maybe sending Eric off to speak to Tim Hendry's first wife isn't such a long shot after all."

CHAPTER TWENTY-FOUR

ERIC SLOWED THE CAR, giving the horses a wide berth as he passed by them. The lead rider tipped her head in his direction, offering him a wave. The estate was sprawling. He couldn't remember how large it was but the network of rambling paths and cycle tracks spread throughout the woods in all directions. In the summertime every car park on the estate was full and even in the off season the locals made daily use of them to walk their dogs or spend time with the children. The Royal family spent the summer here and Eric wondered if Her Majesty was present as he parked the car, the wheels crunching the gravel beneath them.

By the time he got out the riders were approaching. Two of the three continued on past him, their mounts' hooves clattering on the cobbles as they passed under an entrance arch and entered the courtyard beyond. The lead rider came across to Eric, taking his measure. Everyone else who was milling around was dressed for their role, either in equestrian or outdoor clothing, Eric was in his suit and tie, sweating.

"Can I help you?" she asked,

"I'm here to see Victoria Riley," Eric said, reaching up with one hand to hold the horse's bridle and patting its neck with the other.

The rider glanced to her right and gestured towards a row of small cottages a short distance away.

"Vicky has the day off today. You'll find her in the last but one cottage: *The Hawthorns*."

He thanked her and she turned her mount, ambling after her friends in the direction of the courtyard and presumably the stables beyond. Eric locked his car although, in reality, it probably wasn't necessary. The cottages were cosy, that is to say small and were clearly residences tied to working on the estate. Eric knocked on the front door and immediately he heard a dog bark aggressively from the interior. He waited and then heard the dog again only this time louder as it must have come to stand on the other side of the door. He wasn't concerned; he loved dogs and by the tone of this one he thought it must be tiny, whether it was a terrier or one of the yappy sort that seemed popular with film stars and eccentrics, he was keen to know.

Moments later the door opened and he was met with a warm smile by a woman in a loose-fitting pink blouse, her sandy-brown hair tied up, who eyed him expectantly, looking past him. It was so obvious that he followed her eye but was stumped by what she was apparently searching for.

"How did it go? Any problems?" she asked.

Eric must have looked puzzled, his brow wrinkling.

"Have you brought back my car?"

"Um ... no," Eric said, taking out his warrant card. "DC Collet, Norfolk Police. Mrs Riley?"

"Miss." She corrected him and the smile faded to be replaced by concern. "Is everything all right with Michael?"

"Yes, I'm sure it is," Eric said. He had no idea who Michael was. "I'd like to speak with you about your ex-husband, if you don't mind?"

Her expression darkened.

"Which one?"

"Tim Hendry. May I come inside?"

"Tim?" She was surprised. "That's a name I haven't heard spoken in years."

Victoria opened the door, beckoning him inside. The dog, who had been held at bay thus far by its owner's leg, rushed forward to inspect the newcomer. It was a terrier, but not one Eric could identify, and he was usually good with dogs. It was jet black, wiry, in the same way as a Westie, but its nose was longer, thinner and without the whiskers. The animal also belonged to the *bark is worse than its bite* category because as soon as Eric knelt to acknowledge the dog, it turned tail, ducked between its owner's legs and disappeared from sight.

"She gets nervous of strangers. Come through and I'll pop the kettle on."

Eric smiled, righted himself, and followed Victoria through the cottage. The hallway was tight and it opened into a kitchen to the rear that Eric figured was a newer addition at some point because the head height was much improved and the windows larger. The view from the window above the sink was over the manicured grounds towards the stables where Eric had come from.

As his host busied herself filling the kettle, Eric assessed her, wondering what she did on the estate? She was slim, athletic and one of his first thoughts was that she was quite attractive. Becca's image immediately came to mind and he felt a stab of guilt. Brushing the thought aside, he found Victoria looking at him, eyebrows raised, kettle in hand.

"I'm sorry, what did you say?" Eric asked.

"Tea or coffee?"

"Yes."

"Which?" she asked, smiling sympathetically.

"Tea please," Eric stammered, grimacing as soon as she turned her back and set the kettle on its stand. He produced his notebook from his pocket, feeling his face reddening. She turned back to him, leaning against the worktop and folded her arms across her chest.

"What's Tim been up to that could possibly involve me after all these years?"

Eric angled his head slightly, his curiosity piqued by something unsaid in her tone. "Was he often up to something then, in the past I mean?"

She offered him a coy smile. "During our marriage Tim was away a lot – with work – and when I met him, he was quite a party animal, fashionably late but always the last one to make his way home. Unless he got lucky, of course, in which case he'd end up at someone else's home."

"Quite the ladies' man, was he?" Eric asked, returning her smile.

"Before and during our marriage, yes," she said glumly. "I guess it doesn't matter now. It was a long time ago after all."

Eric glanced at his notes. "When did the two of you divorce?"

"My reprieve came through in the August of 2009. It took two years but the wait was worth it … I had a celebratory weekend away with the girls afterwards." Her smile widened to a grin but Eric saw the sadness reflected in her expression, she wasn't quite as upbeat about it as she suggested. The grin faded and her brow furrowed. "What is this about?"

"We're investigating an old case and Tim's name came up, so we're doing some homework on him, that's all," Eric said, not wishing to cloud her memories with the significance of the subject matter. "Specifically, I need to speak to you about an incident that happened a couple of years before you split up—"

"2007," she said flatly. "We'd split by then but it took the paperwork a few years to catch up."

Eric nodded but didn't say anything. Victoria held his eye, taking a deep breath.

"Now that *was* a long time ago," she said quietly, turning her gaze to the window and the expanse of open ground, her casual references to the past forgotten.

"I understand that I'm raking up a difficult—"

"It's not difficult," she said, turning to him, her expression fixed and uncompromising. "I'm glad it happened when it did."

"Why are you glad?"

"Because it reinforced my decision to leave in the first place," she said flatly. "And he would never get the chance to do that to me again."

Eric remained impassive, focussing on the detail. "What brought about the assault, do you remember?"

She stared straight ahead, her lips pursed. The kettle gently rocked on its stand as the water came to the boil and the switch clicked off. Victoria didn't notice.

"Do you remember?" Eric repeated.

"No, not really," she said, sniffing and brushing her hand across the tip of her nose as she turned away from him to pick up the kettle. He wasn't sure but he thought he saw her eyes welling up as she did so. She poured the water into the cups, Eric watched the steam rising from them, curling up into the air. She was taking the moment to gather herself, so he allowed her the time to do it. "Sugar?" she asked without looking round, her voice quivering slightly.

"No thank you," Eric said, feeling bad for forcing her to recall the memory without warning. "I'm sweet enough."

She glanced over her shoulder at his poor attempt at lightening the mood, offering him an appreciative smile. She finished making the tea, turning and passing a mug to Eric, which he accepted, promptly looking for somewhere to put it down because it was far too hot to hold. Victoria suggested a small dining table, only large enough to seat two people, behind Eric in the corner with a flick of her hand and he set it down.

"That was the first time Tim had done anything like that to me, or to anyone as far as I know," she said as soon as Eric turned back to face her. She was still staring blankly ahead. "Don't get me wrong, we'd argued enough over the years: about him being away as much as he was. That was largely down to my mistrust of him and what he was up to."

"Where did that come from do you think?"

She thought about it folding her arms across her chest, now looking at Eric. She glanced at the floor, clicking her tongue against the roof of her mouth.

"A mixture of my own insecurity and his inability to control himself, I should imagine." She sighed. "You know he was engaged to someone else when I started seeing him? I didn't know, by the way. Not at first anyway. I should have walked when I found out but I didn't; figured I was the one for him, you know?" She tilted her head towards one shoulder, eyeing Eric and searching for his approval. "I really should have known better. Anyway ... I had my suspicions about Tim during our marriage; that he was putting it about while he was away. I never had anything concrete to go on, he was very shrewd, but my instincts were shouting at me and, in the end, I listened. It was then that I left."

"He didn't take it well?"

A rueful smile crossed her face. "Tim was used to getting his own way. He never did like it when I asserted myself."

"And that particular night, the night he attacked you, what happened?"

Victoria picked at the fingernails of one hand with the other, an indication of her anxiety. She lifted her head to meet Eric's gaze.

"I went back to the house one night – to fetch a few things – and I thought he was out for the night with friends. I'd organised it with Suzy, a mutual friend of ours, and that would give me the opportunity to slip in and out without speaking to Tim."

"Were you frightened?"

"No, nothing like that," she said dismissively. Eric thought maybe she was detailing a lengthy cycle of domestic abuse but she'd just waved that away. "I just couldn't face yet another argument but I'd been recycling the same three outfits at work for a couple of weeks by that point." She splayed her palms wide and smiled. "A girl has limits, you know?" Eric returned the smile. "Anyway, Tim obviously didn't fancy a night out as his marriage was ending and came home early. Suzy couldn't get hold of me because the signal was so poor where we used to live." Her expression took on a faraway look. "You know, I can still picture the surprise on his face when he walked in and I was standing there with a suitcase in hand. I'm not sure how I expected him to react, looking back. It was like an affront to his manhood or something, I don't know. His ego couldn't take it, maybe?"

"You argued?"

She nodded, pursing her lips.

"And it was then that he hit you?"

"More or less. Like you said, we argued. It escalated as a couple of years of marital frustration boiled over from both of us." She looked Eric directly in the eye. "I'll be honest, DC Collet—"

"Eric, please."

"I'll be honest, Eric, I'm pretty sure I hit him first. I don't recall what he said, but I lost my temper ... then he responded."

"I see," Eric said, averting his eyes from her and scribbling a few notes.

"I think that was one reason the CPS weren't keen to press charges; a case of six of one and half a dozen of the other."

"Only one of you ended up in hospital, though."

She took a deep breath, appearing a little lost.

"That's true, Eric, but I didn't want to go to court, have people staring at me as I described his infidelity only to have it thrown at me that I was imagining it, that I was some sort of basket case. My old mum used to say you should never air your dirty linen in public because people will pass judgement on you and you carry those judgements with you for the rest of your life." She was distant now, dejected. "I just wanted it all to go away."

Eric waited but she didn't say anything further. He sensed that she still fostered similar feelings.

"I'm sorry to press you on this but," Eric hesitated, searching for the right words, "at any point prior to that incident had Tim ever threatened you either physically or emotionally? Did you feel intimidated?"

Victoria stared at Eric.

"What's all this about?"

"Like I said—"

"I know what you said but what *is* this about?"

Eric ran his tongue along the inside of his lower lip. "We're investigating the murder of a young woman. She was found at the site of an archaeological dig where Tim was present, back in 2001, quite some time prior to the events of your marriage."

"And you think it might—?"

Eric held a hand up to stop her. "No, we're just gathering background on those present at the time. Tim is one among many. Did you ever feel threatened by Tim?"

Concern was etched into her expression now, the weight of responsibility clear to see. Then she shook her head but wouldn't meet Eric's gaze.

"No."

There was something about her answer that bothered him, whether it was the speed of the reply or the intonation contained within a two-letter word, he didn't know. He doubted himself as he wracked his brain for a searching follow-up question but one wasn't forthcoming. Instead, he simply wrote a big question mark in his notebook against her reply.

"What about the night he assaulted you? Were you worried then for yourself?" Eric asked, picking up his mug and sipping his tea.

"No, not for myself."

Eric frowned, mug aloft before him. "Then for whom?"

She became agitated, twitchy, looking around as she sought a suitable answer and then she fixed her eye on him.

"I really have nothing more to tell you." She stared at him with her mouth open. To Eric she seemed to be breathing heavily. "I think I would prefer it if you left now."

Eric was caught by surprise, readying himself for another sip of tea. He'd barely touched the contents. Reluctantly, he put the mug down and bobbed his head nervously. He didn't think he'd overplayed his hand and her reaction certainly threw him.

"Okay ... um ... thank you for your time," Eric said. "As well as for the tea."

Holding an open hand out to her left, Victoria encouraged him back to the front door. He opened it and as he stepped out, he took one of his contact cards from his pocket, turning and offering it to her. She glanced at it, hesitated, and then accepted it without looking at the face of it.

"Just in case you think of anything you want to tell me," Eric said, smiling weakly and feeling very much as if he was being shown the door for being rude or ill mannered, even though he knew he hadn't been.

Victoria tucked the card into the rear pocket of her shorts and no sooner had Eric stepped across the threshold, she pushed the door closed without another word. Eric hovered by the front door, hearing a snuffling from the other side; the dog must be there sniffing.

"Yeah," he said to the dog under his breath, "I thought it was a bit rushed too."

CHAPTER TWENTY-FIVE

THE HOUSE WAS IN DARKNESS; he must be asleep. It looked different to how it had fifteen years ago. She could still picture the image from her memory: blooming flower beds in the front garden, a neatly manicured lawn and an elderly man in a pork-pie hat leaning on the boundary, casually chatting to his neighbour. His gardening attire the same every time; a white shirt rolled up from the cuffs and chocolate brown corduroy trousers with braces over the shoulder and a hand-rolled cigarette seemingly glued to his lower lip that had long since gone out. She'd always felt welcome here, but that was a long time ago.

The Bed and Breakfast she was staying in was pleasant enough, only three letting rooms in an imposing old Victorian house set back a couple of streets from the sea front in Sheringham. The couple who owned it were nice, offering her food even though it wasn't what they usually did. They knew the detective inspector; she couldn't recall his name. She'd declined the offer, company had been the last thing on her mind. These past couple of days had passed in such a blur. It was hard to get her bearings. Was it the right choice to come back to Norfolk; to come here tonight?

The hinges of the wooden picket gate shrieked in protest as

she passed through, looking at the house she was unsure if anyone was home. There was an old brass-plated bell with a clapper hanging beside the front door and she rang it. The sound reverberated, carrying in the night, and she looked over her shoulder, embarrassed to be breaching the silence with such a vulgar intrusion. If he didn't answer, she'd already made the decision to leave; part of her hoped he wouldn't and she could do just that.

There was movement inside and suddenly she felt like an athlete having run miles, her chest heaving. A light flicked on in the interior behind the door, shafts of yellow visible from the fanlight above the door. Julia Rose was holding her breath as the door opened. It must have swollen in the current climate because it was stiff and needed some force to pull it wide. A set of dark eyes stared at her with a vacant expression and it took a moment for recognition to follow. She smiled weakly. He stared at her his mouth open.

"Hi Alex."

Alex Hart flinched at the sound of her voice and he retreated half a step, eyes widening.

"It–it's me, Julia."

He bit his lower lip, hesitantly edging forward and looking her up and down. They hadn't seen each other in well over a decade, sharing the occasional Christmas and birthday cards but she'd stayed away. She'd had to.

"Julia?" It sounded like he was questioning himself as much as he was her. She smiled again, feeling her eyes water. She tentatively reached out with one hand, he didn't move to avoid her touch and she slowly, and very gently, touched his left hand, moving to slip her fingers into his palm. Alex curled his fingers around hers, looking at their hands entwined and he smiled, nervously at first before emotion overcame him and he started to weep. Julia pulled him towards her, shocked at how easily he fell into her embrace and light he felt in comparison to how she remembered him. Dressed in a shirt and jeans, his bony frame was uncomfortable pressing against her.

Allowing the embrace to continue for a few moments longer, she eased him away from her but kept her hands on his shoulders. Holding him at arms' length, she tried to look him in the eye but Alex was gazing at the floor, unwilling to meet her gaze. She leaned in closer and they touched foreheads. Then she released her grip on him and he slowly raised his head, wiping both his eyes in turn with the heel of his palm. She continued to smile although now it was artificial, seeking to offer him support.

"You came back," Alex said softly, his voice cracking. She was unsure of what meaning there was behind that simple statement or how she should respond, so she merely nodded.

"I–I'm sorry it's so late. I hope I didn't wake you?"

He sniffed loudly, shaking his head. "I thought I'd imagined you again—"

"Again?"

The comment alarmed her momentarily but he waved it away, stepping back and taking her by the hand to lead her into the lobby. She followed, closing the door behind her, still unsure if she should have come. Alex turned on a light in the sitting room and she was surprised by the odour that greeted her, a mixture of stale air, sweat and junk food, judging by the tell-tale foil containers and white plastic bags on the coffee table alongside the plate. At least he'd eaten from a plate.

Alex was bobbing around the room picking up random items in an attempt to tidy up, most likely for her benefit, but it was all in vain. The house was a tip, akin to the common room in their university halls of residence where they'd first met, only worse, if that were at all possible? Up until now she would have said no. She couldn't help but see the mess and it must have been reflected in her expression, Alex appearing embarrassed.

"If–if I'd known you were coming," he said, running a hand through his hair and glancing around them, "I'd have tidied earlier. I'm sorry."

She waved the apology away.

"Alex, I was so sorry to hear about your father's passing; Gerald was a lovely man." Alex met her eye briefly, his mouth opening slowly and he took a deep breath but didn't speak, licking his lips and glancing away from her. "I feel bad for not coming back for the funeral—"

"Ah ... well ..."

"How have you been?" she asked, unable to keep the edge of fear from her voice. Alex was a shell of the man she knew; the man she'd loved.

He averted his eyes from hers. "I've had better times."

That must have been the largest understatement he could have uttered.

"How about work?"

His head listed from one shoulder to the other, his lips pursed. "Could always be better. Tim pushes work my way whenever he can ..."

"That's good of him," she said, looking away, fearful that he would see through her. It was ridiculous. She and Alex hadn't been an item for years and what passed between her and Tim was but a flash of ill-thought desire, so why did she harbour such shame? Maybe it was having all of it unexpectedly raked over in these circumstances? "Do you see much of him?"

"Yes, quite a bit," Alex said with a shrug. "He lives in his parents' old house near Holt, you remember?"

She smiled and nodded.

"He lives alone, much like I do, rattling around his old place with nothing but a dog for company."

He gestured for her to sit down and she looked around, unwilling to sit on the sofa in case he decided to join her. Her impulsive decision to drop by this night now felt like an error of judgement; she should have left it until tomorrow. What must Alex be thinking, particularly considering the manner in which he was living? Picking up a clutch of magazines that lay on an armchair next to the window, she perched herself on the edge.

Alex had a peculiar expression on his face, watching her. It made her feel self-conscious. He snapped out of it, gathering up the mess from his takeaway and hastily dropping them into the carrier bag he'd brought them home in. She almost couldn't bring herself to mention it but she had to. Psyching herself up, the words came out more bluntly than she'd have liked.

"What do you make of this police investigation?"

Alex hesitated, a foil container poised to go into the carrier bag held in his left hand and glanced nervously at her. He shrugged, stuffing the foil container into the bag and set about the remaining items with gusto, sweeping the leftovers from his plate into another tub before adding that to the bag as well.

"Do you remember her, Tina?"

Alex ignored her, continuing with his clear-up but he was agitated, clumsily dropping a knife and fork. He swore as they bounced from the table onto the carpet. Julia got up from her seat and retrieved them for him. She leant over to put them on the plate and Alex put his free hand on the back of hers. She recoiled, snatching her hand away. Alex was shocked and surprised but said nothing. She sat back down and Alex did like-wise, ignoring his task. He sat with his hands in his lap, his lips pursed.

"I remember her," Julia said. "She was the ..."

"Yeah. I remember her too," Alex said quietly.

"And that night? Do you remember that night?"

Alex shot her a dark look. He held it for a few seconds, then looked away, the action accompanied with a curt shrug. "I don't want to talk about it."

"I think we have to, don't you? Especially seeing as—"

"I said no!"

She was taken aback.

"I'm sorry, Alex, but the police—"

"Are you deaf?" he snapped but she could see pain in his expression rather than anger. "I can't go back there, Jules ... I just can't." He shook his head, lowering it into his hands. She wanted to move alongside him, relieve his burden but she dared not. She adopted a conciliatory pose.

"The police ... they asked me about what happened between us." Alex lowered his head into his hands, slowly shaking it side to side. "I couldn't lie to them, Alex. I had to say. You understand—"

He glared at her, a flash of anger that quickly dissipated as his voice quivered. "I'm scared, Jules. I'm really scared ... no matter how hard I try ... it just keeps coming back at me."

"What does?" She sat forward, her hands clasped in front of her and she angled her head to try to get into his eyeline but to no avail. "What keeps coming back?"

"The past," he said, his voice cracking, "mistakes I made, the things I did ..." He began to cry. Julia abandoned her reservations and knelt in front of him, placing a reassuring hand on his knee. He looked at her with a tear-streaked expression, his lower lip trembling.

"That night," she said, hesitant to press, "where did you go after ... after we ... you didn't come back to our room?"

He maintained his gaze upon her, tears flowing but he didn't seem to notice or care. He slowly shook his head. "I–I don't know."

"But you *must* know or have an idea," she said, taking one of his hands in both of hers and squeezing it tightly. "They think someone ... that someone hurt Tina—"

"I know!" Alex tore his hand from her grasp, wrapping his arms tightly around his midriff and hugging himself as he began gently rocking back and forth. "I was drunk ... and angry. I was so *very* angry." He shook his head. "I walked and walked – it was hot and sticky – I don't know where, I just wandered around I guess, but I don't remember." He gazed into her eyes, imploring her to say something but she just waited patiently, returning her hand to his leg and gently rubbing it as one would a distressed child. "I remember waking – I was in a field – to find the ground hard beneath my feet," he cast his eyes to the ceiling, he was no longer crying, "but my boots were damp and muddy. It was so strange. How on earth did I end up there?"

"Do you remember anything else?"

He glanced at her and away again, absently rubbing at his neck as if it were sore.

"My hands ..."

"What about them?"

"The backs of them were all bloody and scratched, and across my forearms as well," he said, looking at his arm and running a hand up the length of it for emphasis. "The sun was up ... I was hot and felt sick but not from the alcohol, not physically sick ... more lost."

"And?"

He turned the corners of his mouth down, shaking his head and offering her a shrug. "I don't remember. It was like," he looked into her eyes despairingly, "like those times when I ..."

"When you used to scare me?" she whispered.

He nodded, fighting back more tears.

"You know, some nights I still walk out to Beeston ..."

His tone turned icy, distant, and it filled her with dread as she saw the vacant expression he'd greeted her with descend upon him once more.

"You mustn't think like—"

"Maybe it would be for the best—?"

"Alex, you mustn't!" She forced him to allow her to take his hands in hers and insisted he look her in the eye. "You mustn't think that, ever. Do you understand?"

He stared at her, his eyes cold and numb to her words.

"Please, Alex ..." She shook his hands, making him acknowledge her. He managed a feeble smile but it vanished as quickly as it came. "Please, promise me that you won't go back there!"

He closed his eyes and tears fell.

CHAPTER TWENTY-SIX

Tom found Cassie hunched over her desk when he walked into the ops room. Eric hadn't arrived yet. Usually he was the first one through the door and Tom took it for granted that he would be at his desk but recently it wasn't the case.

"Good morning," Tom said.

Cassie mumbled a reply without looking up. She drummed her fingers on the table and then looked round at him with surprise.

"Oh, I didn't see you come in. Morning." She sat back in her chair and stretched. "Tamara's got an early meeting with the chief super, then she'll be in."

Tom nodded, crossing to where she was sitting and putting a cup of takeaway coffee on the desk beside her. She peeled off the lid and smelled the rising steam.

"Hazelnut?"

"Almond," Tom said.

"Close enough." Cassie shrugged, lifting it and sipping. "I made some headway with that mammoth mission you set me."

"What's that, the missing persons' cases in and around our suspects?"

"The needle in a haystack search, aye," she said with a sideways grin. Tom smiled. "But, to give you richly deserved credit, I think you're onto something. Our Indiana-Jones-wannabes have crossed paths with a couple of interesting possibilities—"

"Morning!" Eric said, entering. He shook his head and offered a raised hand by way of an apology. Tom cast an eye over him; Eric looked dreadful, pained. "Sorry, Becca isn't sleeping well at the moment and," he waved the comment away, "it's not great."

"Becca not well?" Cassie asked, concerned.

"Ah, she'll be all right. What have I missed?"

"Coffee," Tom said, thrusting a cup into Eric's grateful hand. He turned back to Cassie, indicating for her to continue.

"Should we wait for the DCI?"

"No, she'll catch up," Tom said, eyeing the board that Cassie had been populating.

Cassie stood up and gathered two printouts from her desk, both had circles drawn on them in blue marker. She crossed to the board. Tom recognised one immediately but he couldn't see enough of the other one to make out where it was.

"2004," Cassie said, pinning the first to the board, "a sixteen-year-old girl goes missing from the southern Norwegian city of *Kristiansand*. Her body was pulled from the water of *Topdalsfjorden*, near a small village on the west shore called *Justvik*. The girl, Anette Larsen, had been attending a friend's birthday party in the city. According to friends she was drinking heavily earlier that night and left the party around ten o'clock, saying goodbye to a couple of friends before heading for home. She never made it. It was thought at the time that she may have fallen into the water, intoxicated, and drowned. The fjord runs a little over seven miles from Kristiansand up past Justvik and ends at a town I'm not even going to begin to pronounce."

"I thought you lot from Northumberland all spoke Viking?" Eric said, his mood lightening as he drank his coffee.

Cassie mock-snarled at him, turning back to Tom. "I didn't think you'd mind if I contacted the locals for more details." Tom shook his head, folding his arms across his chest and concentrating. "Well, I managed to track down an investigator who had access to the file – it's not officially closed but isn't under active investigation – and she told me that the cause of death was originally thought to be drowning but was later changed to a broken neck." Tom's gaze narrowed, potentially that was how Tina Farrow died, or at least she sustained a similar injury. "I thought you'd like that. Anyway, she sent me the autopsy file but I don't understand this particular dialect of Viking," she glanced sideways at Eric, "but Elin ran through it with me over the phone."

"Elin being …?"

"Our counterpart in Kristiansand," Cassie explained. "Now, the deceased girl, Anette, may have fallen into the water because she was drunk – it happens—"

"It does a lot in Amsterdam and Utrecht in The Netherlands," Tom said, frowning.

"Right, yeah, so they looked for signs of assault. The body was fairly well preserved having spent the time prior to discovery in the cold water but they didn't find any indications that she'd been attacked." Cassie double-checked her notes. "Other than the broken neck, which was a clean break, so unlikely from a collision with a car for example, she had no defensive wounds, no scratches or unidentified skin under her fingernails … but – and this is why they didn't close it off as accidental death – she had had sex prior to her death. The pathologist was certain."

"Boyfriend?" Tom suggested. "Someone at the earlier party, perhaps?"

Cassie shook her head. "They spoke to all of those who attended the party and all of her friends said she wasn't dating anyone at the time and no one recalled seeing her copping off with anyone," she saw Tom's expression change and coughed, "recalled seeing her interact with anyone that night."

"DNA?"

"The length of time in the water hampered that but they did recover usable trace evidence from her vagina. Norwegian police took samples from the partygoers … no match. Similarly no hits on their database either."

"Okay, so now you're going to tell us which of our candidates was present in Kristiansand at the time?"

Cassie's nose wrinkled. "Good news and bad on that front. Julia Rose was working on an excavation there, and she was still in a relationship with Alex Hart at that time. I checked against Hart's records and he wasn't named on that particular dig but according to flight passenger records Alex Hart did arrive in the country two weeks prior to Anette Larsen's disappearance and was still there upon discovery of the body four days later."

"Could have been visiting Julia?" Eric said. "Stands to reason."

"Okay, what's the bad news?" Tom asked.

"Not necessarily bad news but it clouds things a little. Professor Cannell was also in Norway attending a conference in Oslo; he was the closing speaker on the Friday afternoon."

Cassie handed Tom a photograph of the crime scene featuring the body of Anette Larsen and even taking into account the paleness of her skin due to her time in the water, she looked a lot like Tina Farrow.

"And how far is Oslo from Kristiansand?" he asked.

Cassie rocked her head from side to side. "Three, three and a half hours, give or take."

"What are the chances of our colleagues comparing the DNA found on Anette Larsen to that of Cannell and Hart?"

"Dicey," Cassie said. "Elin is going to ask the question but they'll need permission from further up the chain, the prosecutor's office or something. I'm not sure how it works procedurally over there but when that happens – if it happens – then there'll be no keeping a lid on it and a story like that, the murder of a sixteen-year-old girl—"

"Yeah, the press will devour it," Tom said. He pointed to the other map, still in her hand. "You've found something in The Netherlands?"

Cassie looked at him quizzically and nodded. Turning away from him, she pinned this map to the board as well.

"*De Spitkeet*," Cassie said, "it's in Friesland, east of Groningen, but don't ask me what—"

"Peat-House, I think," Tom said, "or Turf-House might be better." Cassie stared hard at him. He smiled. "Friesland. It's my grandfather's old stomping ground."

"Ah … right. And you know of De Spitkeet?"

He acknowledged her with a brief incline of his head to one side. "You've got me there, no."

"It's a living museum, of sorts," Cassie said. "Charting different styles of housing throughout the past couple of centuries. Do you know some people dug holes and built up against dykes using turf and stuff for the walls and ceilings; they were like little hobbit-style places?" She looked him up and down. "Not a chance I can imagine you fitting into a place like that. Anyway, back to reality – a nineteen-year-old girl went missing nearby." She handed him another photograph. "Mila van der Berg. She was strangled and her body was dumped on the edge of an isolated park adjacent to some waste ground, and both her and her bicycle were covered with brush to shield them from passers-by. She was found before she was even reported missing. Now, this could be coincidence. The MO is different. The other two disappeared at night after partying in one form or another whereas this girl was just out for a day's cycling. Her neck wasn't broken either and she hadn't been sexually assaulted."

"Maybe her attacker was disturbed before he was able to?" Eric said. Cassie nodded her agreement. "Then he panicked and covered her over before fleeing."

"Who was there?" Tom asked with bated breath. He could feel the adrenalin because Cassie wouldn't have zeroed in on this case unless it was relevant.

She took a deep breath, crestfallen. "All of them."

Tom exhaled and grimaced, a wave of frustration passing over him. "It wouldn't be that easy, would it? Did the killer leave any trace evidence behind?"

"Still waiting to hear." Cassie perched herself on the edge of a desk. Tom sensed there was more but Cassie didn't voice it. Perhaps it was something instinctive she was holding back. He resolved to press her later. He turned to Eric, quietly nursing his coffee.

"How did you get on with Hendry's ex-wife?"

Eric exhaled through gritted teeth, hissing quietly, offering a shake of the head.

"Strange woman, I have to say." He frowned.

"Strange how?"

"Well, she was pleasant enough at first but then ... I don't know, she sort of ... turned on me. Booted me out, just like that! It was a bit weird."

"Before she turfed you out, did she say anything useful?"

Eric's frown deepened. "She's no fan of her ex-husband, that's for sure. From what she described, he comes across as a manipulative control-freak who was used to getting his own way. He couldn't handle the fact she wanted to leave him and ended up putting her in the hospital." Eric's frown switched to disappointment. "I guess you really can't see the real person through a television screen, can you?"

Tom sighed. "They say you should never meet your heroes, Eric. They are almost always a disappointment. Did, what was her name, Victoria—?"

"Think he was capable of being a killer?" Eric shook his head. "Nah. She didn't give me that impression at all. Pretty much threw me out around then as well." He stared into space. "Like I said, weird."

Cassie was still looking at the board, lost in thought.

"What is it, Cass?" Tom asked.

"It's probably nothing ..."

"Try me."

"All right, but don't shoot me down straight away, okay?" Tom nodded. "When I was looking into these missing girls ... I had to pass over most of those who vanished from larger urban or metropolitan centres just because it's far too circumstantial to try and link them but I couldn't ignore the case in Kristiansand and, besides that one ... I found two others in and around locations where these guys were working as undergraduates." She shook her head, frowning. "It's too much of a coincidence for my liking."

"You know what you're inferring, don't you?"

She bit her lower lip. "Yes, I do ... I think one of these guys is a serial attacker and when Elin calls back, we might have enough evidence to start building a case to prove it."

Tom nodded solemnly. "Eric, have a look into this conference that Cannell was speaking at, see if you can determine his movements, specifically if he visited Kristiansand. Drop in on Julia Rose, see if she can recall him visiting her on the dig." He indicated Cassie. "We should wait until your Norwegian counterpart comes back to us but, dependent on what she says, I think we may need to speak to Alex Hart – formally."

CHAPTER TWENTY-SEVEN

Tom and Cassie watched Alex Hart, sitting at a table in the interview room chaperoned by a uniformed constable, via the monitor streaming the feed from the camera in the corner of the room. He was clearly agitated. Whether that was a result of being picked up unannounced from home, an hour earlier, or purely the anxiety of being held in relative discomfort in a sterile, windowless room. Depending on your point of view, his body language either exhibited nervous tension or fear of discovery.

"He looks scared," Cassie said, not taking her eyes from the monitor. Tom agreed.

"Doesn't mean he's hiding something, though." Tom glanced sideways at her. "And he declined legal representation?"

She nodded. "Surprisingly, yes. He must be supremely confident—"

"We'll see."

"It will be interesting to gauge his reaction, though, won't it? Do you think he'll see it coming?"

Tom didn't answer, scooping up the files from the desk and heading for the door, Cassie a half step behind. Striding purposefully into the interview room, Hart stared at them wide-eyed as Tom pulled out a chair opposite him without a word and set the folder down in front of him. Cassie swapped places with the constable, off to Hart's left and in his peripheral vision, leaning against the wall and folding her arms across her chest. Hart glanced nervously in her direction before focussing on Tom. Tom put his elbows on the table and brought his hands together beneath his chin in a prayer pose. He allowed the suspect to watch for a few moments, maintaining an impassive expression and patiently observing how on edge Hart appeared to be. If he was confident then he did a good job of concealing it.

Casually, Tom opened the folder on the table. Removing two photographs he set them down on the table, reversing them and sliding them across in front of Hart. He lowered his eyes, scanning them before lifting his gaze back to Tom.

"It's a nice place, Kristiansand, isn't it?" Tom said.

Hart looked puzzled. Whatever he'd expected the opening comment to be, it certainly wasn't that.

"Excuse me?"

"Kristiansand, the fifth largest city in Norway and, of great interest to historians and archaeologists alike, occupied since prehistory ..." Tom glanced at his notes, lifting the next page from the folder and eyeing it, "... to the south and west of *Oddernes Church* lies one of the largest pre-Christian burial grounds in southern Norway. But you already know that don't you?"

Hart swallowed, noticeably appearing to have difficulty with the action but didn't speak.

"Tina Farrow and Anette Larsen," Tom said gently, pointedly tapping each photograph in turn as he said the name. Hart pursed his lips, as again his eyes darted to the images but they lingered on neither. "Tina Farrow – murdered in late August 2001. Anette Larsen ... sixteen years of age ... abducted and later murdered in Kristiansand, 2004." Hart wouldn't meet Tom's eye, instead he glanced at Cassie but broke away from her intense gaze as well, flicking to the pictures of the smiling girls and away again. His chest heaved. "Look at them." Hart stared at Tom. Tom leaned forward, pushing the pictures closer and repeated himself. "Look at them!"

Hart looked down eyeing the two girls in turn.

"You know them?"

"I knew Tina," Hart said quietly, reaching up slowly with his left hand. His fingertips brushed over her image carefully, deliberately, and then moved to Anette's. He pointedly pushed the picture back towards Tom. "But this other girl; I don't believe I know her."

"You're sure? You've never met her?" Tom said, picking up the image and holding it aloft in front of Hart, pointing to her face with his forefinger. "You're certain you've never come across her?"

"Yes, I'm certain. I've no idea who she is."

"Julia Rose participated in an excavation during the July of 2004, in Kristiansand. Do you recall that?"

Hart shrugged. "Yes, that rings a bell. So what?"

"Anette Larsen went missing walking home from a night out with friends ... and her body was pulled from the fjord four days later near the village of Justvik." Hart tried to swallow but couldn't.

"May I have some water—?"

"Her neck was broken," Tom continued, ignoring the request, "and she may have been sexually assaulted."

Hart forcefully shook his head refusing to meet Tom's gaze. "Not me ... not my fault," he mumbled.

"Coincidence that both girls, teenagers, were to die in similar circumstances ... in the same way. Pretty girls aren't they?" Tom placed Anette's photograph back alongside Tina's and pushed both into Hart's view; he closed his eyes to shut them out. "Look at them!"

Hart shook his head vigorously, clamping his eyes tightly shut. "No ... no ... not my fault. I didn't do anything."

"We know you attacked Julia, she told us," Tom said. Hart looked up, glaring at him as his eyes began watering. "Your girlfriend at the time told us how you beat her—"

"It wasn't like that!"

"Then how was it?"

"I didn't mean to … you have to believe me," Hart said looking between Tom and Cassie, imploring them. "When it happens, I don't recall it afterwards, not really. I–I lose myself … but not anymore."

"What do you mean *not anymore*?" Tom asked. Hart dropped his head into his hands.

Cassie sighed. "He means he doesn't kill anymore—"

"No! That's not what I mean." Hart snapped in her direction in an uncharacteristic display of lucidity, holding up his hands in a placatory gesture. "I am … ashamed of what I've done in the past to people I love." He nodded towards the photographs. "But I didn't do this."

Tom sat back, leafing through the folder and taking out another piece of paper.

"You were not very clear about your time in Kristiansand, did you help Julia with the excavations?"

He shook his head. "I visited the site a few times, out of professional curiosity, personal interest, as well as to support Jules."

"I should imagine the digs blend into one, don't they?"

Hart shrugged. "Some are more memorable than others."

"But let us be clear, you have no recollection of meeting Anette Larsen?"

"No. I've already said so—"

"Are you sure about that?"

Hart's mouth fell open under Tom's piercing stare, his eyes widening. Tom waited, watching as Hart's lips moved but he said nothing. Tom took another picture from the folder and put it down on the table on top of the photographs. It was a picture taken from a traffic camera, time and date stamped on the night of Anette's disappearance, depicting a blue saloon car passing through a red light. Tom double-tapped it with his finger.

"This car ran a red light in the area of the docks, where the ferries depart Kristiansand for Denmark, coincidentally the same area Anette had to traverse to reach her parents' waterside apartment and where her mobile phone and purse were found several days after her body was discovered. You recognise this car?" Hart stared at the image, it was black and white, grainy and generally low quality but the registration plate was visible. "During the investigation into Anette's disappearance Norwegian police gathered all the images they could from traffic cameras, CCTV, both from private enterprise and public transport hubs ... and this image was one among hundreds. A needle in a haystack; until we fed your name into the data." Hart glared at him but Tom remained resolute. "The car was traced back to a hire company who'd leased it out at the time, and it was leased to you."

Hart slowly shook his head, squinting at the image. "B–But I–I ... it can't be me ..." he stammered. "I would remember, wouldn't I? I mean, it can't have been me."

"You would remember," Tom said.

"Yes, of course I would, surely—?"

"But you just said that you *lose yourself*," Cassie reminded him. "Maybe you lost yourself that night in Kristiansand?"

"No," he shook his head firmly, "I was ill in Kristiansand and hardly drove the damn car. I–I certainly didn't get any ... bloody traffic tickets for running a red light! I barely left the apartment. Ask Julia! Yes, you should ask her. It can't have been me."

"Just a coincidence," Tom said. Hart nodded. "And Tina Farrow ... also a coincidence—?"

Hart slammed his fist on the table. "I didn't hurt her! I liked her for crying out loud."

"She teased you ... just like she teased the others," Tom said, "and when you pressed on, thinking you'd pulled, she knocked you back and you didn't like it!"

Hart swung his head from side to side. "No, it didn't happen like that ... it wasn't my fault."

"And then she laughed at you, just as she laughed at Billy and you went for her, didn't you? That's what happened. You went for her and you killed her. How dare she do that to you!"

"No … that didn't happen … I don't remember …" Hart said, clamping his hands against the sides of his head, trying to block out Tom's accusations.

"Was it the same with Anette? Only she was easier to dispose of – you'd learnt by then – you could throw her in the water but Tina … you had to come back for her the next day, dragging her to the site, knowing the freshly backfilled soil would be easy to dig. That's where you buried her, safely hidden from view!"

"No! I didn't do that!" Hart balled his fists and hammered them down on the table, glaring at Tom.

"Where did you stay that night, the night of Tina's disappearance because you didn't go back to your room, did you?"

Hart closed his eyes, leaning his head back and breathing hard through his open mouth. Slowly righting himself, he shot Tom a despairing look. "I walked … and I walked." Shaking his head, his brow wrinkling as he seemed to be recalling painful details from memory. "And I can't tell you where I slept. I really don't recall." His eyes were vacant now, his spirit deserting him. "I woke the next day, aching and stiff with a thumping headache; that was common for me back then. When it all got too much I just sort of zoned out. With my medication things are different now. The next morning I found my way back to the Crown – Julia had already left for the site – and I didn't have an access card for our room." He shook his head. "I lost mine at some point the previous night. I had to get one of the staff to let me into our room – I don't remember who – and then I showered, gathered myself as best as I could and went to join the others at the dig."

He gently placed both hands on the photographs before him, staring hard at them and spreading his fingers wide to get maximum purchase, pushing them slowly across to Tom. He was still breathing heavily, his expression strained but he was focussed. "I have no recollection of what you are telling me …" He glanced between Cassie and Tom "… and in all honesty I can't tell you that I did something when I have no memory of having done it." His voice was cracking as he spoke, his lower lip quivering and shoulders sagging. "I just want to go home," he said in a whisper, hanging his head.

TOM ACKNOWLEDGED the constable who stepped into the interview room as both he and Cassie left. Cassie leant her back against the wall in the corridor, blowing out her cheeks. She raised her eyebrows, tilting her head in Tom's direction.

"You know, I'm pretty sure he's telling us the truth."

"Which part?" he asked.

"I'm not convinced he knows what's real and what's fantasy," she said chewing on her lower lip. "Hell of a temper for a guy who looks like he'd snap in the wind though."

She had a point. Alex Hart's medical history detailed multiple occurrences of delusion and psychotic episodes over the years. However, provided he kept to his regimen of drugs then the professional medical opinion was that his condition should be manageable. With that said, Hart was clearly struggling at the moment.

"Maybe we should get the on-call doctor to check him over before we let him go home."

"Let him go? Seriously?"

He nodded, inclining his head to suggest they walk back to ops. Cassie fell into step alongside him.

"We have no more reason to hold him now than we did this morning."

"But the car—?"

"Taken from a traffic camera in 2004 in the same area a girl, who went missing, was last reportedly seen in ... and that's it. And we can't even prove he was driving it because he's not visible in the camera shot. Plus," he said, rounding a corner and sidestepping a uniformed officer who was in a hurry, "I'm not up on international law but unless the Norwegians put out an arrest warrant then we have no grounds to hold him anyway."

"Elin says they'll want to speak to him."

"Absolutely, I would too if I were them. Any word on the DNA?"

"Still waiting," Cassie said. "But if what was found on Anette Larsen is matched to Hart then Elin will be on the first available flight."

Tom laughed. "It still doesn't quite fit though." He glanced at her, reading her quizzical look. "If Hart is our man then it strikes me that Tina's assault was a result of his mental condition, a sporadic assault brought on by a psychotic episode."

"Agreed. So what?"

Tom stopped, turning to face her. "Anette Larsen looks more like a pre-planned attack; a hunter out on the prowl who found a vulnerable target and took advantage. That's what you get when dealing with a serial offender." He resumed his walk. "The two scenarios are very different."

"That's true," Cassie said. "Listen, serial killers often like to keep things from their victims, right?"

Tom nodded. "Yes, trophies: personal effects, mementos ... why?"

"Do you think we could get a search warrant to go through Hart's house. Maybe he'll have something from one of the victims?" She read Tom's placid expression as unenthusiastic. "Come on, I know it's a long shot but it's got to be worth a look, right?"

Tom resumed his walk back to ops, glancing back over his shoulder, he saw she was still standing still, concentrating hard.

"Find out if any of our potential victims were missing anything special to them when they were found and then we'll see."

Cassie realised he'd moved off and she hurried to catch up with him, coming alongside as they entered ops. Tamara was there and she beckoned them over, no doubt keen to hear what Alex Hart had to say. Tom heard Cassie muttering something about *this case being so weird* under her breath. He could appreciate the sentiment.

CHAPTER TWENTY-EIGHT

JULIA ROSE MET Eric on the porch as she closed the door to her guest house, glancing up at the sky. The clouds were moving at pace and a quick look out to the horizon over the North Sea showed the long-awaited storm was threatening to finally make its appearance. The day felt close and muggy.

"Thank you for seeing me at such short notice," Eric said.

"That's okay," Julia replied, walking alongside him as they set off away from the house. They could have stayed indoors to talk but the guest sitting room was far from private. Julia cut a dejected figure. "It's not like I have anything much to do anyway. I'm not even sure why I've stayed on."

"Why have you?"

"To be here for Alex if he needs me, maybe?" She shook her head. "I don't really know, to be honest. I have a ton of things I should be doing in Svelgen."

"Have you seen Alex since you came back?"

"Yes, of course."

"How did you find him?"

Julia fell silent, looking at the ground where she walked. Her reticence was obvious.

"Not good," she said after a few moments, glancing sideways

at Eric. "I knew he was struggling ... I've always known he was struggling, but what was I supposed to do, stay with him in spite of everything?"

"I don't think anyone can attach blame to you for his condition," Eric said. "I think you've had to cope with a lot over the years—"

"That's not what I meant," she said, smiling weakly in appreciation of Eric's reassurance and touching her hand to the back of his, hanging at his side between them.

Eric returned her smile, feeling awkward at her touch and reddening as her hand lingered on his, Julia looking into his eyes. He wasn't supposed to be counselling a witness; no one else in the team ever stumbled into this type of situation. Was it his youth? He'd always been considered to be younger than his years, despite his muscular physique. Some would say he was fresh-faced but his mum, much to his embarrassment and a source of great hilarity for his friends, always labelled him as baby-faced. He'd tried to grow a beard when he joined the police; an idea that generated more mirth and did little to age him. He'd abandoned that plan very quickly.

He gently withdrew his hand. Julia Rose noticed the awkwardness in his expression, smiling apologetically.

"I'm sorry. You remind me a lot of him."

"Who? Alex?"

She nodded. He was surprised.

"When he was in his teens," she said, clasping her hands in front of her as they walked. He was in his twenties and about to embark on a new chapter in his life and he still looked like a kid. "You have a fresh face."

Eric winced.

"I need to ask you about one of your projects in Norway," Eric said, keen to change the subject. She looked sideways at him quizzically. "Specifically, the work you did around Kristiansand."

"Wow! That's going back a little. What is it you want to know?"

"You were still with Alex around then weren't you?"

Julia concentrated hard. "That would have been early two thousands—"

"2004," Eric said.

"Yes, yes it was. We were together then but," she frowned, "it was getting difficult by that time. We'd split up a couple of times previously but we came back to each other the Christmas before." She sighed. "I always find that time of year very hard. My father passed away in December and the holiday season is always hard for me because of it. Less so now, to be sure. Time is a healer, or, at least, it helps soften the pain." She looked directly at Eric. "Have you lost a parent?"

He didn't want to bring himself into this, certainly not now he'd managed to shift the conversation where he wanted it to go. She noticed his reluctance to speak.

"I'm sorry. You're the policeman and get to ask the questions."

"Oh ... it's not that—"

She waved away his denial. "What is it you want to know about Kristiansand?"

"Did Alex visit you while you were working there?"

"Of course. He came to stay with me for a few weeks." Her eyebrows met as she tried to remember specifics. "He may have come across twice. He wasn't working at the time, not anything regular anyway. He found work hard to come by after the fallout of Brancaster and the waste of his doctorate."

"Right. We understand William Cannell was also in—"

"Oslo, at the time," she said, nodding her head and moving the hair away from her eyes as they walked. The wind was picking up. "Yes, I remember. Billy was a guest speaker at an event in Oslo. He offered me a ticket to go and see him speak." She tilted her head to one side. "Billy was like that – always trying to get his peers to come and watch him present. It was as if he loved basking in some perceived adulation of the crowd, but it only counted if his peers were there to witness it. He was a bit of an arse for that type of thing."

"Did you go?"

She shook her head.

"Because you were busy on the excavation or because you didn't want to give him the satisfaction?"

"No, it was nothing like that. I could have easily spared the time; Oslo is only three to four hours from Kristiansand, and it would have been an interesting talk. Billy can be tiresome in many ways but he really is a genius." Eric raised an eyebrow; he had found the man to be quite pompous when he'd interviewed him alongside Tom. Julia must have read Eric's expression because she smiled. "A genius can often be flawed ... but they are still a genius in their field. No pun intended." It took Eric a moment to get the joke, and then he also smiled. "No, I couldn't go because I had Alex staying with me at the time and Billy wouldn't have offered him a ticket even if I'd asked. They weren't speaking any more by that point."

"I understand that was because of what happened between them here in Norfolk?"

She nodded. "Alex blamed Billy for throwing him under the bus over the debacle at Brancaster and for his part, Billy thought Alex had tarnished his reputation." She laughed but it was a bitter laugh without genuine humour. "The pair of them were a night-mare in altogether different ways. Why are you asking about this anyway?"

"Oh, we're looking into an attack on another teenager out there at the time—"

"And you think Alex did it?"

Eric heard the fearful edge to her voice and immediately regretted telling her. He shouldn't have and he felt his face flush; Tom was going to kill him. He backtracked.

"It's not that we think he did it ... it's j–just that it happened at the same time as he was there, that's all."

"He couldn't have," she said, dismissing the suggestion. However, her expression didn't convey the same confidence. She caught him eyeing her and she tried her best to lighten her tone. "It couldn't have been Alex. He was with me most of the time—"

"But you were on the dig, weren't you?"

"Y–yes, that's true but even so … Alex was rather unwell during his stay and was largely confined to my apartment. He only came to site a couple of times."

"Another way of looking at it is that he had plenty of opportunity to go out and about alone, then?"

"I'm sure it wouldn't have been Alex."

She sounded less sure now and averted her eyes from Eric's.

"Why are you asking about Billy as well?"

"Because he is also a suspect in the attack on the sixteen-year-old girl in Kristian—"

"Sixteen?" she said, visibly deflating. Eric feared she was about to faint and reached out to offer her his arm for support. She took it and he helped her over to a nearby bench at the edge of the path and overlooking the sea. Eric sat down alongside her and once she'd had a moment to gather herself, she turned to face him. "He came to visit me on site, too, and—"

"William Cannell was in Kristiansand?" Eric asked, excited. Julia nodded. "At the same time as Alex?"

"Yes. Like I said, Alex was ill and Billy came down to see me on the site—"

"When was this?" Eric said, eagerly taking out his notebook, keen to record every detail accurately. Julia thought about it.

"It must have been that weekend after he'd given his speech at the conference because he was flying back to the UK on the Saturday afternoon, I think." She took a deep breath, her complexion was pale and Eric was still concerned about her.

"I could run and get you something to drink?" Eric said, looking around to see how he could achieve it. She put a restraining hand on his forearm.

"No, thank you, you're very kind but I'll be all right."

Eric frowned through his concern but didn't press it. "William Cannell – you were saying?"

She took another deep breath, exhaling slowly and bobbing her head. "It must have been the Friday. He arrived late afternoon, early evening. I remember he joined us on site and then a few of us went for dinner."

"And Cannell went with you?"

She nodded. "Absolutely. We found a little restaurant near the harbour; where the catamaran leaves from, heading for Denmark."

"And Cannell was with you? Until what time?"

She blew out her cheeks, slowly shaking her head. "I guess it would have been until ten-ish … maybe later. Once we all get chatting time sort of passes by without any of us noticing."

"But Alex wasn't there?"

She shook her head. "No, as I say he couldn't have been because he was—"

"Unwell. Yes, you said," Eric replied, trying hard not to break into a grin. He could place William Cannell in the area of where Anette Larsen was last known to be alive. It was a big part in building a case and Eric knew it. Maybe it would be enough to temper Tom's wrath when he found out he'd blabbed about the parallel investigation; but probably not.

"What happened to the girl … the one in Kristiansand?"

Eric sank back on the bench. It was too late now; he couldn't really dismiss her question.

"She was sixteen – a local girl – heading home from a friend's birthday party. Someone attacked her, and she was found dead a few days later." He turned his body to face her, she looked lost and he considered not saying anything but she smiled weakly at him and he chose to anyway. "Listen, I shouldn't have mentioned the Kristiansand case really. It's just … a set of coincidences but the killer was never caught—"

"And you really think Alex or Billy could have done that to her, I mean, really believe it could have been one of them?"

Eric nodded. "I'm afraid so, yes. It is a possibility. Our counterparts in Norway are looking into it, but please," he implored her, "don't speak about it to either Alex or William Cannell. I know you have some personal loyalty—"

"I have none with Billy!" she said aggressively. "I owe him nothing."

"Well," Eric inclined his head to one side, "as I say, if you could refrain from contacting him, I'd appreciate it."

She nodded slowly, offering him a glum smile. "What about Alex?"

Eric took a breath. "He is being interviewed at the moment."

Julia gaped at him, then raised a hand across her mouth. Eric felt awkward again, splitting the moment by checking his watch. He wanted to get back to the station and go through this development with the team because it might alter their plans. His mobile rang and he searched his pockets for it, answering as he stepped away from the bench.

"Eric, it's Cassie. Are you still with Dr Rose?"

Eric glanced back at the bench; Julia remained transfixed on the view out to sea. Colour was returning to her cheeks but she still looked ready to cry at any moment. He hoped she wouldn't.

"I'm almost through here," he said, turning his back on Julia and not noticing her focussing on him. "You'll never guess—"

"The DCI wants you back here pronto. My contact in Norway has come back to us with some new evidence. The word is out over there and an eyewitness came forward following a piece on the television news last night to say she reckons she saw Anette Larsen getting into Alex Hart's car on the night she disappeared."

"Into Alex's car?" Eric said, glancing over his shoulder. Julia Rose looked away. He wasn't sure if she'd heard him or not as the wind was picking up even more now. He lowered his voice. "Is she sure ... that it was Alex's car?"

"She saw the traffic camera footage, so yeah, she was confident. Not only that but the witness picked Hart's photo out of a line-up that Elin showed her this afternoon."

"Right," Eric said, hearing the disappointment in his own voice. "That's ... erm ... pretty damning."

"Isn't it?" Cassie said, her tone upbeat and excited. "Anyway, we're waiting on you getting back here, so get a shifty on, yeah?"

He hung up, turning back to Julia.

"I have to get back to the station," he said apologetically. She didn't react, looking to be in her own little world. "Can I walk you back to your lodgings?" He was still concerned about her, not because he feared her speaking to Cannell, although that seemed not to matter much now in any event, but because she seemed overawed by all of this. Just a short while ago he feared she was about to faint. She looked over, reading the concern in his face.

"I'll be all right, Detective Constable Collet, thank you." She smiled again. "I think I'll just stay here a while."

Eric looked at the gathering storm clouds. She ought not stay here too long or she'd be caught in the coming storm but he figured it was at least an hour or two away from making landfall.

"Okay," he said, nodding in her direction. "Thank you for your time. If you need anything, anything at all, please do call me." He reached into his pocket and took out one of his contact cards but she declined it as he approached and made to pass it to her.

"Thank you but I already have one from your DI Janssen. You are all very caring, you know? I appreciate you thinking of me."

Eric flushed with embarrassment making her smile again. He turned and walked away, quickening his pace as he felt the first drops of rain on his face.

CHAPTER TWENTY-NINE

JULIA ROSE WATCHED the young detective constable stride away, experiencing a sinking feeling in the pit of her stomach. He'd definitely said something about Alex's car and the tone he used, was it surprise or disappointment? Maybe it was both? She hadn't slept well for days and all of this made her head spin. She'd meant what she'd said about Billy, he'd turned his back on all of them some time ago, unhappy with them apparently riding on his coat tails. But now there was all this. She racked her brains trying to recall her time at Kristiansand and the events of that Friday in particular. The way the detective had seized upon Billy's presence that night, she desperately tried to recall how he'd been during her company; was there anything he'd said or done to make her think him capable of what was being suggested.

Then there was Alex. He'd been largely left to his own devices that visit. She'd been so caught up in her work that she hadn't made time for him, hadn't wanted to if she was honest. He was spiralling into a pit of depression, his outbursts becoming more frequent and sustained. By that time she'd realised the rekindling of their relationship was a grave error on both their parts.

But this? This was too much for her and she sank forward, head in her hands. She felt her chest tighten and she struggled for breath, ignoring the rain. Taking out her mobile she clutched it tightly. She couldn't call Alex, she promised she wouldn't, but even if she did, what would she say? How could she ask him? But she needed to know, to hear herself ask the question at least. Staring at the mobile screen, she steadied herself and opened her contacts list, scrolling down, her finger hovering over the name. She tapped it and placed the mobile against her ear. There was only one person who might understand what she was going through.

Tim Hendry answered the call immediately.

"Julia, this is a nice surprise! Alex told me you were in the area … I thought about calling but, what with everything that's going on, I thought it might … complicate things."

"I–I know, I thought the same."

"Is everything okay, Jules? You sound … upset."

She couldn't hold back the wave of emotion anymore; that one question broke the dyke and her voice cracked, tears falling. In between the sobs she was able to outline much of what Eric had told her, her fears about Alex and the questions surrounding William Cannell's visit. Tim Hendry listened to her without interrupting until she'd exhausted everything she needed to say.

"Hold on one moment, Jules," Hendry said. She heard him tutting as he typed away at a keyboard in the background. Moments later he offered her his full attention. "I have it here, I just googled it. A girl from Kristiansand called Anna – no – Anette Larsen. She was … dear God … she was murdered in 2004."

"Yes, that was what they told me."

Hendry sighed.

"This is awful. And they think either Alex or William did this—?"

"No, not for certain … but … maybe," she said, hearing desperation in her tone. "They couldn't have done it. Neither is capable of such a thing, surely? I know Alex could be … violent but not like this. Please tell me I'm mad to think it."

Hendry hesitated and she picked up on it.

"Tim, you don't think one of them could, do you? I mean they were our—"

"No, no, of course not. It must be the police doing their thing. It'll all be cleared up soon enough, don't worry."

She sniffed, wiping her nose with the back of her hand. He was reassuring. Tim was always the safe pair of hands to go to when you needed support.

"Thanks, Tim. I needed to hear that."

He chuckled.

"They've told me not to speak about it to either Billy or Alex but they're talking to Alex today … and I'm worried about him, Tim. This could push him over the edge. I'm sorry to come at you out of the blue and ask you this, but do you think—"

"Of course, I'll pop across to see him as soon as I can."

She smiled into the phone, feeling a weight lifting off her shoulders.

"He wasn't in great shape when I last saw him," Tim said, "so I imagine this will not do him any good at all. Are you outside? I can hear the wind."

"Yes," she said, nodding furiously and casting an eye up at the rolling clouds. "There's a storm brewing."

"You'd better get inside, Jules. I've got a couple of things to tie off here first and then I'll head over to Alex's place and make sure he's all right."

"And you'll let me know how he is?"

"I'll call you later. I promise."

"Thanks, Tim, you're an absolute star."

CHAPTER THIRTY

Eric walked into ops and Tom beckoned him over to join them. Cassie was in mid-flow of her briefing but paused to offer Eric a warm smile before Tom encouraged her to pick up where she'd left off.

"The police in Kristiansand have confirmed Anette Larsen's personal effects were not found on her person when she was pulled from the water in Justvik. They suspected at first she'd possibly been the victim of a robbery gone wrong rather than attacked by someone with a sexual motive—"

"But she had recently had intercourse, though, right?" Tamara asked.

Cassie nodded. "But they have been unable to determine if that was consensual or forced. Her body was in a good state of preservation because the water temperature in the fjord is consistent in that it rarely alters more than a degree throughout the course of the year. It's something to do with the depth as much as the location. However, after detectives retraced her presumed route between where she left her friend's apartment back to her home they came across her purse and mobile phone, therefore discounting robbery as a motive."

"She still had cash?" Tom asked.

"Yes, her purse contained just shy of three hundred Krone, around twenty quid in old money."

"You said earlier," Tom glanced at Eric, obviously reiterating something for the DC's benefit, "that you would check to see if anything was missing—"

"I did. Elin wasn't aware, and there was nothing specifically mentioned on record, but the pictures they obtained from the family around the time of the original investigation pretty much all had Anette wearing a necklace." She reached to her left and retrieved a picture from her desk. It was a segment of a photograph that had been enlarged to A4 size. Cassie held it aloft so they could all see it and then stuck it to the board behind her. It was a delicate silver chain and attached to this were two small hearts entwined with one another. "This wasn't found with the body and Elin got in touch with her parents to ask the question. Apparently their daughter wore it everywhere – it was a gift from her father for her sixteenth birthday – and it certainly wasn't left at home."

"Looking at it, it could easily have broken off during the assault or when she went into the water," Tom said.

Cassie agreed. "But if we can execute a search warrant then we have something worth looking for. If our killer is a repeat offender and likes to gather trophies this will be as good as any."

"What about Tina Farrow?" Tamara asked. "Are we aware of any personal item missing from her?"

Tom nodded "Her sister, Angela, spoke of a heart-shaped pendant that Tina always wore; a gift from an aunt, I think." He caught sight of Eric looking glum in the corner of his eye. "What is it Eric?"

Eric started to shake his head but Tom persisted and he cleared his throat.

"Are we sure then, that it is Alex Hart we should be looking at?"

Cassie rolled her eyes. "Eric, the eyewitness puts them together—"

"Nearly twenty years ago!" Eric didn't mean to be so forthright. It caught Tom by surprise. Eric held up a hand in apology. "I'm not saying it isn't him but we know how unreliable eyewitnesses can be at the best of times and we have to take this man at his word?"

"Woman," Cassie said, correcting him. "And besides, we know Hart was in the area and no one can vouch for his whereabouts at the time—"

"Although," Eric cut in, "Julia Rose says he was ill during his visit to Kristiansand ..."

"Seriously, Eric—"

"Pack it in, both of you!" Tamara said. Both Cassie and Eric fell silent. Tamara indicated Eric with one hand. "You have a point, but an eye-witness identification is enough for us to proceed with."

"But Julia Rose told me William Cannell was also there that night," Eric said.

"Where – in Kristiansand?" Tom asked.

"Not only in the city," Eric said, "but *in* the area where the girl went missing. He was having dinner in a restaurant near to the harbour with Julia and her colleagues."

Tom's curiosity was piqued and he glanced at Tamara who seemed equally interested. Tom told Eric to continue.

"Julia recalls Cannell leaving the restaurant around ten o'clock. How does that fit into your timeline?" he asked Cassie who had been glaring at him up until now but her stance softened. She checked the board.

"Anette was walking home at that time, it's true," she said looking at Tamara.

"We still have the witness. How strong was the line-up shown?"

Cassie shrugged. "I've no idea but she did pick out Alex Hart."

Tamara took a deep breath, folding her arms across her chest. "If she struggled then she might be guessing but if she went straight for him then it's a different matter."

"Where are the Norwegians with the DNA samples you sent across?" Tom asked.

Cassie splayed her hands wide. "No news on that but they're working on it. Maybe the results will come back tomorrow."

"And the arrest warrant?"

"Won't be issued until after the DNA tests are returned." Cassie looked at Eric and nodded. "Seemingly, their prosecutor isn't a fan of eye-witness testimony either."

Now it was Eric's turn to roll his eyes at her.

"It's not that I'm not a fan—"

"Chill, Eric," Cassie said, waving a hand and dismissing his reply.

"Wind your neck in," Eric replied using one of Cassie's favourite phrases.

"Stop bickering, the pair of you," Tamara said. "It's like being at my sister's and listening to her kids." Both Cassie and Eric looked sheepish. "Now, here's what we're going to do—"

Tamara was interrupted by her mobile phone ringing on the desk beside her. She glanced at the screen and scooped it up. Stepping away she looked at Tom. "Chief Super—"

Tom rubbed at his eyes. It'd been a long day and wasn't over yet. His instinct was to follow Cassie's plan and execute a search warrant on Alex Hart's home address. If they didn't find anything, then they still had an eyewitness who could place him with one victim and by the time they got around to interviewing him after the search, they could well have DNA evidence to back it up. That could provide enough leverage to press him on Tina Farrow's murder.

"What? No one has spoken to me!" Tom heard Tamara exclaim, spinning on her heel. She snapped her fingers and drew everyone's attention. Covering the mouthpiece with her hand she hissed at Eric, "Get the BBC news channel up on your computer, now!"

Without asking why, Eric hurried over to his desk and opened up his Internet browser, navigating to the BBC website. Tom and

Cassie followed Tamara over to stand behind Eric, looking over his shoulder. She was still talking.

"Yes, of course, sir," Tamara said. "I'll—" She took the mobile away from her ear, the chief super having hung up on her. She looked ashen. Tom was concerned.

"What's going on?" he asked.

"Oh bugger!" Eric whispered as the live stream started to play.

Tom looked down and read the headline displayed beneath the feed – *Local men implicated in second teen's murder*. The live stream was on the national news channel. Tom glanced at the clock; it was the headline report at the top of the hour. The anchor-man crossed to a reporter. Tom ran a hand through his hair, pleased to see the reporter was standing on the steps of the police station in King's Lynn. At least he wouldn't have to manage the press on his exit from the station. No one spoke as the reporter detailed the case.

"One of the men lives here in King's Lynn while the other is believed to live at an address in north Norfolk. We understand that both men are being treated as suspects in the rape and murder of a sixteen-year-old girl from Kristiansand in southern Norway – a brutal slaying of a teenager from a small, low crime city, that rocked a nation some fifteen years ago and may yet reach a conclusion in Norfolk. More questions are being asked tonight about how this may link to the murder of Tina Farrow whose remains were uncovered this past week in Brancaster, and whether either, or both, of these men are responsible for her murder."

"Initially, the focus was on Professor William Cannell, an academic of great renown in the field of medieval archaeology, who operates a high-profile consultancy from his office here in King's Lynn. He is a former lecturer at Cambridge. When we called at his home this evening, a couple of miles from where I am now, he was unavailable for comment but I did speak to his wife who emphatically denied her husband's involvement in any of these events."

"These events are moving swiftly tonight, Clive, as the attention in the investigation moves to another man – former archaeologist Alexander Hart. We were unable to reach him for comment this evening.

However, we were able to speak to some locals who know him, one of whom described Alexander Hart as an oddball character, who is unemployed and lives alone having spent the past couple of years caring for his elderly father who passed away this time last year.

So far, police have been unwilling to comment on the two cases, notably regarding the original inquiry into the disappearance of Tina Farrow and how the police in Norfolk may have allowed a serial killer to elude capture for so long. The investigation continues ..."

Tamara turned away in disgust. Tom pointed at the screen.

"Eric, switch that off will you?"

Tamara stalked the office. She wasn't one to overreact, always being very controlled but he could tell she was furious.

"Well," Cassie said softly, nervously watching the DCI pace the room muttering under her breath, "Elin did say they wouldn't be able to keep it quiet and if it was on the Norwegian news last night—"

"Then it stands to reason it will have crossed the North Sea by tonight," Tom said, rubbing his cheeks. They could have done without the extra scrutiny for another couple of days at least. They'd lost the element of surprise.

"Of all the bloody irresponsible things to do!" Tamara said, barely keeping herself in check in front of the team. She glared at Eric's monitor, waving a pointed finger at it even though he'd already navigated away from the news channel. "Don't they know what they've done with that report?"

Tom shook his head, feeling dejected. "We should have moved on it this afternoon. I didn't think they'd catch onto it so soon." He exhaled with a sigh. "Bloody daft of us really."

Tamara was in no mood to shoulder responsibility, or to assign blame either. Tom's phone rang and he answered without checking the screen.

"Hello ... i–is that DI Janssen?" The voice was flustered, speaking quickly and he thought she sounded scared although it was hard to discern due to the background noise.

"Yes. Who is this?" he asked, stepping away from the others to enable him to hear better. "I'm sorry, I can hardly hear you."

"It's Julia, Julia Rose," she said, almost shouting to be heard above the roar of the wind. "Please, you said I should call if I need to—"

"Yes, of course." Tom gestured with his free hand to get Tamara's attention. Eric and Cassie stopped their spirited discussion and looked over. "What is it?"

"It's Alex!" she said, desperation in her voice. "Please, you have to help me, help him!"

CHAPTER THIRTY-ONE

TOM CLAMBERED out of the car, drawing his coat about him and turning the collar to the wind. The rain was almost horizontal now, coming at them in sheets off the North Sea. Tamara got out and came to stand beside him, repeatedly pushing the hair away from her face but to no avail. The wind was ferocious, lashing the rain against their faces as they shielded their eyes from the sting. The roar of the sea crashing against the rocks below carried in the brief interlude between gusts, the taste of salt was prominent with sea spray flung into the air around them.

"I should go alone!" Tom all but shouted to be heard. Tamara shook her head emphatically. He dismissed her protestation, frantically waving a hand at the police cars now queueing up behind them, the darkness punctuated by the pulsing blue lights. "If we all tear about in the dark it will only make matters worse!"

Tamara looked past him to see the numbers gathering. Eric and Cassie got out of their car and hurried over to them. Behind them were half a dozen uniformed constables, almost everyone on the late shift was present. Tamara looked up the path and into the darkness. To their right were sparkling lights of the houses in Beeston Regis, dropping away on a gentle slope from the cliff top.

To the left was the inky blackness of the North Sea, raging as the late summer storm hammered the coast.

"And you're sure this is where she said they were?" Tamara asked.

Tom nodded. "She said he'd gone to the Bump." He gestured with his thumb over his shoulder. "That's Beeston Hill. The locals call it the Bump. If he's as distraught as Julia Rose says he is, then if he sees all of us piling up the path mob-handed it will make things worse not better."

The rain was streaming across Tom's face now, his hair stuck to his scalp as he squinted to keep it from his eyes.

"Fine!" Tamara said. "But you're not going alone." Tom made to protest but she waved away his argument. "And I'm coming with you." She turned to Cassie who looked displeased at her decision. "The two of you stay here. If you don't hear from us in fifteen minutes, come after us." She turned on Tom "No arguments. We can't be out here all night and if we can't talk him down by then ..."

Tom accepted her call and turned, heading along the well-trodden path up to the high point without checking that she was with him. Beeston Hill had been a listening station during the war, part of the building's foundations were still present as was a simple three-metre tall wooden cross erected to overlook the sea. The hill had been one of two carved from the coastline by the retreating glacier at the end of the last ice age. Now only one remained, the other long since pulled into the water by the brutal battering offered up by the tides.

With only a couple of hand torches to light their way, the two of them hurried along the path. Reaching the steep steps up to the point, Tom checked with Tamara. She was wet through, much as he was. It was incredible to think he was already missing the dry humidity that'd been plaguing them for the past week or so. The early rain of that evening had been a relief, a precursor to more tolerable conditions but not before this weather front finally made landfall.

They made eye contact, Tom eager to see if Tamara was prepared for what they might face. She nodded and they set off for the summit. A gust of wind caught Tamara off balance, virtually lifting her off the ground and Tom caught her before she was blown from the path. Undaunted, they pressed on. They couldn't see anything beyond the beam of their torches, driving rain shooting across their path and making the going treacherous. The ground, a mixture of sand and shingle, had been baked hard over the previous weeks and now the deluge was coming down with such speed it didn't have a chance to soak in and was cascading across the ground at their feet along the path of least resistance.

Tamara, holding tightly on to Tom's hand, was being practically dragged up by Tom who was ploughing on regardless, so keen was he to reach the top.

"You go on!"

He looked sideways at her and she nodded vigorously. He seemed reticent but did as she asked, releasing his grip on her and setting off, striding up the hill at pace. The rain momentarily eased as he approached the summit, gifting him the briefest of reprieves and allowing him to take in his surroundings properly. Two figures were present. Dr Julia Rose stood roughly four metres away with her back to him, her coat and hair billowing out behind her. Alex Hart stood in front of her, a few steps away, the gale force winds swirling around them. Tom stood still, buffeted by the wind, assessing what was passing between them. Hart was dressed in a chequered shirt and jeans, completely drenched and ill-prepared for the conditions. His face was contorted but not as a result of the driving rain that now returned with increased intensity. His eyes were red-rimmed and bloodshot, his expression was maniacal and he spat at Julia Rose as he barked at her. Tom couldn't make out what was being said, the words drowned out and carried away on the howling wind.

Tom moved closer, careful not to angle the beam of his torch at anyone directly. He approached Julia and she must have seen the torchlight in the corner of her eye or sensed his presence because she turned to face him, instantly recognising Tom and stepping forward to clasp both Tom's hands tightly within her own. Tears streamed, carrying her eyeliner and make-up with them, mixing with the falling rain.

"Please!" she screamed at Tom, glancing towards Alex Hart who seemed poised to run, but where to, Tom could only guess. "You have to stop him, please!"

Tom tried to release himself from her grasp and move in front of her, but she was reluctant to let him go as if doing so would be a failure on her part to convey the gravity of her need. Her presence worried Tom. Hart was clearly distressed and having someone present who was emotionally tied to him, even one from so many years ago, could be more detrimental to the situation than beneficial by triggering intense memories when what was needed was calm.

Managing to free himself, Tom eased himself past her, putting himself between the two of them. Hart scowled at him, his eyes dancing in the flickering light of the torch.

"Alex!" Tom called. "It's me, Tom. You remember? We spoke a couple of times this week—"

"Leave me alone!"

Spittle flew from Hart's mouth as he spoke, his upper lip curling into a snarl as he shifted his weight onto the balls of his feet. Tom half expected him to launch forward with an attack but instead he leapt away from Tom, awkwardly climbing over the simple wire fence stopping people from walking too close to the cliff edge. Tom followed but at a steady pace, eager not to alarm Hart. He kept his hands out in front of him, wishing he could dispense with the torch because the flickering light seemed to agitate his quarry but without it they would be plunged into darkness.

"Alex, please don't!"

Tom glanced back over his shoulder upon hearing Julia's desperate plea, happy to see Tamara reach her and place a supportive, and restraining, hand on her shoulder. The second beam from the torch sparked another tirade from Hart.

"Black Shuck!" he screamed, his eyes widening in horror and his anger turning to fear in an instant. Tom was momentarily thrown. "You won't take me!" Hart screamed, looking behind him and moving another step away from Tom. Carrying out a quick calculation in his head, Tom considered how quickly he could close the gap between the two of them. He figured it was less than three metres of open ground, easily traversable provided he didn't lose his footing on the long grass between the fence and his quarry. But the fence was the problem. He couldn't spring a surprise advance and get over the fence quickly enough without Hart having a chance to react. Hart's eyes fixed on Tom. Perhaps he read his mind because Hart backed away, perilously close now to the cliff edge. In between gusts, Tom could hear the roar of the sea hammering away at the cliff face some sixty metres below them. He daren't advance much closer.

Holding out one hand, palm up, Tom sought to make eye contact with him, the only way he thought he might be able to convince Hart that he wasn't a threat.

"Alex," he called, loud enough to be heard above the wind but hopefully soft enough not to cause alarm. "I'm here to help you, Alex." He beckoned towards his chest with his raised hand. "Please can you come away from the edge?"

At mention of the cliff edge, Hart looked behind him and down. To Tom it looked as if he must be peering down into the dark and foamy fury of the water itself. He stared down at it and Tom silently cursed the presence of the safety fence, confident that with a clear run he could get the drop on him before he could react. Hart was in a state, evidently borderline psychotic but certainly not thinking properly. Any decision making he had would be impaired but that could be just as dangerous because it was also more likely to be impulsive.

"Alex!" Tom called again, reaching out to him with an open hand. Alex stared hard at him, blinking rapidly with his lower lip visibly trembling. Was it an attempt to clear the rain or salt spray from his eyes or was he crying? Tom couldn't tell.

"I'm so sorry," Hart said, sobbing. His shoulders appeared to constrict, his hands coming together before him. "I–I'm so sorry … It wasn't my fault." His jaw was slack, his upper body seemed to sag down to his right and he teetered. Tom wondered if he was about to collapse.

"Alex, please come towards me!"

Tom slowly took a couple of steps forward.

"I'm so sorry," Hart mumbled, almost inaudible now, but the wind carried his words directly to Tom. Hart clamped his eyes shut, attempting to shut out the world.

"Alex, please listen to me," Tom said, chancing a glance at the fence and calculating whether he could make it after all. He caught sight of Tamara in the corner of his eye and cast a sideways glance in her direction. She had both hands holding firmly onto Julia Rose, stopping her from coming forward. Looking back at Hart, he implored him, "Alex, I need you to come towards me. Please. I don't want you to fall. No one wants you to fall."

"It hurts so much," Hart said, opening his eyes and looking straight at Tom. He didn't seem to register Tom's presence at all, staring through him and into the darkness of the storm. "It has to end. I'm so sorry."

"Alex!" Tom barked at him now, using a tone far more aggressive and trying to grab his attention. It worked and Hart's eyes grew wide, focussing on Tom. "Alex, step towards me or you'll fall. I don't want you to die, Alex."

He held Tom's gaze, ignoring the offered hand. He slowly swayed from side to side, making little attempt to brace himself against the wind.

"Alex. Can you hear me? I'm here to help. I have to get you to safety."

Hart maintained Tom's gaze, appearing to register the words. He slowly nodded and Tom took that as tacit encouragement, inching forward. He was barely half a metre from the wire of the fence now, Hart less than that on the other side. Tom held the eye contact, desperate to maintain their connection. He only stopped his advance when he felt the wire of the fence pressing into his abdomen. Hart's mouth was open, his jaw slack and he was crying. Tom reached out, if Hart did likewise, he would be able to take hold and he was confident he'd have him.

Alex Hart closed his eyes and took a deep breath, the sobbing subsided and Tom kept his hand extended to him. Opening his eyes, Hart lifted his right hand slowly towards Tom's.

"That's it, Alex. I've got you," Tom said, offering him an encouraging smile despite the stinging rain lashing against his face. "Take my hand! It will be okay, I promise you."

Hart met Tom's eye, his proximity to Tom's grasp tantalisingly close.

"I'm so sorry," Hart said, shaking his head. "I–I'm so sorry ..."

"Don't worry about that now, Alex. Take my hand. It will be okay," Tom called reassuringly, nodding towards his outstretched hand. "Just take my hand ..." ˙

A gust of wind blew across them, momentarily knocking Tom off balance, and in the blink of an eye Alex Hart was gone.

CHAPTER THIRTY-TWO

JULIA ROSE HELD the cup of tea before her in both hands, the plume of steam rising past her face which was given over to a thousand-yard stare. Tamara placed a blanket around her shoulders and drew it around her front but Rose didn't react, continuing to stare straight ahead at some far-off point on the other side of the room. Tamara pulled out a chair and sat down. They'd returned to the station leaving Cassie to marshal the uniformed presence, close off Beeston Hill, and await the coming of dawn when the investigation team would comb the area for the inevitable independent inquiry. Any death where the police were present, particularly when involving a suspect, would need to be referred to another constabulary to carry out an investigation.

Tamara sat forward, elbows resting on her knees. Tom perched himself on the edge of a nearby table. They were in the refectory, no one else was present, the shutters pulled down over the serving hatch until the day shift came in. Tom glanced up at the clock; it was approaching midnight now. Julia Rose hadn't said a word since she watched Alex Hart fall from the cliff and disappear into the foaming mass of dark water below.

The coastguard had been called immediately, but there's no way they'd be able to get close enough to the cliffs to search for

Hart; the gale force wind associated with the storm as well as the tidal surge swiftly put paid to any rescue attempt. They would remain out there, searching as best they could but everyone knew, even if they wouldn't say it openly, that Alex Hart was dead. With luck they could retrieve his body from the water at sunrise but even that was not a given.

Tom cast an eye over Julia Rose. Her hair was drying slowly now they were safely indoors, but she was still a bedraggled figure. There was a fresh cut across her eyebrow, above her left eye. The paramedic crew who'd examined her when they came down from the cliff top staunched the flow of blood and secured the skin in place with several sterilised medical strips. The cut was shallow and not deemed to be too serious.

"What happened tonight, Julia?" Tamara asked gently. For a moment both Tom and Tamara thought the question hadn't landed, Julia's expression remained vacant, staring ahead. Then she blinked, her lips parting slightly, and she slowly turned to Tamara.

"I–I was worried about him ... about Alex."

Tamara leaned in closer, drawing Julia's eyes to her own.

"So ... you went to see him?"

She nodded. "He didn't react well when I saw him the other day. I was concerned I'd made matters worse by coming, rather than better." She shook her head, her fingers curling around her cup more as she straightened her back. "Alex ... is quite a complicated man."

"But you care for him."

Julia looked deeply into Tamara's eyes, tears welling, but she blinked them away and lifted her cup to her mouth with trembling hands. Tamara glanced at Tom and he took a breath, allowing Julia the space to sip at the sweet tea he'd given her before asking his question.

"You went to his house?" She glanced sideways at him and nodded. "And what did you find when you arrived."

She opened her mouth fully to draw breath, the intake of air stuttering on its way in. Her brow furrowed as she sought to remember the detail.

"There was no answer when I knocked – at the front – and so I went around the back." She closed her eyes tightly, pursing her lips.

"Take your time," Tom said softly.

She smiled weakly in his direction and nodded. "The back door to the kitchen was wide open, which was odd because it was raining and had been for an hour or two." She tilted her head to one side, running her tongue along the top of her lower lip. "There were no lights on ... the house was in darkness but I went in. By that point I was fearing the worst ..."

"What did you think might be going on?" Tom asked.

She shrugged. "I–I don't know really, just that it wasn't right, you know?" She looked between them, Tamara smiled supportively. Tom was watching her intently now, keen to understand how they ended up at Beeston cliffs.

"Go on," Tamara urged her.

"The place was a tip – really untidy – even more so than it had been on my last visit. Alex ... clearly wasn't taking care of himself and as I walked through the house – calling to him – I started to think maybe he'd done what he'd threatened to do ..."

"Which was?"

She stared at Tom blankly, obviously reticent to say the words. "I thought – what with all the pressure he was under – that he might have ... taken his own life."

"What made you think that, tonight especially?"

Julia sighed. "After I spoke with your detective constable, I went for a long walk before heading back to my lodgings. The owners ... they were talking about it. It was all over the news about Alex and Billy and this whole thing in Kristiansand—"

"You don't seem surprised?" Tamara asked.

She shook her head. "No, well DC Collet spoke about it to me, but I was shocked to see it on the news like that. I mean, he said you weren't sure either of them had done it."

Tom exchanged a look with Tamara whose eyebrows knitted together momentarily.

"Anyway, I wanted to make sure he was all right. I had visions of reporters and paparazzi chasing him across West Runton ... so I went to see him, but he wasn't there."

"He'd already gone over to Beeston Hill?" Tom asked.

"Yes. He'd left a note in his house. I read it ... and knew where to look for him."

"What did it say?" Tamara asked.

Julia turned the corners of her mouth down and slowly shook her head. "That he was sorry," she said, lifting herself upright and adjusting her seating position as if she was numbing out. "That ... he wished it could have been different, that no one would have been hurt ... and that none of it had happened—"

"None of what had happened?" Tom asked.

"I genuinely don't know ... his illness maybe?" She looked at Tamara, frowning deeply. "How he treated me ... others ... I don't know. It didn't say."

"Was it addressed to you?" Tamara asked. She shook her head, staring into her lap. "How did you know where to go?"

Julia lifted her head, frowning. "Alex had talked about ... about ending it all from time to time. I never thought he actually meant it, he just wanted the pain to stop and sometimes ... he thought that would be the best way. Beeston Bump was his go-to place – he'd walk out there late at night under the light of the moon and stare at the sea, picturing the peace he'd find below." A painful smile glimpsed her face, her words catching in her throat. "And even when the weather was terrible, he'd listen to the waves crashing against the cliffs ... it was his release." She looked at both of them in turn. "For a while he used to harm himself – a long time ago, back when we were together – and the pain, the sharp pain it caused him he described as his release. He came to view the sea in the same way; watching, listening to it ... the thought that the water could carry his pain away." She sat back, nursing her cup and staring at the liquid. She spoke quietly, barely above a whisper, "So yes, I knew where he would be."

"And you found him at the top of Beeston Hill?" Tamara asked.

"Yes. I knew he'd be there and when I approached him ... I could see in his face that this time was different." Her eyes darted to Tom. "I tried to speak to him, but he immediately flared up at me. I–It was like he didn't recognise me at all. He backed away towards the cliff edge and I reached out and grabbed him, taking as strong a hold of him as I could, begging him not to do what I thought he was planning to do."

"How did he react?" Tom asked.

A solitary tear ran from the corner of her eye but she didn't appear to notice.

"He lashed out at me." Her voice cracked as she spoke. "Trying to free himself but I clung on to him, dragging him back from the fence." She looked at Tamara. "Alex is so slight now – I probably weigh more than him. I managed to drag him back, it was hard because he resisted so much, and the ground was slippery what with the rain and all ... and he kept on lashing out at me ..."

"Is that how your face was cut?" Tom asked, pointing to her eyebrow. Julia reached up, tentatively touching the area of the wound and probing with her fingertips as if it was the first time she'd been aware of it. Lowering her hand, she nodded.

"Alex was screaming at me ... calling me all manner of names, much of it I couldn't understand." Her voice dropped away. "That's when I called you, Inspector," she said, glancing sideways at Tom. "He's gone, isn't he? Alex?"

Tom read the despair in her eyes as she sought for any glimmer of hope that he might provide. He couldn't lie to her; it wouldn't be fair.

"They will keep looking," he said. It was all he could offer her. She held his gaze and he knew that she'd already accepted the reality; Alex Hart wasn't coming back.

The doors opened and they turned to see Eric's arrival with

Tim Hendry at his side. He rushed past Eric and hurried to Julia's side, dropping to his haunches and clasping her outstretched hand with both of his own.

"Jules, I'm so sorry," he said, freeing one hand and placing the flat of his palm against her right cheek. She leaned into him at the feel of his touch. He glanced furtively at Tom and Tamara before meeting Julia's eye. "How awful for you to have witnessed that."

"He's gone, Tim. Alex is really gone ..." Her head sank and the repressed emotion of the night flowed from her. Hendry took the cup of tea from her and placed it on the table, allowing Julia to fall forward into his embrace.

Tamara exchanged a look with Tom and the two of them stepped away to give them a moment alone. Without family in the area it had been Tim Hendry whom Julia had asked for when they suggested calling someone to support her. Aside from Alex, Tim was the only person she was acquainted with. Tom dispatched Eric to find him when they'd left Beeston Hill. Eric lingered in the background and Tom silently requested he keep an eye on the two of them as he and Tamara walked to the far side of the room.

"Do you think the news report was the final straw for him?" Tamara asked Tom as he watched Tim Hendry comforting the crumpled form of Julia Rose, clinging to him and openly weeping.

"That it was all too much for him?" He shrugged. "Maybe he couldn't handle it and the pressure led to a psychotic episode, I don't know. Something wasn't right." He glanced sideways at her and mock grimaced. "Perhaps."

"What was that he shouted at you – *Black Sheep* or something, wasn't it?"

Tom smiled wryly. "Shuck."

"I beg your pardon?"

"*Black Shuck*," Tom repeated, turning to face her and reading her puzzled expression. "I think he was hallucinating. It's a figure from folklore. Black Shuck – a massive, terrifying hound who prowls the fields and hills of north Norfolk. It's said that should you be unfortunate enough to set eyes on the beast then it is a precursor to death."

Tamara exhaled deeply, raising her eyebrows. "Cheery thought."

The hint of a smile crossed Tom's face. "Apparently – following a holiday hereabouts – the legend inspired Sir Arthur Conan Doyle to write his *Hound of the Baskervilles*.

"He should come back here," Tamara said out of the corner of her mouth. "Plenty more where that one came from."

Cassie entered, acknowledging Eric and then seeing the two of them to her right. She came to join them, Eric did likewise.

"Well, I guess that's that then," Cassie said.

"What's what?" Tom asked.

"Well, it's over isn't it? Mystery solved."

Tom raised his eyebrows, taking a deep breath and looking at Tamara who winced.

"I'm not so sure," he said.

Cassie frowned. "It follows though, right? A prime suspect in multiple murders – on the verge of discovery – can't see a way out and commits suicide rather than face the music. What's not to like?"

Tamara inclined her head to one side. "Did your Norwegian contact come back to you yet regarding the DNA we sent across?"

Cassie replied through gritted teeth. "Inconclusive. They couldn't match either sample to the victim, but that doesn't mean it wasn't Alex Hart."

Tom's face wrinkled in thought. "Therefore, it follows that it could just as easily be William Cannell though, doesn't it?"

Cassie scratched the side of her head, looking between the two senior ranks. Tamara was concentrating hard. She levelled her eyes at Cassie.

"You think it was Alex Hart?"

Cassie nodded. Tamara looked at Eric who shrugged, indicating he wasn't sure.

"What about you, Tom?"

"Hart would certainly make it neat and tidy."

"I like neat and tidy," Tamara said, pursing her lips.

"You'd never guess from the inside of your house," Tom replied. They all smiled. "But … tonight …" He looked over to where Julia had recovered her composure and Tim Hendry had taken Tamara's vacated seat, still holding Julia's hand in a supportive grip. "Have we secured Hart's house?"

"Yes," Eric said. "Uniform are there and will stay until we tell them otherwise."

"Make sure they don't touch anything," Tom said. Eric nodded and Tom flicked his hand towards Tim Hendry and Julia Rose. "Make sure they get home safely, would you? Then get yourself off home; plenty to do in the morning." Eric nodded to all three of them and crossed the room. "You too, Cass. Get yourself home and get some sleep."

"Okay. Night you two," Cassie said, turning to leave.

"What do you expect to find at Hart's house?" Tamara asked.

Tom's eyebrows met briefly at the bridge of his nose. "Answers. I expect to find answers."

IT WAS APPROACHING one in the morning by the time Tom arrived home. The worst of the storm had passed them by now, the wind was still gusting but the rainfall was sporadic and light in stark contrast to what they'd faced earlier. Usually when he arrived home, irrespective of the time, he was met by Russell – Saffy's terrier – almost as soon as he set foot in the hallway. But not this night. The dog had no desire to go for his late-night mooch around the garden, no doubt put off by the deluge earlier in the night. Tom was happily able to creep upstairs to bed. He'd looked in on Saffy, snuggling up with her current favourite: *Santa Paws*, a cuddly stuffed pug with a Santa hat stitched on, her favourite despite it being late summer – and kissed her forehead gently, before making his way quietly into the bedroom he shared with

Alice. He was pleasantly surprised to find Alice asleep in their bed. With Saffy in her own, which made a change, he hoped they might have turned a corner.

Saffy was still coming to terms with the loss of her father and no one really knew how long that would take for her to process, or how the trauma would manifest itself. Alice had slept in with her daughter every night for nigh on two months and now, although she was called through more nights than not, the gap was certainly widening. Alice had mumbled something as he'd slipped between the sheets they used instead of a duvet in the hot sticky nights of this summer, but she hadn't woken and he'd drifted off into a restless sleep.

He woke with a start, bathed in sweat; the pitter-patter of gentle rain drumming on the bedroom window. It was still dark and Alice was no longer beside him. Having no idea how long he'd slept, he picked up his watch from the bedside table and focussed on it, angling the face to pick up what little reflected light came from outside. It was barely three o'clock. He rubbed at his cheeks trying hard to shift the image from his mind's eye of Alex Hart vanishing from view, along with the shrill scream of Julia Rose – isolated in his memory from the roar of the howling gale – as she despaired, watching Alex die. Only, in his dream, it hadn't been Julia screaming but Alice … and it was himself who he saw falling to his death.

A figure appeared in the doorway and as his eyes adjusted, he recognised Alice. She came to the bed, lifting the sheets and sliding in alongside him. He put his arm across her and held her tightly as she backed into his embrace.

"Whatever it is, Tom, you're safe now."

He lay there with his eyes open, knowing sleep would not come.

CHAPTER THIRTY-THREE

JULIA ROSE HOVERED on the doorstep underneath the shelter of the canopy. The rain was falling steadily today but nothing like the previous night. She felt numb to the world. Had it not been for the after-effects of a dreadful night's sleep, she probably wouldn't feel anything at all. A dog barked from the other side of the door and she hurriedly stepped forward and pressed the bell, hearing a muted chime indoors. A figure appeared, visible through the obscured glass, unlocking and opening the door. Tim Hendry glanced up at her from a hunched position, one hand gripping the dog's collar, the other holding open the door.

"Julia. How are you?" The dog, satisfied to have seen who was waiting outside, turned and Hendry ushered it back indoors and out of sight.

"Hi, Tim," she said wearily. "I'm sorry to call round unannounced—"

"No, no, don't be silly. Come in, come in."

Hendry held the door wider allowing her room to pass. Tim was always so polite and willing to help, but a nagging concern told her she'd put upon him too much already. However, she also had no one else to turn to locally and sitting in her room at her guest house any longer would drive her mad. She entered, wiping her feet on the mat and smiled appreciatively. Before he was able to close the door she was already apologising.

"You're probably sick of the sight of me by now," she said. He waved away the comment. "We don't see each other for a decade and ... now we have all of this to contend with."

Hendry led them through to the kitchen in the rear of the house. The smell of freshly brewed coffee permeated the air. He picked up the jug and offered it to her, reaching for a cup from a nearby shelf. She nodded and he poured it out as she wandered into the breakfast area with her hands in her pockets. A newspaper lay upon the table, Tim's glasses set down alongside it, no guesses as to what the lead story was. A photograph of Alex Hart was on the front page beneath the headline *Death of a Monster*. She felt her eyes glass over and she blinked away tears. Hendry appeared next to her, passing her a cup of coffee.

"Still take it black?" he asked.

She smiled weakly, nodding and accepting the offered cup. He glanced at the newspaper, frowning apologetically and reaching for it.

"I'm sorry. I'll move—"

"No, don't," she said placing a restraining hand gently on his forearm. "It's important to know what people are saying, to prepare ourselves."

She wasn't sure he agreed but he tilted his head off to one side and reluctantly acquiesced.

"I just can't believe it, Tim ... none of it. How c–could he be all of these things ... and still be my Alex? I can't get my head around it."

Hendry sighed, shaking his head and pinching the bridge of his nose with thumb and forefinger. "I don't get it either. How could none of us know?" He walked back to the coffee machine and poured himself another cup.

"So, you believe it?" Julia said, pointing to the paper as he turned to face her. "All of this, about Alex being," she shook her head, struggling for the words, "a monster?"

Hendry took a deep breath, lifting himself upright. He met her eye, straight-faced. "I'm sorry, Jules ... but at some point we may have to face facts."

"What facts?" She was irritated, and knew she was coming across defensive.

"That – maybe – Alex wasn't who we all thought him to be?" She scoffed at him and he shrugged. "Let's be honest, we know he was messed up—"

"Yes, but—"

He held up his hand and she let her protest drop.

"Alex is – was – very troubled and trust me because I've been around him a lot more than you these past few years, he was getting worse." He shook his head despairingly. "I used to push as much work as I could his way and he was grateful, but he was ... somewhat erratic with his behaviour. You didn't see him like this, not like I did. I don't think you knew him as well as you think you did. Do we ever really know people?"

She shook her head, feeling the burning of rising anger in her tightening chest.

"I knew Alex," she emphasised herself by jabbing a thumb into her chest, "and *I* still believe in him."

He must have sensed it because he adopted a more conciliatory tone.

"Look, Jules, people can hide their real selves from the world – and just maybe – those closest to them are the last to see who they really are." He shook his head. "Maybe I am wrong? Maybe the police are wrong? They'll investigate properly and figure all of this out. We should be patient and not jump to conclusions—"

"Like this lot?" she said, pointing at the newspaper. "They're not waiting."

"The papers! Honestly, does anyone really care? By tomorrow they'll be on to the next story and Alex will ..."

"Be forgotten?" she asked accusingly. Hendry held up both hands in apology. Julia turned over the front page following the story into the double page spread on pages two and three. They already had images of Alex working on dig locations. She wondered how they'd got to them so soon, the university websites or social media, presumably. The chosen images annoyed her too. Not one of them depicted Alex smiling, in every shot he was sullen and removed from anyone else around him. It was almost as if they wanted to find a way to portray him as a loner, a serial attacker who struggled around people. That wasn't Alex. It wasn't *her* Alex, who was always quick with a joke and a smile, setting people at ease. The article covered his background, where he grew up and went to school. They'd already quoted anonymous school friends who painted him as aloof. That wasn't true. She was certain they were making it up. His body hadn't yet been recovered and here they were destroying him without trial. There wouldn't be a trial. Not now.

The story continued on the next page as well, charting his career and pointing out the locations of missing girls and whether it was suspected Alex was present or not. Each location had a shot of some waste ground along with a smiling picture of the victim, young women, pretty. Besides Tina Farrow, one was in The Netherlands, another in Kristiansand. Her eyes lingered on that one. The date must be wrong. Tim Hendry must have seen her expression change because he spoke to her but she didn't register his question. He came alongside and gently touched the back of her hand as he placed his cup down on the table.

"Jules? What is it?"

She looked at him, her eyes narrowing as she tried to remember. "They must be wrong."

"Who? The police?"

She shook her head, pointing at the paper. "There. It says the girl who died in Kristiansand ... it says she was abducted on a Friday night and a witness saw her getting into Alex's car ..."

"Yes, so?" Hendry's eyebrows met, puzzled.

"Well ... Alex was ill on that visit. That's why I couldn't understand why the detective constable was asking about it ... it couldn't have been Alex. You remember, he had appendicitis and it very nearly ruptured. He was recovering in my apartment following the surgery. There's no way he could have been driving that hire car ..."

Tim was staring at her intently. She looked into his eyes. "It can't have been, Alex ... but—"

The doorbell rang and the dog barked. Tim Hendry held his gaze on her. She felt the speed of her breathing rapidly increasing, as if she'd just completed her morning jog. Tim's expression clouded and she thought she saw his upper lip twitch.

The doorbell chimed again.

CHAPTER THIRTY-FOUR

THERE WAS something very odd about trawling through the belongings of the deceased. Tom always thought so. Returning to his mother's house in the days after her death, the place seemed to have lost its soul, even though in that instance he'd only been there that very morning. He'd been staying at her place while she'd been in hospital those last few weeks. Leaving her house with a change of reading matter and some toiletries, he'd found it very peculiar returning later that day knowing she'd passed on. The house felt cold and even more empty. He'd never been able to shake that peculiar feeling, and he felt it now.

They were notified that the lifeboat crew out of Wells had recovered Alex Hart's body from the sea. Official confirmation would follow but the account transmitted from the crew described Hart as in a bad way, most likely smashed against the cliff face by the punishing power of the North Sea. Tom could still picture him falling from view. Did he fall or did he jump? He didn't have an answer, no matter how many times he was asked the question.

The ticking of the clock broke the silence, followed by two officers entering the sitting room having just searched through the dining room. Tom allowed them to pass and then stepped out into the tight hallway and climbed the stairs. Officers were rummaging through clothes drawers, searching for anything that could make sense of all of this. Because it didn't, none of it.

Tom entered the bathroom, glancing around. The towels on the heated rail were grubby, dirt showing against the pastel colours. He opened the cabinet above the basin and found the bottles of tablets Tamara had spied on their earlier visit. All those present were less than half full and Tom examined the dates printed on the labels. They were fairly recent. He read the dosing require- ments along with the contents listed and did a quick mental calcu- lation; Alex Hart didn't appear to be skipping his medication. He would need to ensure a proper analysis was done to confirm his theory but, for now at least, Hart seemed to not be ignoring his doctor's instructions.

"Thoughts?" Tamara asked, appearing behind him having emerged from one of the bedrooms.

Tom took a plastic evidence bag from his pocket and shook it open before putting the medications inside.

"I don't think he was skipping his meds."

Tamara looked surprised. "But you thought he was halluci- nating last night—?"

"Yes, I did. He wasn't all there, that's a given," Tom said. "Maybe he'd slipped recently?"

"Or perhaps his dose needed increasing? The impact of medication can deteriorate following prolonged usage, can't it?"

Tom shrugged, sealing the bag and making a note on the tag. "I guess so. We'll have to check."

"What is it, Tom? You've been quiet all morning."

"Ah, it's probably nothing."

"Which means it's *something*."

Tom smiled. She knew him well. He folded his arms across his chest, still holding the bag in his right hand and biting his lower lip. He couldn't articulate his unease, but he'd had it since he'd awoken during the night and had been unable to shake it.

"I don't know," he said, frowning. "It's just—"

"Tom!"

Both of them stepped out onto the landing and looked over the bannister to the bottom of the stairs where Cassie was looking up at them. She beckoned them down.

"You guys need to see this."

They made their way down and Cassie led them through to the rear yard and out into the garden. They were greeted by another constable standing at the gate offering access to the lane at the back of the house. Journalists and camera crews were crawling around the area trying to get shots of the inside of the house and the police at work for their next editions. Their presence and scrutiny was more of an irritation than actually hampering the operation though. Squeezing between the old moss-covered car and the exterior wall of the brick garage, Cassie led them inside.

The garage was barely two metres wide, far too small to house a modern car and even if it were large enough it was still full of junk. Old bicycles that couldn't have been ridden in years, rusting tools and boxes full of who knows what were stacked everywhere. Tom touched a stack of nearby cardboard boxes that were bowing under the pressure of the contents. The cardboard outers were soft to the touch, probably due to the moisture in the air; the smell of damp was strong despite the recent spell of hot and dry weather punctured by the previous day's storm.

Cassie lifted a small rectangular box from a bench in front of her and set it down on a homemade wooden trellis table at the centre of the garage for them to look at. At first glance the exterior appeared to be leather-lined but was in fact brown plastic. It was aged and covered in dust. It reminded Tom of his father's old shoe-care kit, a small box where he'd stored his boot polishes and assorted brushes. Cassie nodded towards it, suggesting they look inside.

Tom exchanged a look with Tamara and lifted the lid. The inside was lined with purple velvet but it wasn't this that caught his eye. Tom picked up a student photo-card identification; the picture had aged with time but he could understand many of the words and definitely recognised the girl from Cassie's briefing. He held it up, turning it to show Tamara.

"Mila van der Berg. The murdered girl from Friesland."

Tamara's mouth opened and her expression echoed his sadness. He put it back in the box and carefully lifted out a necklace on a fine silver chain – two entwined hearts. It belonged to Anette Larsen, their victim in Kristiansand. Beside this necklace lay another. He lifted it out; a silver heart-shaped pendant on a chain just as Angela Farrow described one belonging to her sister, Tina. Tom pursed his lips and Tamara sighed.

"Trophies," she said softly, leaning over to look inside the box. "How many different—"

"Seven objects," Cassie said flatly. Tom closed his eyes.

"Seven?" Tamara whispered.

"It doesn't necessarily mean there are seven victims," Cassie said, "but ..."

Tom continued his inspection of the contents. There was a small silver ring with an inset black stone. He thought it might be jet, bringing to mind jewellery he'd seen in and around Whitby over the years. He found an NUS card but water had penetrated the seal at some point in the past and where the type used to be was now a mixture of blurred print and mould, as if they'd been laminated intentionally. The university might be Warwick but he couldn't be sure. The photo was of a young woman with a broad smile and sandy-brown hair hanging to her shoulders. Her smile struck him as warm and friendly. Every victim they knew of could be similarly described.

He looked at Cassie. "Have scenes of crime check all of this stuff, photograph and catalogue it. Then you need to feed it into the system and start trying to put names to these belongings."

Cassie nodded solemnly. "Will do."

"This is going to take some time. Have Eric help you with it," he said, looking around. "Where is Eric anyway?"

"You remember all those old case files relating to Brancaster the two of you brought back from Tim Hendry's house?" Tamara asked. Tom nodded. "Well, we don't need them, so I wanted to get them back to him. Seeing as Eric has been itching for his autograph, I figured he may as well be the one to take them. He had a personal errand to run afterwards."

"Everything okay with him?" Tom asked.

Tamara shrugged. "As far as I know, yes. Why do you ask?"

"No reason. He said Becca hasn't been sleeping well that's all."

They left the garage, Tom feeling deflated. His job was to catch killers, not to piece their lives together after the event and work out just how much they'd got away with over the years. They hurried back into the house as the rain started falling again. They stopped in the kitchen where two officers were emptying the cabinets in the hunt for any more items of interest. They both shook their heads to indicate they'd found nothing worthy of a mention.

CHAPTER THIRTY-FIVE

ERIC PUT the archive box on the ground at his feet and rang the bell for a third time. The dog barked again but it didn't sound close; it must be in a closed room somewhere else in the house. Eric pressed his face close to the obscured glass and tried to make out the interior. He couldn't of course but he hated the idea of a wasted trip. He'd been cutting it fine anyway, too fine as it turned out. He'd barely be able to stay for more than five minutes before he'd need to be off. It was a shame. He was looking forward to picking Tim Hendry's brain on any number of subjects that had come to mind over the past few days. He might never get this opportunity again.

Deciding to give it one more try, he reached for the bell but a shape loomed into view and Eric released his finger without pressing the button for a fourth time, he'd been too impatient. He hoped Hendry wouldn't be irritated. Backing away from the door, he smiled as Tim Hendry opened it, eyeing Eric warily.

"DC Collet," he said, surprised. "What brings you here?"

"Oh, right," Eric said nervously, glancing at the box at his feet. He dropped to his haunches and hefted it up with both arms. Exhaling at the effort required, he smiled across the top of the box. "I'm returning the files you lent us."

For a moment Hendry seemed reticent, glancing back inside but then his face split into a half-smile and he opened the door fully. "Of course, thank you. Do bring them inside," he said, beckoning Eric in.

Eric didn't stand on ceremony, striding past him into the hall and looking around. There was nowhere suitable to put the box down and the golden retriever he recalled from their first visit was making its presence known around Eric's legs and he decided that putting the box down might be too tempting for the dog not to investigate. Spying a table in the kitchen at the end of the hall, Eric set off for it.

"I'll pop it on the table for you," Eric said before Hendry could object.

"It's very decent of you to bring these back for me, Detective Const—"

"Eric, please," he said over his shoulder, trying to turn but catching the box on the panelling lining the hall. "Oops ... sorry."

Hendry seemed irritated but Eric just resumed his course into the kitchen. The room opened out in front of him and Eric placed the box on the table, eyeing the newspaper and a half-drunk cup of coffee alongside it. Tim Hendry followed him in. Eric glanced at the paper, pointing to it with a flick of his hand.

"How are you after last night?"

Hendry shifted his weight between his feet, rocking sideways. "I'm okay. Really, it was Julia who suffered the most. I just helped her after the fact." Eric nodded. "Tell me, is there any word on ... on Alex?"

"Yes. I'm sorry to tell you Alex's body was recovered from the sea early this morning. He was pronounced dead at the scene," Eric said, anticipating the next question. Hendry looked glumly at the floor.

"It is an odd sensation, Eric ... to find someone you thought you knew so very well is in fact someone completely alien to you." His eyes looked up at Eric and away again. "Very odd indeed. My rational head tells me I should not mourn him but ... I do. I miss him very much." He fixed Eric with a stare. "Is that something you can understand?"

Eric smiled weakly. "I can only imagine, but it makes sense."

Reading the sadness in his expression, Eric realised now would be a terrible moment to start talking about his favourite archaeological documentaries. The best he could hope for would be to come back another time. Besides, looking at the clock on the wall, he had to go. He hesitated, struggling to think how he could engineer a return visit. Avoiding Hendry's strangely intense gaze, Eric noticed a spillage on the floor on the other side of the table, along with some shards of broken cup. Hendry followed Eric's eye and moved to pick up the pieces of smashed ceramic.

"Oh, let me help," Eric said, ignoring Hendry's protestations, moving around the table and kneeling to help clear up the mess. Eric saw the dog sniffing at a door off the hallway, about halfway down it, probably to an under-stairs cupboard or cellar. It tentatively scratched at the base of the door with its paw before casting a sideways glance into the kitchen. Eric turned his attention back to collecting the broken pieces just as Hendry picked up the last piece.

"No harm done," Hendry said, taking the pieces from Eric into his cupped hand and crossing the kitchen to drop them in the bin.

"Butter fingers, this morning?"

"Accidents happen," Hendry said, watching the dog approach, "the furry one here got under my feet just as you rang the bell and I tripped, dropping my cup."

The comment piqued Eric's curiosity. Just then a telephone rang in another room off the kitchen. Looking in that direction through an open door, it looked like a study. Hendry stood where he was and Eric awkwardly nodded towards the sound of the ringing phone.

"Do you ... want to get that?"

Hendry's mouth formed an O, looking between the study and Eric. "I suppose I should." The phone was still ringing, the caller was persistent and didn't seem likely to give up. "Would you mind?"

Eric shook his head, glancing at the clock. "I need to be off anyway. I have somewhere I need to be."

"Right you are," Hendry said. "Would you mind seeing yourself out?"

"Not at all but," Eric quickly looked around, "could I use your facilities before I go?"

Hendry hesitated, the phone still trilling in the background. "Yes, by all means. It's the first door off the hall by the entrance."

Eric smiled his thanks and Hendry begrudgingly went to answer the phone. The retriever came to Eric and nuzzled his leg. Eric dropped to his haunches and ruffled its head, scratching behind the dog's ear as he saw Hendry standing in his office lift the receiver on the call, one hand on his hip. Rising, Eric looked at the half-drunk cup of coffee on the table. Hendry had his back to him and Eric quickly took a couple of steps to his right and touched the cup; it was still warm. Something wasn't right here. Walking towards the hall the dog passed him and went to a door set beneath the stairs, stopping to scratch at the foot of it and then glancing at Eric.

"What is it, boy?" Eric asked quietly, coming alongside the animal and lowering himself to its head height. He ran a hand along the dog's back. "What have you got in there?"

He stood up, nudging the dog to one side with his knee and eased the door open. The door opened to the cellar head which was narrow with limited head room due to the staircase passing overhead. A set of concrete steps led down into the darkness of the cellar itself and Eric felt a draught of cool damp air pass over him from below. The dog pushed past Eric and ran down the stairs with an excited bark. Eric grimaced. The dog would give away his snooping. He glanced back over his shoulder towards the kitchen, hearing Hendry's muffled conversation in the study. Looking around for the light switch, Eric found a dangling pull cord and tugged it. The cellar head was bathed in yellow light, some of it casting down into the cellar below to reveal peeling white paint from the walls in the stairwell.

"Come here, boy!" Eric called in as an assertive tone as he could whilst refraining from raising his voice. He considered whistling but thought better of it. He couldn't really hold a note and he didn't know if that would work anyway. He'd always liked the idea of having a dog but wouldn't have a clue how to manage one. The dog didn't appear in any event and Eric cursed. He walked to the top of the stairs, searching for another pull cord. He found a switch and pressed it. His mouth fell open.

Julia Rose lay unconscious at the bottom of the stairs, the dog standing over her. Blood poured from a wound to the side of her head. Eric rummaged in his pocket for his mobile phone. He hit the speed dial for Tom's mobile but there was silence. Glancing at the screen he saw he had no signal, enclosed on all sides as he was by thick brick walls. He had to call for help.

Spinning on his heel, he met Tim Hendry standing directly in front of him. Eric felt pressure in his stomach like he'd been punched but this was different. Then there followed another similar blow and his legs went numb, the mobile slipping from his fingers and clattering to the floor. Not that he heard it. He reached out, open mouthed, trying to grasp hold of Hendry's shirt but all strength ebbed away from him and his knees buckled. Hendry, eyes wide and with gritted teeth, stepped forward and shoved Eric backwards. The numbness in his stomach vanished to be replaced with searing pain and he gasped just as he felt the floor disappear from under him and he tumbled backwards down the stairs.

The light flickered and then everything went dark.

CHAPTER THIRTY-SIX

TAMARA WAS LOOKING at the pictures on the mantelpiece above the fire. Tom came to stand with her. One in particular stood out to him. The same one that'd caught his eye on his first visit where he'd mistaken Tim Hendry for Alex Hart. It seemed odd to him that Hart kept a photograph of his ex-girlfriend on show, especially one where he wasn't in shot with her but with his friend and competitor for his lover's affection. But then again, Hart was unaware of that fact. He stared at the image of Tim Hendry smiling at the camera with his arm around Julia Rose. The snap took on a new light in Tom's mind now that he knew the two of them had had a relationship of sorts behind Alex's back. Was their relationship during one of the couples' periods apart or was it adulterous? Neither was likely to tell him and he didn't really need to know. That picture, the two of them with the steep mountains set as the backdrop behind them falling away into the water. They were both well wrapped up for the climate; it looked cold, north European.

"Did Elin ever come back to Cassie?" Tom asked. Tamara looked at him inquisitively. "Regarding the DNA?"

"Yes. It was inconclusive, remember?"

"In regard to Alex Hart and William Cannell, yes," Tom said. "Did we ever send anyone else's?"

Tamara didn't get to answer, Tom's phone interrupted their conversation. He kept his eye on the photograph, not even looking at the mobile screen Julia looked so happy and Tim Hendry along-side was grinning broadly beneath his orange woolly hat.

"Tom Janssen," he said flatly. Casting an eye along the line of photographs they all appeared to be taken at archaeological dig locations rather than on holidays. He picked up the picture he was focussed on and passed it to Tamara, tapping the image when she had it. She stared at it, unsure of what he was getting at.

"Hi Tom ..." He recognised the voice but she sounded distant and concerned. There was an echo and he could hear muffled voices behind her.

"Becca. Hi, what can I do for you?"

Tamara lifted her head upon hearing the name but returned to the photograph.

"Um ... I'm really sorry to bother you, Tom, but ... by any chance do you know where Eric is?"

"Eric?" Tom said, turning the corners of his mouth down. "Er ... no, not really. He had to drop some files off nearby and then he had an errand to run but I'm afraid I don't—"

"That was me," she said. He could hear frustration in her voice along with a touch of irritation, or maybe it was anger, he couldn't tell. "Eric was supposed to meet me and he's not here."

Tom looked at the clock. "Maybe he's running a bit behind? Have you tried calling him?"

"Yes, of course but his mobile cuts to voicemail. Eric always has his phone on."

Tom had to admit that was true.

"I'm sure everything is fine. He'll be there as soon—"

"No, you don't understand. He wouldn't be late, not for this."

"Becca," Tom said, hearing a beeping sound in the background, "where are you?"

There was a pause where all he could hear was the background noise. The voices sounded officious, professional. She hesitated for a moment longer.

"I'm at the hospital, Tom. It's my twelve-week scan."

Tom snapped his fingers to get Tamara's attention. She looked at him expectantly.

"Tom?" Becca asked.

"Yes, I'm here."

"Can you find him for me? He should be here. I don't understand because he's talked about nothing else all week."

"I had no idea—"

"I'm sorry. We didn't tell anyone. We didn't want to jinx it, you know?"

"Yes, of course," he said, rolling his tongue across the inside of his cheek. "Leave it with me. And don't worry – his car has probably got a flat and he's out of signal range or something."

"Okay, you're right … it's just … you know?"

"I do. Listen, you do what you need to do and I'll chase Eric up and give him a friendly kick in the backside, okay?"

"Thanks, Tom. I'm sorry to have bothered you."

"No trouble. And Becca – congratulations! I'm very pleased for you."

Tom held the mobile in his hand, touching the tip of it to his lips. Tamara looked concerned. She made to speak but he held a hand up to stop her and began scrolling through his contacts to find Eric's number. Just as with Becca, the call passed straight to voicemail.

"What is it, what's going on?" Tamara asked.

"Eric was dropping by Tim Hendry's and then running a personal errand, right?" She nodded. "Well, Becca is pregnant," Tamara gaped at him, "and Eric hasn't shown up for the scan."

Tamara chewed her lower lip. "That's unlike Eric. Do you think he just got talking with Hendry? I mean, you know what he's like when he gets going—"

Tom shook his head. "I don't know but," he tapped the photo in her hand, "where would you say that was taken?"

Tamara eyed the picture. "By the sheer angle of those cliff faces dropping straight into the water, I'd say Scandinavia. Maybe Norway."

"Dig sites?" Tom queried.

Tamara nodded. "Yes, I should think so."

"But Tim Hendry never worked in Scandinavia. That's why we focussed on William Cannell, and Alex Hart because of his connection with Julia Rose. And we never sent Hendry's DNA sample to Norway for comparison—"

"Because he never worked there."

"But did he visit – much like William Cannell did?" Tom said, as he felt his stomach flip momentarily. "They were a tight group and even Cannell called in on Julia's dig in Kristiansand. Hart came over as well, so ..."

"Why not Hendry?" Tamara finished for him.

"He was in Norway—" he pointed to the picture in her hands again. "With Julia Rose and he was visiting Alex Hart regularly." Tom cast an eye in the direction of the garage as if he could see through the walls. "The net is closing in, so why not place a few trophies where we can easily find them to divert attention away from himself? He told Julia and us, that he didn't make it over to see Alex Hart last night like he promised he would, but we only have his word for that."

Tamara shook her head, her eyebrows knitting and held up a hand to Tom. "Hang on. There's no way Hendry could have known Hart would die yesterday—"

"No, but you met Hart. He had no idea what he had or hadn't done most of the time. He looked on the verge of confessing to anything and everything on the grounds that he didn't know whether he'd done it! Think about it. Who would believe him if he were put on the stand? The man didn't look like he believed himself!"

Tamara exhaled heavily. "And Eric is ..."

CHAPTER THIRTY-SEVEN

THE DOOR creaked half open and Tim Hendry first looked beyond Tom and then eyed him up and down, apparently surprised to see him.

"Detective Inspector Janssen. I wasn't expecting to see you again so soon."

"Expecting or hoping?" Tom asked.

"Whatever do you mean?"

"May I come in?"

Hendry looked back over his shoulder into the house, hesitated, and then checked his watch. "Well, I do have a call coming up—"

"I'll not keep you long," Tom said, smiling broadly. "I promise."

Hendry frowned, lips pursed and reluctantly agreed, pulling open the door and gesturing with an open hand for him to enter. Tom stepped in, turning sideways on to face Hendry and glanced around the interior as the door was closed by his host. Hendry turned to Tom and raised his eyebrows in query. Tom said nothing.

"I'm sorry to sound a little rude, Inspector ..." He glanced nervously towards the kitchen as his dog appeared. "What is this regarding? I wasn't present last night until after the event—"

The dog moved along the hall, stopping by the door to the cellar and sniffing at it.

"D–Do come through, Inspector, please."

Hendry led the way, taking the dog by the collar and guiding him assertively back to the kitchen and instructing him to sit on his bed in the far corner of the room.

"There's no need," Tom said. "I'm quite used to dogs."

Hendry dismissed the comment with a flick of the hand, turning to face Tom and standing in the middle of the breakfast room. He rested one hand on the table and the other on his hip. "Not everyone feels the same way, Inspector. I seldom have visitors at the house, so it generally isn't an issue."

Tom nodded, looking around. His eyes lingered on a familiar archive box set down on the floor beside the French doors leading out on to the patio.

"How about today?"

"Excuse me?"

"Visitors," Tom said, staring hard at him as Hendry registered a blank expression. "Have you had a visitor today?"

Hendry stood upright, putting both hands to his side, his lips parting ever so slightly.

"No. Today has been very quiet." He looked towards his study. "I've had a couple of work things to finish up and," he shrugged, "I've pretty much had my head down. What's this all about?" he asked, his brow wrinkling.

Before Tom could answer, Tamara appeared on the other side of the French doors, making eye contact with Tom. Without waiting to be bidden entry, she tried the handle and the door opened. The dog leapt off its bed and ran to inspect the newcomer. She bobbed her head in Tom's direction – it was the signal he'd been waiting for and he stepped forward, took a hold of Hendry's shirt and spun him and shoved him face down across the breakfast table. The dog started barking. Hendry howled in protest as Tom forced his arm around his back and twisted his hand up towards his neck, the howl was stifled, morphing into a yelp of pain.

"How dare—"

"Where's DC Collet?"

"I–I ..."

Tamara stepped forward, slamming the flat of her hand down on the table beside Hendry's head. He blinked furiously before his face contorted in pain as Tom exerted more pressure. "Eric's car is in your double garage!" Tamara said. "Where is he?"

Hendry said nothing, gritting his teeth as Tom put even more of his body weight on Hendry's stricken frame. He shrieked, a tear escaping one eye, but as Tom eased off Hendry sucked deep gasps of air into his lungs and instead of answering the question he laughed. It was a twisted chuckle that incensed Tom.

"Right!" Tom said, reapplying pressure to Hendry's twisted arm and grasping him by the collar. He hoisted him upright, manoeuvring him into the kitchen at speed. Hendry didn't find this so amusing and protested just as Tom slammed him into the cast-iron cooker, face down on the plates.

"Tom!" Tamara shouted at him but he ignored her. He took out a set of handcuffs and slapped one around Hendry's right wrist, doing so with such force that it elicited a scream of pain. Tom slid the other cuff through the stainless-steel bar running the length of the cooker's front. Dragging Hendry unceremoniously back, he attached the second cuff to the wrist of his free hand. Hendry was secured in place. Tom looked at Tamara.

"Now we'll tear this house apart."

Tamara nodded, taking out her radio and summoning Cassie and the uniformed officers waiting nearby but out of sight. Hendry shot Tom a wicked smile and without a word, Tom kicked out with his right foot and side kicked Hendry's knee. The man's legs buckled and he sank to the floor with a groan, the smile vanishing. Tamara headed across the room to the study and Tom hurried to open the front door for Cassie, his intention to search the upstairs rooms. He reached the front door, pulled it open and grasped the bannister. The dog barked again and Tom hesitated, seeing it standing in the hall staring at him. It wasn't aggressive but when he made to climb the stairs it barked again, spinning round and on the spot, its front paws lifting off the ground with each bark. Instinct made Tom stop and then Cassie appeared in the doorway breathing heavily. She looked at him, hope in her expression.

"Eric?"

Tom shook his head and walked towards the dog which held its ground, tail wagging. As he approached it turned and moved to the cellar entrance, barking once more. Tom opened the door to the cellar head and the dog went to the top of the stairs, looking back and barking excitedly. Tom exchanged a look with Cassie who rolled her eyes.

"We're taking Lassie's lead now are we?"

Tom ignored the sarcasm, pulling on the light cord and stooping low to avoid banging his head. Throwing on the second switch he immediately reacted to what he saw. "No, no, no!" he said, setting off down the stairs and calling back over his shoulder to Cassie as he negotiated the steep, narrow descent. "Call an ambulance, now!"

At the foot of the stairs he found Eric unconscious. Julia Rose was kneeling over him, her hands and feet secured at wrist and ankle with multiple layers of gaffer tape. Blood had been flowing from a wound at the side of her temple but seemed now to be clotting and drying amongst her matted hair. The blood had run down the side of her face and over another length of gaffer tape wrapped several times around her head – covering her mouth – so much so that she couldn't have removed it without a blade or a pair of scissors. She was visibly sweating, her eyes wide and red-rimmed, and she was applying pressure to Eric's abdomen – his shirt sodden and wet through with blood – trying to stem the flow of blood from Eric's midriff.

Tom didn't have time to free her, Eric was the priority. He could see two bits of cloth wedged in place beneath Eric's shirt.

Unbuttoning the shirt, Tom saw they were once light coloured but had now absorbed a great deal of fluid turning them a dark shade of crimson. Julia Rose had interlocked her fingers and was attempting to stem the flow of blood from what must have been a third wound higher up. Tom couldn't tell what had caused the injuries, there was too much blood and it was clear Eric was bleeding out; his face was pale and he was completely unresponsive to calls of his name. The darker the blood, the more serious the condition – that was what Tom had always been told – and even taking into account the gloom of the cellar this blood was very dark indeed. Easing Julia's hands out of the way, Tom applied pressure of his own. Eric groaned which Tom read as a good sign.

"Stay with me, Eric."

He heard someone descend the stairs behind him and Cassie knelt alongside.

"Geez, what do I do?" she asked, her hands poised above Eric but unsure of what was required.

"Pressure there," Tom indicated with a nod, and Cassie grimaced as she put the flat of her hands on both of Eric's wounds. "I think they're knife wounds."

"You're sure?"

He shook his head. "No, but if they were bullets, I think he'd be dead by now."

Julia Rose had slumped back against the wall and cried possibly out of relief, or from shock.

"Ambulance is on its way!" Tamara called from the top of the stairs. "How is he?"

Tom glanced up over his shoulder. That was a question he didn't want to answer. The look alone was enough. Tamara closed her eyes.

CHAPTER THIRTY-EIGHT

TOM STOOD with his back to the wall. Tamara sat alongside Becca in silence, holding her hand supportively. Becca stared blankly ahead. She'd been crying. In truth, they'd all been crying. The double doors opened and all eyes turned towards them as a nurse came through but she wasn't there to see them, she removed her face mask as she walked by. Cassie rounded the corner at the end of the corridor. She lingered at the nurses' station before catching Tom's eye and hurrying towards him. He moved to intercept her, reluctant to have a conversation in front of Becca bearing in mind what had just happened. Tamara nodded to him silently, her eyes darting to Cassie.

"How is she?" Cassie asked, looking past Tom and observing the DCI and Eric's fiancée sitting in the chairs at the side of the corridor. Cassie's expression was fixed, her usual upbeat manner completely absent. Tom could see she, too, had been crying.

Tom sighed, shaking his head. "Bearing up, under the circumstances. How did you get on?" He was eager to have something else to think about right now.

"I had the lab send Tim Hendry's DNA samples over to Kristiansand. Elin is keen to have the analysis done, so they're hurrying it through."

"It'll match," he said, meeting her eye.

"You're confident."

Tom nodded. "There's no way Alex Hart was driving that car. Julia Rose told us Alex Hart was at her apartment, unwell. He was recovering from having his appendix removed. There's no way he picked up Anette Larsen in his hire car but he wasn't the only one visiting. Hendry was there too. A friend's reunion of sorts ... Cannell drove down from Oslo because he knew Alex Hart wouldn't be present—"

"Because he was bedridden?"

"Exactly. The relationship between William Cannell and Alex Hart never recovered after Brancaster, but he would have been willing to visit Julia's dig along with Tim Hendry and then join them for dinner."

"So, you reckon Hendry borrowed Alex's hire car?"

"Julia confirmed it while you were taking Hendry back to the station," Tom said, putting the heel of his palms to both eyes and pressing hard. The relief was fleeting. "And that's why he attacked her today. She saw the newspaper report on his breakfast table – read the dates surrounding Larsen's disappearance and murder – and she knew Alex couldn't have done it. Hendry was using Hart's hire car while he was recovering. It was the only possibility left." He swore under his breath drawing a cursory glance from a passing nurse making his rounds. "I blame myself for this!"

"Don't be daft!"

He shook his head. "We were so hell bent on thinking it was Cannell or Hart that we never stopped to consider what was right in front of us—"

"Nonsense," Cassie chided him. "We were on the right path and would have got there in the end."

"Yeah, maybe," Tom said.

"Here's something else of interest," Cassie said. Tom looked at her. He needed something to cheer him up right now. "I showed the drugs you took from Hart's bathroom to Fiona Williams – she

was at the station taking a blood test from some drunk driver –
anyway, she found the drugs curious."

"Curious how?"

"The pills were branded but with a different stamp to those
listed on the label." She fixed her brow in consternation. "The lab
are going to test them but like I say – curious."

"He switched them," Tom said quietly. Cassie looked at him
inquisitively. "Hendry – he switched the tablets. That's why Hart
deteriorated so quickly. That's why he was hallucinating the night
he died – he wasn't knowingly off his medication, Hendry
ensured he was, knowing what would happen." Tom shrugged.
"All he would need to do is find a tablet that looked similar
enough to be missed by Hart when he took them each day. He
could have made the switch days ago."

"The crafty sod! Just like planting the trophies for us to find—"

"Hendry's a sociopath … as cold and uncaring as they come. I
wouldn't be surprised if he'd buried Tina Farrow at the Branodunum dig site because it gave him some perverse pleasure to
see if he could get away with it. He stashed her wherever he killed
her and then returned the following night. Tina was in the wrong
place at the wrong time," Tom said. "Did you take a look at the
report Eric wrote after he'd spoken to Hendry's ex-wife?"

"Yeah, Victoria. I was just going to say – you remember Eric
said she was really nice and then turned on him when he
mentioned what we were investigating?"

"Yes. Eric figured she still harboured some misguided loyalty
towards him and didn't want—"

"Not to Hendry but to Michael, her son." Tom's head snapped
round to look at her. "She mentioned him to Eric when she opened
the door, thinking he was there about Michael but we never
picked up on it. Michael is her child, her only child, and a brief
check on the police national computer shows he was born a mere
seven months after she split from Tim Hendry."

"Nothing in our investigation showed up that Hendry had a
son."

"I don't think he knows. Smart on Victoria's part, don't you think? She put up with his violence for who knows how long but then she found the courage to leave him, possibly around the same time she learnt she was pregnant." Tom glanced over at Becca. "The strength of a mother to be, eh? She wasn't protecting Tim. She was protecting her son from exposure to who and what his father was. One thing I don't get, though, is how did Hendry realise we might be on to him?"

Tom sighed, rubbing at his face to get colour into his cheeks. "That one's on Eric, at least, in part. He told Julia about Kristiansand and she ..."

"She told Hendry." Tom nodded solemnly. "Damn it! Sometimes I could brain that little doofus!" Cassie said, immediately regretting saying so.

"Hendry had all of us fooled," Tom said. "Not just us but everyone throughout his entire life – like I said – a monster hiding in plain sight."

A doctor stepped out from a side door, casting a glance around and making a beeline for Becca. Tom and Cassie hurried over. The doctor appeared pained, wearily coming to stand before them. Becca shot up to her feet, Tamara alongside.

"How is he?" Becca asked, her voice cracking as she spoke such was her fear of the answer.

"Eric's lost a great deal of blood ... and his body has suffered a severe trauma." Becca reached for Tamara's hand and squeezed it tightly as Tamara leaned into her. "I'm afraid we had to remove his spleen and one of the stab wounds nicked his pancreas." Becca gasped. "He is in a critical condition ... but he is stable. The surgery went well and he is in the most capable hands. He is in recovery and we will be moving him up to ICU in a few minutes. You can go and sit with him if you like?" Becca nodded and the doctor smiled at Tamara and Tom before gesturing for a nearby nurse to escort Becca to where Eric lay in the post-surgery recovery room.

The doctor turned to walk away but Tom touched his forearm

to hold him back. Once Becca was out of earshot, he asked, "How is he doing?"

"Your colleague is very ill, but he is young, strong and otherwise healthy."

"What odds would you give him?" Cassie asked. The doctor looked at her, tilting his head to one side.

"I'm not a betting man—"

"Well, it's not your money, is it?" Cassie hit back. Then she apologised under Tamara's piercing gaze.

Tom met the doctor's eye. "We just want to be prepared. Please, what's your gut telling you?"

He took a deep breath and released it slowly. "No guarantees, but if it *were my money*," he looked at Cassie, "then I think it would be safe to bet he'll make a good recovery. He's got through the worst of it by getting to hospital and then surviving the operation. I think he'll make it, I do. Whoever it was who initially stemmed the flow of blood – your colleague owes them his life."

The doctor offered them a polite smile and Tom thanked him as he walked away, and they all exchanged welcome glances, breathing a collective sigh of relief. The doctor may well have been reticent, an approach they could relate to in their line of work, but he also carried an air of confidence that only came from experience.

Tom saw Cassie wipe her eye with the back of her hand, avoiding eye contact with anyone. Tamara exhibited similar signs of relief and Tom felt the tightness in his chest loosen.

"Right," he said assertively, "who's staying here with Becca and who's coming back to the station with me to nail a serial killer?"

CHAPTER THIRTY-NINE

Tim Hendry sat quietly in the interview room, one hand resting on the other on the table in front of him. He didn't register a flicker of emotion or change in expression as Tom Janssen entered the room and took a seat opposite him and next to Cassie. Hendry had barely spoken since his arrest, remaining resolutely silent the entire time he'd been in custody. Tom placed a folder on the table in front of him, opening it and setting out several documents neatly beside each other. Tim Hendry maintained his expression, staring straight ahead.

"Up until now, you've refused legal representation, Mr Hendry," Tom said. "I intend to remind you of your rights before we—"

"I have no need of representation."

Hendry's tone was flat, monosyllabic.

Tom inclined his head. "As you wish."

He started the recording, identifying himself and indicating for Cassie to do the same. He picked up a photograph of Anette Larsen, laying it in front of Hendry. The archaeologist's eyes lowered to it briefly and then lifted to meet Tom's gaze.

"Anette Larsen, sixteen, heading home from a friend's birthday party, but she didn't make it home because she met you, didn't she? You borrowed Alex Hart's hire car several times that week, most notably for us on the night Anette went missing. A witness came forward recently, following a television appeal, claiming to have seen her getting into Alex's car, and picked his photo out of a line up offered to her. I must admit that threw me initially. That is, until I remembered seeing a picture of you and Julia standing alongside each other in a photograph on Alex's mantelpiece taken on your visit to see Julia at the Kristiansand excavation she was working on. At first glance, I thought it was Alex in the shot. The two of you looked very similar back then."

Hendry sniffed but said nothing.

"We sent your DNA profile to our counterparts in Norway," Tom said, putting another document down alongside the photograph. "And we've heard back. The police in Kristiansand are eager to speak to you."

"Are they?" Hendry said. He shrugged. "Are you expecting a confession from me; a dose of *mea culpa*?" He reached up and lightly touched the right side of his face where his cheek had reddened, a result of the impact when Tom had flung him across the cast-iron cooker in his kitchen. "I'm afraid I am disinclined to assist you, Detective Inspector."

"Oh, you misunderstand my intention here," Tom said. Hendry's eyes narrowed. "I don't require a confession. We already have enough on you with the assault on Dr Julia Rose, her false imprisonment, and the attempted murder of Detective Constable Collet to ensure a conviction. The attention of the Norwegian police – your DNA matches what was found on Anette Larsen, by the way – will only add to your time inside."

Hendry took a slow, deep breath. "Then, what is the point of all this? Vanity?"

Tom fixed him with a stare. "I wanted to look into your eyes, to see if there is any conscience there at all."

He scoffed, shaking his head. "Please, Inspector. What is it with you – or society as a whole – where you feel the need to assign rhyme or reason to every event?"

"To try and understand the world we live in, and our place in it, perhaps?"

"Naive," Hendry said, disparagingly. "Some things *just are*, and it goes no further than that." He took another breath, slowly fixing his eye on Tom. "I think I understand the situation I'm in quite well." He interlocked his fingers in front of him, gently tapping his thumbs against each other and frowning. "Now – provided we can discuss matters in a grown-up manner – I will answer your questions. However–" he looked at Cassie "–if not, then I will be more than happy to sit here in silence until you lose patience and call time on this conversation."

Tom nodded almost imperceptibly. "Why?"

"Why kill?" Hendry asked. Tom nodded. "Why does the sun come up or the rain fall?" He leaned forward, exhaling from his nose. "Because they *just do*."

"I'm not buying that."

"Really?" Hendry smiled. "Would you rather I told you how my father beat me, every day, for years, while my mother did nothing? Or perhaps how I learnt that pain is in your own mind, a call for help, that if it goes unanswered forces you to face the reality that you alone are responsible for what you do in this world."

Tom inclined his head. "I was thinking more along those lines, it's true."

"But, of course, none of that is true. My parents were wonderful people, church goers and highly respected. As are my two brothers."

"So, what happened with you?"

Hendry ran his tongue slowly along his lower lip before answering. "Lucky, I guess."

Tom refused to rise to the bait. "And what of your friends? You had a fleeting relationship with Julia Rose and Alex Hart was a lifetime friend—"

"True enough. Julia was a distraction, someone I tried to love.

She and Alex made quite a couple at one time. I wanted to see what the fuss was about—"

"With Julia?" Cassie asked.

Hendry looked at her. "Not necessarily, more the art of a meaningful relationship." He rolled his lower lip beneath the upper, then shook his head. "I still didn't understand the fascination people have with it, especially after I tried living with someone."

"Yes, we spoke with your ex," Tom said.

"Victoria? A dull woman, to be fair. But aren't they all?"

"She was less than encouraging about you, too," Cassie said.

Hendry smiled briefly. Was he amused or annoyed? It was impossible to tell.

"What of your friendship with Alex?" Tom asked. "Julia told us how you found him work, supported him. That doesn't fly with switching his medications and trying to frame him for murder—"

"Friends are a necessary irritation, I'm afraid. Alex… was like a little lost boy at times, clinging to those around him. Sadly, we need people around us in order to function. No man is an island and so on."

"I think the meaning to that phrase is lost on a man like you," Tom said.

"Yes, I could have walked away at any point and," Hendry continued without faltering, "to be quite honest, I could quite happily never see or speak to any of my friends ever again, and I would be comfortable with it."

"Why Tina Farrow?" Tom asked.

"Ah, Tina." He smiled warmly, looking up, as if recollecting a fond memory. "Now, she was an interesting girl. She could control and manipulate as well as me, albeit in a different way."

"You followed her from the pub?"

"No, not at all." He shook his head. "I recall it was stifling inside that night – any night around that time – and I wanted to get some air. Tina … just happened across my path. A curious girl."

"Curious, how?"

Hendry frowned, thinking hard. "Intuitive. I spoke to her… and it was almost as if she knew. I can't explain it any better than that. She could read people. To be the type of girl she was, she would need to have that talent. I think I saw it in her eyes – as the life drained out of her – the understanding of who and what I was."

"And why did you choose to bury her at Branodunum?"

He smiled. It was chilling.

"To see if I could get away with it. Aside from the practical benefits, a sparsely populated location, freshly backfilled soil that was quick and easy to dig … I found it amusing."

Tom sensed Cassie tense alongside him, but she controlled herself, maintaining her composure. Hendry noticed anyway.

"Detective Sergeant Knight, I should imagine you to have more fortitude within you." Turning back to Tom, he shrugged. "I couldn't leave her where she was. She would have been discovered soon enough. The heat being what it was, she would have attracted attention within a day or so. I had to be in London the next day, returning to Norfolk in the evening. It was easy enough to meet up with the others and say goodbye before returning to collect Tina and disposing of her at the dig site once everyone else had left. I even chatted with a dog walker that night when I parked the car beside the access gate. A lovely chap, had me there for fifteen minutes before he went on his way."

"What about Mila van der Berg?" Tom asked, putting a photograph of the girl on the table. Hendry gave it a cursory glance, screwing up his nose.

"I'm not sure I recognise her?"

"In The Netherlands—"

"Oh, yes. Of course." He paid more attention to the photograph now. "Her hair was lighter when I met her."

"When you killed her," Tom said.

"Now, now, Inspector. I don't care for your tone," Hendry said, sounding parental. "I will have to put you on notice for that one, particularly following on from your *man like you* comment before."

Tom was undeterred. "Did she come across you by accident as well?"

"She had come to the park on her bicycle, as I remember. She was sitting on the grass reading a book." His brow furrowed. "I don't recall which book."

"And there are others," Tom said. "We found the seven trophies you left for us at Alex Hart's home."

"Good to know that tax-payers' money has been well invested, Inspector. Although, I did think you weren't going to join the dots."

"Why would you think that?"

"Public servants … limited intelligence—"

"We caught you, though," Cassie said, smiling. "Perhaps we're not quite as thick as you might have thought?"

Hendry tilted his head to one side in acknowledgement of that fact. Now, Tom was certain he was irritated. He might be a man without a conscience, but he definitely possessed an enlarged ego; the misplaced belief in his own superiority. Hendry drew himself upright, raising his chin.

"And I think we will end things there, Inspector Janssen, seeing as the two of you are clearly incapable of basic civility."

Tom smiled, maintaining eye contact with him. "No matter. We have more than enough to ensure you never see the light of day beyond a prison wall."

Tim Hendry was escorted back to the custody suite where he would soon be charged with murder. Tom felt only emptiness inside, despite knowing they'd taken an extremely dangerous man off the streets it still left him with a bittersweet sensation. Hendry operated in plain sight, presenting an image to the world that few could see through. These people were terrifying because they could genuinely be anyone.

"I hope I never have to come across anyone else as cold as him again," Cassie said, leaning against the wall behind her. Tom nodded, his phone ringing. It was Tamara.

"Eric's come round," she said. He could hear the happiness in her tone. "He's worried about all the fuss we're making."

"That sounds like Eric," Tom said, smiling at Cassie to relieve the concern on her face.

"I think he quite likes the attention, though."

"Tell him from us that he can milk it for as long as he likes," Tom said.

"I will. How did it go with Hendry?"

Tom glanced at Cassie. "We nailed him. It's over."

FREE BOOK GIVEAWAY

Visit the author's website at **www.jmdalgliesh.com** and sign up to the VIP Club and be first to receive news and previews of forthcoming works.

Here you can download a FREE eBook novella exclusive to club members;

Life & Death - A Hidden Norfolk novella

Never miss a new release.

No spam, ever, guaranteed. You can unsubscribe at any time.

Enjoy this book? You could make a real difference.

Because reviews are critical to the success of an author's career, if you have enjoyed this novel, please do me a massive favour by entering one onto Amazon.

———

Type the following link into your internet search bar to go to the Amazon page and leave a review;

http://mybook.to/kill-them-cold

———

If you prefer not to follow the link please visit the sales page where you purchased the title in order to leave a review.

Reviews increase visibility. Your help in leaving one would make a massive difference to this author and I would be very grateful.

A DARK SIN - PREVIEW
HIDDEN NORFOLK - BOOK 8

PASSING the larger of the two car parks, preferring the shelter from the surrounding copse of trees at the edge of the woods in the smaller one, he drove the car further down the hill, slowing to make the turn. The excited snuffling from behind the cargo net signified Bodie realised they were at their destination. He glanced in the rear view mirror.

"That's right, boy, we're nearly there."

There were no other cars present. In the summer there would be several. He wasn't the only local to get out for an early morning walk before the rest of the county came out to go about their daily business. The cold was keeping them home now, he was certain. The larger car park he'd just driven by had a solitary vehicle in it; not one he recognised but it was still dark, still early. Switching off the engine triggered the interior lights to burst into life, the signal for his dog to make himself ready to leap from the car. Bodie let out an excited bark.

"All right, all right. I'm coming."

Cracking open the door let in a blast of freezing air and the warmth of the heated seat and steering wheel would, no doubt, soon become a distant memory. The protection from the wind offered by the trees, even though not in leaf, was still of benefit.

Perhaps the path around the woods would be more pleasant rather than braving the open ground of the common up to the high point overlooking Grimston Warren Reserve. Zipping up his coat, he waggled a foot beneath the rear bumper and the electrically operated tail lift raised the boot lid. Bodie immediately made to leap from the car but his owner was ready, as always, grasping the dog's collar firmly and reaching up to clip the lead in place.

The dog hustled past and jumped to the ground, nosing the earth and taking in the fresh smells that accompanied a heavy frost. The mud of the car park was churned up by visiting vehicles but had subsequently frozen. The winters here could be harsh and none more so in living memory than this one. Several crows cawed to one another from the nearby trees as the inky darkness of the night sky slowly shifted towards a slate grey as dawn approached.

They set off through the gate and on into the woods beyond, Bodie pulling as they went; keen to get moving. Once in the sanctuary of the woods and within the fenced reserve, safely away from the road, he pulled the dog back, making him sit down before releasing the lead. Dogs were supposed to be kept under control but he often chose to ignore that rule if there was hardly anyone else around. One of the car parks here was well known as a location for some rather salubrious night-time activities that the police didn't seem to bother trying to stamp out, so why shouldn't Bodie be allowed to run free?

The dog took off along the path ahead, tail in the air and nose to the ground. He wouldn't go too far. The trees were thinning as he approached the access to the open ground of the common, the bracing freshness of the crisp breeze gathering pace against his cheeks. They felt numb and his head was cold. Only now did he realise he wasn't wearing his woolly hat. Glancing back through the trees towards the car park, he considered nipping back for it, envisaging it on the passenger seat where he'd left it to be warmed by the heated seat. It never worked but he still tried it most days. Maybe there needed to be weight applied on top. There's a thought. He'd try that tomorrow.

"Bodie!"

He waited. The dog didn't appear. He whistled. Still there was no reply. Muttering under his breath he carried on, quickening his pace. Who knew what the dog would be up to if he left him to his own devices and went back to the car. He was irritated to find the gate out of the woods was unlatched.

"Bodie! Here boy!"

An excited bark carried to him from a distance. He recognised it. Bodie must be halfway across the common. Hopefully he hadn't come across anyone of a nervous sensibility. Most dog owners, the only people daft enough to be out here at this time in sub-zero temperatures, would be okay with Bodie; but there were others who turned their noses up at a large Doodle charging across the field towards them, particularly if they had one of those miniature dogs who were often a little skittish in the presence of a larger cousin.

Clearing the woods, a gentle hum of early morning traffic from the distant Queen Elizabeth Way broke the silence and he scanned the gently undulating common for an overexcited hound, seeing him a few hundred metres away bounding back and forth, barking at something. With no one else in sight, the second car park sky-lined off to his right was now visible and looked empty from this distance but, admittedly, his eyes weren't what they used to be. Bodie must have chased down a rabbit or forced a squirrel back into one of the two trees standing proudly and isolated in the centre of the reserve.

"Bodie!"

His shout was one born of a forlorn hope. If the animal hadn't returned after the first round of calls, he wouldn't do so now. In fact, the dog didn't even look back at him which he would usually do just before ignoring the call once again. Instead, the barking continued. He hurried across the field, taking care to avoid the cow pats deposited in random places among the wild grass. A sheen of frost disguised them from the human eye in the diffused early morning light, and the cold masked the smell, but the contents beneath the surface was just as unpleasant. It was okay if wearing wellies, as he was, but it was still a pain to deal with before getting back into the car.

Bodie must have sensed him getting nearer because the barking was growing in intensity, almost continuous now, as he approached, carefully picking his route across the uneven surface. Upon reaching the dog, panting heavily with its tongue lolling to one side as a result of his noisy efforts, he quickly reattached the lead before the dog saw fit to take off again. The dog nuzzled his hand and barked once more. He ruffled the top of the dog's head with his free hand. Bodie whimpered.

"What is it, boy? What's all the fuss?"

Looking to his left, his mouth fell open. Shielded from view on his approach, he hadn't seen it. He hadn't seen him. The breeze felt colder now, biting. A nearby collection of saplings were fenced off to protect their growth, and he decided to tie Bodie to one of the posts, almost tripping over the creature as he stepped forward. Cursing, he gathered himself, hurrying the two of them over to the nearest post, securing the dog in place and returning to the trees.

The body swayed gently in the breeze, the ageing branch it hanged from occasionally creaking under the strain. The teenager's facial expression could easily be judged as one befitting that of a deep sleep if not for the tinge of black to his lips and the noose around his neck, forcing his head to rest offset at an awkward angle. The discolouration of the boy's skin disturbed him as he came to stand beneath the child. Not only was he understandably very pale, but his skin was blotchy with a green or bluish hue to it; in this light he wasn't sure which. Tentatively removing his glove, he reached up, slowly placing the palm of his hand on the boy's right leg. The body felt frozen, the skin stiff and rubbery to the touch. He had been dead for hours. The dog whimpered again but his owner didn't hear him. He couldn't take his eyes off the boy; what was he, fourteen, fifteen at a push, maybe?

Easing his hand away, he slowly backed off whilst rummaging in his coat pocket for his mobile phone.

What a waste of a young life.

The next book in the series;

A Dark Sin
Hidden Norfolk - Book 8

ALSO BY J M DALGLIESH

The Hidden Norfolk Series

One Lost Soul

Bury Your Past

Kill Our Sins

Tell No Tales

Hear No Evil

The Dead Call

Kill Them Cold

Life and Death*

*FREE eBook - visit jmdalgliesh.com

The Dark Yorkshire Series

Divided House

Blacklight

The Dogs in the Street

Blood Money

Fear the Past

The Sixth Precept

Box Sets

Dark Yorkshire Books 1-3

Dark Yorkshire Books 4-6

Audiobooks

The Hidden Norfolk Series

One Lost Soul
Bury Your Past
Kill Our Sins

The Dark Yorkshire Series

Divided House
Blacklight
The Dogs in the Street
Blood Money
Fear the Past
The Sixth Precept

Audiobook Box Sets

Dark Yorkshire Books 1-3
Dark Yorkshire Books 4-6